D1011448

Books by Pamela Hansford Johnson

DÊ NOVELS

Cork Street, Next to the Hatter's

Night and Silence Who Is Here?

An Error of Judgement

The Humbler Creation

The Unspeakable Skipton

The Sea and the Wedding

Corinth House

DÊ CRITICISM

The Art of Thomas Wolfe

Cork Street,
Next to the
Hatter's D3

Pamela Hansford Johnson

CORK STREET, NEXT TO THE HATTER'S

A NOVEL IN BAD TASTE

New York

CHARLES SCRIBNER'S SONS

TO

Dr David Sofaer

Contents ᴅⱻ

Cork Street,
Next to the
Hatter's D3

1

IN WHICH MISS MERLIN INTERVIEWS
THE LATEST DOCTOR OF HER CHOICE,
AND LEAVES HIM IN A CERTAIN DEGREE
OF DOUBT, ON HER PART AND ON HIS.

A pretty sight, the confrontation of Dorothy Merlin and her new doctor. They glared at each other,
rampant, like supporters on a coat of arms, with the
desk as shield between them. Dorothy, a little griffin in
an abusive shade of emerald green, bulged her eyes at
him till her skin stretched, and the fuzzy black hair,
pulled tightly enough already into a little bun which
she called a *chignon,* looked as if it might start breaking
off at the roots. Dr. Hubble, an altogether heavier animal, a rhinoceros perhaps, glared back at her.

"I am not," he said, "a grocer, and I don't deal in
grocery orders."

He was her fourth new doctor in as many months,
which was why she felt her knowledge of medical men
—and, indeed, of medicine itself—was wide-ranging
enough for her to play the game according to her own
rules. Again she pushed the long list of pills under
his nose. She had listed sixteen items, including pills to
reduce her blood pressure, pills to reduce the weight the
pills put upon her, pills to relieve the depressive activities of the first lot, pills to send her to sleep, pills to
wake her up, pills to vitalize her, pills to quieten her
down.

"Look here," she said, "this is *all* I want from you. Do I make myself clear?"

"I should shay sho," said the doctor, in the unthinkingness of pure rage reverting to a vulgarism of his youth, when he had lived as a poor medic in Brixton, and not, as now, as a rich G.P., in the best house, in the best square, in the best of all possible boroughs—as he thought it—Kensington.

"*What?*" Dorothy half rose.

It was a warm day, very warm. In the heat she appeared to pulsate from head to foot: perhaps she did. Outside in the square the tawny houses seemed to pulsate also, inhaling and exhaling the sweet London mingling of petrol-fumes and lilac.

"I should never think of giving you half this shtuff without making a proper examination."

Having recollected himself, he was trying to cover the initial slip by a pretense that there was an impediment in his speech. Then he regained his dignity, and gave her a Messianic frown.

"You must understand, Mrs. Hines—"

"Miss Merlin."

"You said Mrs. Hines."

"I told you Miss Merlin was my professional name."

"—understand that it would be unprofessional of me to give out drugs of this nature to a patient of mine of whom I as yet know nothing, without first finding out whether they are necessary at all."

Dorothy, in anger reverting to her own origins, retorted that she understood her case perfectly and knew damned well what she wanted when she felt crook. "I am simply asking you to treat me as a person of perhaps rather more than normal intelligence," she added, quickly changing her manner. She even gave a little laugh.

He restrained himself from telling her she had done nothing whatsoever to prove this: rather the reverse.

"At all events," he said, with considerable self-mastery this time, "I'd like to know what symptoms you have. What, in fact, is the trouble?"

"No trouble," said Dorothy, "that my pills don't cure. I get headaches, if you want to know—"

"Naturally I want to know."

"Especially at weekends, just when I'm pining for a rest. And my ankles swell in the evenings. The pink pills fix that, though."

"I shall need to take your blood pressure, for a start."

An able diagnostician, with, he thought, more than a touch of black magic when he was compelled to make guesses, he would have bet a fiver that he was going to take a very high reading. The character of the pills she had extorted from other physicians told him that, and so did the breathy character of the patient herself. She was a woman of forty-seven, and he did not expect the results of an examination to be encouraging. Indeed, his better nature began to mourn for Dorothy, even if his worst did not.

"I thought I made it clear," she said, "that I have *had* my blood pressure taken. Quite recently. At least six months ago. And everything else that opens and shuts."

"Not by me."

"I can give you any further information you—"

"I prefer to gather my own information. Now, Mrs. Hines—"

"Miss Merlin."

"—if you will come and sit here and let me have your arm—"

Dorothy wreathed her lean, speckled arms before her and gave him a smile of infinite understanding. "Dr. Hubble, I suppose, as a very busy man, you have little time for reading."

He glanced, offensively, at his watch. "I have very little time for anything."

"Then do forgive me if I tell you that in my own field, I am not entirely unknown."

If a smirk could hold sweetness, Dorothy's did. One might envisage amber in a fly, rather than the reverse.

She went on: "I am a poet and dramatist of no small reputation. Indeed, there are those who consider, though it is not for me to say whether they are right or wrong—"

"May I have your arm, please?"

"No, doctor, you may not. Why do you keep on pressing me when you *know* it's no good?" Had he known her better, he would have recognized the whooping rise and fall so indicative, to her friends, of patience exhausted. "If you knew how dead weary I was of—"

Dr. Hubble swept his well-filled sleeve over the desk, knocking Dorothy's ultimatum to the floor. With a grunt, he retrieved it and handed it back.

"Sorry. But, Miss Merlin—"

A concession. Dorothy's sweetness returned.

"Either I give you a thorough examination, or you may take that list of yours elsewhere. That's all. Would you like to think it over?"

She rose decisively. "I do not *think* I shall think. I am accustomed to being treated as a sentient person."

"Nobody denies that you are sentient. Nor am I. And I feel that we are getting nowhere."

She bestowed upon him the kind of bow that is used either in contempt, or in awe of a royal personage.

"I must confess," she said, "that I am disappointed."

"So you were by my predecessors, I gather."

She blushed a little at this. She was one of those rare people who, recognizing their legal rights, have the spirit to change doctors as often as seems to them desirable. But even she wondered how disagreeably those same doctors might speak about her behind her back, one to the other.

"I should, perhaps, like to think this over," she said.

"Do." He consulted his watch again and pressed the bell on his desk.

Dorothy stowed her list away in her bag and quick-stepped to the door before he could usher her there. Such small triumphs, she felt, were hers.

Walking in the fumy heat towards a taxi-rank, she slowed her pace. She was by no means sure that she had seen Dr. Hubble for the last time.

Why was she not sure? Perhaps it was a new experience for her to be pushed around. Perhaps she even liked it. Perhaps, being convinced of her ultimate capacity for survival, despite uncalled-for fits of depression and a disinclination to visit friends who persisted in living five flights up, she felt it as well to be in the wise, if ham-like, hands of somebody.

She found a taxi and went off to Cork Street. This was her day for the accounts. And whatever Dorothy would have had known about herself, there was one thing she passionately concealed, as being degrading to her art, degrading to her entire poetic *mana*: she was a good hand with figures.

2

THE READER HEREWITH IS MADE AC-
QUAINTED WITH A BOOKSHOP, WITH A
PHOTOGRAPHER, AND WITH A YOUNG
WOMAN OF PECULIAR COUNTENANCE.

London in high summer, when summer does happen to be high, has the sweet, pulpy, aromatic softness
of the flesh of an over-ripe watermelon. Even now, despite recent excrescences, a low-built town, it seems to
squat in sunshine as villages squat when shadows are
purple and motionless in leafy lanes and tar melts on
the roads. In winter, nothing much is left of the fanta-
sies of a Wodehouse world: but summer brings the
people to saunter along the Mall and St. James's Street
as if time has stopped, and valets, high in penumbrous
chambers, are still laying out white ties and tails for
evenings to come. In Cork Street, dealers and art-lovers
(some are both) mooch in and out of Roland, Browse
and Delbanco, Redfern and other galleries. The symbolic silk hat, the only object in the hatter's window,
has been brushed and glossed and polished like a cat
prepared for the show at Olympia, and young men
pause to gaze at it, possibly with some unconscious degree of atavistic yearning.

Next door to this hat, Cosmo Hines, a tightly but-
toned man, stood looking out of the window of his
bookshop while his wife Dorothy slogged away in a
back room. Cosmo was sixty-two now, and stuffed out
his clothes rather more than he had done half a dozen

years ago; but his middle-parted hair was still white and thick, and his pale blue eyes, which had always seemed a little mad, had got no madder.

This was a slack time for most booksellers, but for Cosmo, whose shop was the smartest in W.1, all seasons were much the same, except for the Christmas rush and the annual roosting of American visitors. There were seldom customers in crowds, but those who did come in were well-heeled enough to buy three or four books at a time, for which they never, of course, paid spot cash. On this hot day the coolness of the shop was delicious. A peer and a diplomat were browsing through Nancy Mitford and Evelyn Waugh, an elegant elderly woman was thoughtfully balancing on the palm of her hand a book of royal reminiscences (written by a Royal's second cousin twice removed) as if she were proposing to buy by poundage, or was guessing the weight of the cake at some rural junket. A few shafts of sunlight caught in their rays thistledowns of dust from the higher bookshelves and set them spinning. Cosmo turned to adjust a display of new novels and poetry on the center table, deplored the fact that he was obliged, at a dead loss, to stock Dorothy's last book of playful verses for children, then resumed his watch along the street.

He saw Duncan Moss, stouter than ever but looking younger than his forty years, enter the building across the way, where he had opened a new photographic studio on the first floor, and he sighed. Duncan and Dorothy were, at bottom, no longer even on the dubious terms that characterized their relationship when they had all—with Matthew Pryar—gone on holiday abroad together in the spring of 1957. Duncan had become more famous in his line and was therefore less inclined to take Dorothy's lip, though when they met he would still go through the usual forms of exclamatory affection. It was a pity, really, that Duncan could not have found a studio somewhere else.

Cosmo wondered, seeing a resemblance in a passer-by, what Matthew was doing these days. Matthew had, to everyone's stupefaction, married the most famous, and certainly the liveliest, of American multi-millionairesses, and, since Dorothy had been misguided enough at the time to hail his good fortune with contumely, had paid only one fleeting visit to Cork Street since and had afterwards confined himself to communication by Christmas card. A pity. Cosmo, in so far as he was capable of liking any human being, had liked Matthew. He wondered whether he had retained the pink plastic egg acquired at a very frank representation of *Leda and the Swan*, which they had been privileged to witness one scabrous night in a street on the outskirts of Bruges: and, if so, what Matthew's wife thought about it.

At that moment, he knew the shock of eyes staring straight into his own, and he retreated into the shadows so that he could better study the extraordinary appearance of the starer.

He imagined that she must have come from one of the galleries, either as spectator or exhibitor: if not, there was no excuse at all for her presence in Cork Street.

She was a small, stocky young girl who wore, above a short tartan skirt and stockings of quite a different tartan, a long, hot, hairy black sweater. Her head was small, the dust-colored hair hacked off crudely, except where a lock flopped down over her bulging forehead. Below her eyes, it seemed to Cosmo, she had less of a face than a muzzle: pug-nose, short upper lip, mouth squashed up almost against her nostrils, square, narrow chin. But the eyes that stared were superb, as green and pale as bottleglass washed up by the sea, rocketing up at the outer corners, the pupils very black, the lashes pale, but thick as plumage.

(It must be borne in mind that Cosmo had purely classical ideas of beauty which, of course, he could never have applied to his wife Dorothy.)

The girl hovered. She scowled at the books displayed in the window and seemed to sneer. She made as if to walk on—and she did walk on: but she must only have paused to scowl at the silk hat, because in a second or two she was back again. She made a dash in the direction of the door handle, retreated. Cosmo realized that though he had seen her eyes, she could not have seen his. She took a decision. Squaring her shoulders, she marched straight into the shop.

Cosmo said good-afternoon and walked away. It was not his habit to accost potential purchasers: they were all—even this girl—to be made aware of freedom to choose, of timelessness, and of the negative role played by money in such a shop as this.

Having cast one apprehensive glance at him, she began to make a round of the shelves with a curiously uncertain, almost crippled gait. Because she gazed so blindly at the dazzling spines, Cosmo knew she had come for a purpose, and that this purpose was not to buy. At last, like a kind of doddering butterfly, she came to rest by the new novels.

She picked up one or two and, in the arcane fashion of people in bookshops, stared first at the back of the jacket, then opened the volume at random, flicked through a few pages and stuck it back into place, the wrong way round. The somewhat conspicuous apple in her throat moved up and down like the wooden bun at the end of a yo-yo. She approached Cosmo.

"Madam?"

"I don't seem to see the new Pringle Milton."

He was, for once, caught napping. "The new—I beg your pardon? I'm afraid I can't for the moment—"

Flushed to the roots of her hair, she said tartly, "But you must know! Her latest novel. It's had the most fab notices!" Her accent was sub-cockney.

Even now, he did not understand.

"It's called *The Sick Ones*."

"You say her latest? Do forgive me, I—"

"*Actually*, it's a first novel."

He remembered. He had seen, pushed away in a corner of *The Times Literary Supplement*, a note on a book by a girl of seventeen. He remembered, also, the tail-end of that note, a sting by someone old enough to have shown more charity—"Shows some minimal promise."

"I'm afraid I haven't got it in stock, but I could order it for you."

"I can't understand you not having it in stock. Everyone, simply everyone I know, is talking about it."

He explained, indulgently, and without truth, that in such a shop as his, one kept relatively small stocks.

"I hear it's fab," said the girl, standing her ground, but now as red as a beetroot, "*m'hav'lous!*"

"So I have the pleasure of meeting Miss Pringle Milton," Cosmo said suavely.

Her mouth opened and shut. She replied, ridiculously, "I suppose so."

"Let me welcome, then, a very young acquisition to the ranks of literature."

"I don't believe in literature."

"I beg your pardon?"

"I don't write *literature*. I just write."

"Oh, I see."

What would have happened next Cosmo was not to know, for at that moment Dorothy emerged, incensed, from the back room.

"Do you realize that skunk Breckenridge has owed us fifteen pounds eleven shillings and sixpence since last July—? Oh."

"My dear, let me introduce to you the latest very young, but very welcome, acquisition to the ranks of literature, Miss Pringle Milton. Miss Milton, my wife: Dorothy Merlin."

"Oh. Nice to meet you, Miss Merlin. Of course I've heard of you."

"It would be quite extraordinary if you had not, wouldn't it?" Dorothy said, her eyes protruding, and half her mouth stretched in a teasing smile: but only half.

"You must look in and see us often," said Cosmo quickly. "We like to think we encourage the young, as well as the established, writers."

"Well, you haven't got my novel. I don't call that encouraging."

He made a soothing noise.

"Well, but you haven't."

"Your name," said Dorothy, "simply can't be Pringle."

"It's my second name. If you'd got my first one, you wouldn't use it either." Miss Milton picked up

Dorothy's book, pretended to look at it. She said, "Are you working on anything at the moment, Miss Merlin?" She sounded very grown-up.

"How charming of you to ask. In fact, I am writing a play. An Anti-Verse play."

"Anti-Verse?"

"Yes."

"You mean a play in prose."

"I don't mean a play in prose," Dorothy said furiously, "I mean something entirely different!"

"Poor me," said Pringle, "always dropping clangers."

Dorothy's amiable and handsome debtor came strolling in out of the sun, looking as if it had gilded him permanently.

"My dear Lord Breckenridge!" Cosmo cried, and Dorothy was all smiles now, though they were not her most brilliant ones.

"How y'both?" He had picked up his speech-habits from his aunt, Mrs. Jones. "Feel quite a stranger these days."

"Never, never a stranger," Cosmo insisted.

"Been in America. Fantastic place, isn't it? Saw Matt Pryar. Got a place up the Hudson, now." He saw Pringle, and his eyes widened. Cosmo thought they had widened in horror.

"Y'ever been in America, Miss—"

"This is Miss Pringle Milton, whose novel I'm sure you must have read. A very young acquisition to—"

"How j'do, Miss Milton?"

"Miss Milton, let me introduce Lord Breckenridge."

At this she stiffened, flushed again, and planted her feet as if squared for battle.

"How do you do. I think I ought to tell you—"

"Cosmo," said Dorothy, "when you are free I should like a word—"

It came in a rush. "I think I ought to tell you I don't believe in lords."

Miss Milton might have been about to cry.

After a second of pure puzzlement, Breckenridge laid his large, navvy's hand on her shoulder.

"But you don't want to worry on that score," he said warmly, "so long as they believe in you."

She twitched away and made towards the door: she collided with someone coming in. That someone was about to murmur an apology and step aside, when he suddenly, in one visual and mental operation, swept her into his full consciousness. "I *say!* No, don't go."

Taking her by the upper arm, he drew her further into the shop. "I say, Cosmo— Hullo, Dorothy, what a sweetie you look today, all in green! —Hullo, Wulfric, haven't seen you for ages. —I say, Dotty, seems a silly thing to ask, but could you lend me a ledger? A huge, fat ledger, red if humanly possible. I want to pose a girl on it."

"My dear Duncan," said Dorothy, "of course we *can*, but doesn't it smack of chichi?"

"Hi, Duncan," said Breckenridge. "V'you met Miss Pringle Milton?"

"This one?" Duncan realized that he was still gripping the girl tightly. "No. I want to."

"Let me introduce Mr. Moss," said Dorothy frostily, "the photographer."

"I think I ought to say—" Pringle began.

"No, no, don't," said Breckenridge. "I am sure y'believe in photographers. Mr. Moss is quite corporeal. Too much, I tell him."

"I shall make her believe in me." Duncan spoke tenderly and with unction. He let Pringle go, and she rubbed her arm.

"Mr. Hines," Breckenridge said, "I want that marvelous new collected Surtees, with the plates. V'you got it?"

"Complete set, thirty-two guineas," Dorothy said tightly.

"That's what I want. Send it round to me, will you, m'dear chap?"

"Lord Breckenridge," Dorothy intervened, "I wonder if you could spare a moment—"

"Nothing to say that can't be said in public. Y'send me the Surtees and I'll settle up for the whole shoot. Honest Injun."

Not pausing for her reply, he waved his hand benignly at everyone, and left the shop.

"Now Cosmo, he is *not* going to get—"

"Yes, my dear, we'll talk about that later on."

"I want to talk about *you*," said Duncan to Pringle, with an air of playful mastery, "and when darling Dotty's got me my ledger, I shall do so."

Despite his fat, despite the flowery sweetness of his eyes, he had managed to frighten her a little.

"I don't know what there is to say."

"I want to photograph you."

"No, you don't!" She backed against the door.

"Dear girl, not *that* kind of photograph. Don't be silly. It shall be sweater and all—if you must. I want the head, that's all. Come along, I only work across the street."

"I don't know you, and I won't."

"Cosmo," said Duncan, "do tell this enchanting creature that I am perfectly reputable, will you?"

"Mr. Moss's reputation could not stand higher," Cosmo said obediently, though he thought Duncan was mad.

"Miss Milton," Duncan persisted, "I think—I am not sure, but I think—that you have got an absolutely new face. Do let me try and prove it to myself."

"You're having me on. I don't want to be photographed. I don't care about my face. I'm a *novelist*."

He assured her there was no rule against novelists having faces; some had quite nice ones.

Dorothy, who had retired, came out to bang a ledger down in front of him. "Will that do?"

"Dotty, you are the sweetest, loveliest—"

"And mind you bring it back."

By the time he turned round, Pringle had gone. He tore to the door and opened it: somehow she had contrived to vanish, as if the street had swallowed her up. "The hell, she's got away! Cosmo, I've got to get her back again. It is a supremely new face, I'm sure of it. By God, I'm sure!"

"I think she's a rude little gargoyle," said Dorothy, "and entirely hideous."

"Dotty, pet, I bow to your judgment in all other things, you know I do, but I do know a face when I see one. This girl is going to set a trend that will be 'with it' with something that doesn't yet exist, I do assure you."

"You could write to her publisher," said Cosmo, with the grin of a satyr. He suspected Duncan's motives, though in this he was wrong.

"God, so I could! Do you know who they are?"

"I can find out."

"Duncan," Dorothy said, her face tightening up like a screw beneath the screwdriver, "she is only one of those awful little squalid girls you are always picking up. You only want her to be disgusting with. When I think of the years I've spent trying to teach you something about taste—"

"Cosmo, you've got to find it for me."

"Why do you say you want to take photographs when you know you don't?" Dorothy demanded, with a rip in her voice which rose to a tiny scream. She thumped the ledger and dust flew.

"But I do want to take photographs, you stupid woman," said Duncan, simply.

3

MISS MERLIN ATTENDS A THEATRICAL PERFORM-
ANCE WITH A FRIEND WHO IS NEW TO US. THIS
FRIEND SUFFERS A DEGREE OF SHOCK, SOMETHING
DEMONSTRABLY GOOD FOR A GIGGLE WITH OTHER
PERSONS, BEING NOTHING OF THE KIND WITH HIM.

Tom Hariot had taken Dorothy Merlin to the
theater, in recompense for a little kindness she had
shown him—or so she thought. In fact, she had been a
deadly nuisance.

She was in no way given to showing little kindnesses,
but one morning, on her way up to the studio of Duncan Moss, she had noticed, outside the door of an ad-
joining set of chambers, five untouched milk bottles.
Inflamed by an addiction to detective stories, which
she had concealed from everybody, she immediately
jumped to the conclusion that the occupant was dead.
It is true that she tried to test the matter by ringing the
bell: but finding nobody answered, she tore off to telephone the police, who arrived with gusto.

What had really happened was this: Tom had gone
off to Paris for five days and had forgotten to notify the
milkman.

So there they were, new acquaintances, Miss Dorothy Merlin and Mr. Hariot, lecturer in structural linguistics at King's College, London, assisting at a performance of something the critics had hailed as a
comedy. It was Dorothy's own choice: she had been
naturally attracted by one of the notices, which read—

"The dialogue hisses gloriously with spite, like a drop of water spilled on a red-hot stove."

There seems no reason to delay explanation of what a lecturer in structural linguistics was doing with rooms in Cork Street, since there is nothing suspenseful about the matter. Tom was the son of an ancient family (one of his ancestors had read mathematics with Sir Walter Raleigh) and he had both money and a social conscience. He believed he should do a job of work. He was generally clever, with some small literary talent: but the talent would not have been enough, he thought, to provide him with a satisfying career. Graduating with a good degree, he thought he might teach. The normal course of the English schools had seemed to him far too soft an option, so he chose something more difficult and more trying to his pupils. He worked very hard and with scant results: often, he was correcting papers until midnight. And so, his conscience assuaged, he saw no reason why he should not spend his private hours in the comfort, and the ambiance, to which he had always been accustomed: he had settled in Cork Street, in two nice rooms with bath.

(Why had the daily woman not discovered the milk bottles? Because he had given her five days' paid leave —fair's fair.)

He was a very tall, lean young man of remarkably pale complexion, whose limbs seemed to dangle. Conscious of his height, he had adopted a permanent stoop which, far from giving an impression of age, made him look like an overgrown boy of eleven attempting to play Polonius. He was, by the way, thirty-two. He had a long head, hair straight and neat, features delicately tilted, eyes round and brown. His mouth was soft and cordial, the lips always a little parted. He had not married: he had never been in love with anybody at all. He was a happy, natural hermit.

"I say," he whispered ingenuously to Dorothy, half-way through the third act, "isn't it awful?"

She started, then gave him a smile of brilliant estrangement. He realized that they were by no means thinking as one.

The play concerned three psychopathic siblings, who lived with their old mother who was deaf and dumb, in a suburb of Basildon New Town. They had taken as a lodger a psychopathic prostitute of lesbian tendencies, with whom they felt themselves in sympathy: but she, whose trouble was gerontophilia, had a fancy for the old lady. At the end of Act II she had fought with her —since her advances did not appear to be returned— had heaved her out of her wheelchair onto the scullery floor and beaten her to death with an Indian club, partly in view of the audience but mostly, to be just, behind a dismantled gas-stove. The *dénouement* would, apparently, deal with the question of whether the siblings should conspire to take the blame for the murder if the prostitute would agree to distribute her ambiguous favors between them, *privatim et seriatim*, before they rang 999. Since all three siblings had always wanted to be hanged, each took a ritual jab at the corpse with a bread-knife to ensure this pleasurable outcome.

They were busy arguing it out; the audience, which had a large admixture of clergymen and elderly ladies, was laughing obediently away with a puzzled expression on its collective face.

"But it is so true," Dorothy whispered in return, relenting a little since she was his guest, "it is so inconceivably *true!*"

She whispered again later, under cover of the general merriment, "It is almost—I don't say quite—Anti-Verse." She wriggled out of both shoes, partly in delight, and partly because her ankles had swollen with the heat.

Tom had a depressed feeling that the play might run for some months. A small theater, a cast of five, one set, consisting of three blank walls with a hole in one of them, a table, a gas-stove and a wheelchair. The overheads could not be prohibitive. Preferring not to watch the stage, he watched Dorothy, who sat upright in her stall, head uplifted, teeth bared, never distracted for one moment from her enjoyment except when she stole a quick look around to see if anyone had recognized her.

"If you only knew," cried the heroine, "how the lot of you makes me want to *crap!*"

The word was brought out with such exquisite timing that all the clergymen and ladies went off into renewed gales of mirth, then stopped laughing abruptly and, with lowered eyes, let the smiles fall away as if they had dropped them into their laps. Tom imagined the floor littered with fallen smiles, to be swept up later with ticket-halves and chocolate papers.

"It is true," Dorothy murmured, clutching painfully at his knee, "you have to *see* that!"

When it was all over, and they were outside in the blessed freshness of a rust-colored, dazzle-strung London night, he asked her hastily about her children. He hoped it would head her off the play. He had never seen them, since Dorothy's sons (. . . with their quaint Victorian names, Albert, Augustus, William, Frederick, Wilfred, Percival, James) were always away at university, public school, prep school, or Grannie's:

but they were a great topic with her, or rather, the fact that she had borne them was a great topic.

"They're all right," she said shortly. "I ache for them sometimes, but do they ache for me? Ought I even to want them to ache for me? We won't talk about it."

"Let's go round to the Arts and have a drink." After all, he had to ask her, and they walked through the crisscross of streets, Dorothy limping a little because her shoes always hurt her worse once she had allowed herself to slip them off. Though the weather was still hot there was a sharp breeze from the river, which smelled of Dickens and the sea, Rogue Riderhood and Yarmouth beach. It was not altogether an agreeable smell, but at least it was a cool one.

In the Arts Theatre Club it was pretty warm again. When they found a table, and Dorothy had waved buoyantly to a number of total strangers in order to give the impression that everyone knew her, she returned to the charge.

"Tom—if I may call you Tom?"

"Do."

"I am so enormously excited by that marvelous play. Black comedy—yes. But above all, True. Surely you must have felt it."

"The general situation was rather outside of my own experience," he replied courteously.

"Ha!" She pounced. "Your outer experience or your inner experience? You were regarding it from what level?"

"Well, any old level."

"And it seemed so strange?" The little, light laugh, the upward flick of the brows, just a touch of the Tease. *Echt* Dorothy.

"Awfully strange. I say, is that drink all right? It looks very weak."

"But why, tell me why? Can't you face the belief that all of it—all—is a part of you? Or a potential part of you? Tell me, Tom"—the laugh even lighter—"are you a *cowardy-custard?*"

He pondered this for some time, then said "No." Surreptitiously, he looked at his watch.

"But you're afraid of your own unease, aren't you?"

"I wasn't uneasy. I just thought it wasn't any good. But I'm so glad you did."

"Oh, Mi-chael!"

She jumped up, waving furiously in the direction of a gaggle of men who were talking by the bar.

All four, after a moment of doubt, waved back.

"Are they all called Michael?" Tom asked.

"No! The short one, with red hair—that's Michael Wing, the director. I'm sending him my Anti-Verse play."

"I know the one next to him slightly," said Tom, "that's Michael Shaughnessy. He's a director too." He tried waving to his own acquaintance. Again, all four waved back. "That proves it. They are all called Michael."

Dorothy, who had hoped to be approached by one man and perhaps introduced to the others, fell into sulks and pushed her drink away with the flat of her hand, rocking the glass as she did so. Tom steadied it.

"Shall we go?" he asked her.

"We may as well. Why not?"

She sulked in the taxi all the way back to Cork Street. Only when he was about to send her off to Kensington, where she lived, did she remember to thank him for the evening. Clutching at his sleeve, she thanked him at length, while the meter ticked up.

"You mustn't allow yourself to be shocked by things, Tom."

"I couldn't be, after teaching *Puss in Boots* for six years. It's a most lubricious story, if you really think about it."

"*Puss in—*?

"It makes a useful exercise in my subject. Good-bye, and thank you so much."

"—but you *mustn't* be shocked! We can only be purged and made clean by being forced to confront the worst in us and to laugh at it, yes, laugh! Humor is holy, holiness is humor."

"I expect I'm all wrong. I usually am. Well, it's been so nice—"

"But listen, Tom, I do want to explain. I—"

The driver, perceiving the suffering of a fellow-man, suddenly let out the clutch. Dorothy, only just relinquishing in time her grasp on Tom's sleeve, nearly fell out of the door. "Whoopsy, ducks, you've got to be careful!" the driver shouted through the glass. "Too few like you for us to spare 'em."

Tom returned to his rooms and sat for a while in thought. Then, although it was a quarter to midnight, he dialed a number.

"Harold. You're not in bed?"

"No, of course not. How are you, old boy?" Vivacious now as at seven in the morning, his friend's voice came light and clear from the heights of Highgate, a voice that implied in the owner blue eyes, good looks, slight stature, and implied these things correctly.

"I think I'm all right. How's Zena? And the children?"

"Fine. Why do you only think you are?"

"I went to the theater tonight. You know I don't go often. So perhaps I'm out of touch."

"What did you see?"

"I saw something called *Good for a Giggle*."

"What on earth for? You didn't have to."

"It wasn't my choice. Have you seen it?"

"One and a half acts. Did it end in a ritual murder, by the way?"

"I suppose one might say so. It looked like a real one. Except, of course, the participants were so strange. There was a deaf and dumb grandmother—"

"I know, old boy. I got that far. Zena stuck it out as far as the second interval. Why don't you forget it and go to bed?"

"You mean, you want to go to bed."

"You shouldn't sound *louche*, it's unbecoming. No, I don't want to go—Zena does. But she'll like me all the better if I make her wait."

Harold Boulton had been to school and university with Tom. He was a Lloyd's underwriter, fond of the arts, felicitously married, with two boys and two girls who all seemed to be much the same age.

"Harold. Do you remember that I wrote a one-act play for amateurs, years ago? I still get royalties on it. I should say it brings me in anything from seven and six to fifteen shillings per annum. Is the Lord Chamberlain very permissive these days?"

"I read that thing of yours, it's as clean as *Cranford*. Why on earth should you want permission?"

"No, not for that play. But I've been wondering. You're something of an ideas-man, aren't you?"

"Something of. Why?"

Tom said slowly, "Do you think it would be possible

D3   26

to write a play so nauseating that it could not, in any circumstances, be allowed on any stage?"

"What would you do with it, then?" Harold's voice was still vivacious, but held no surprise. As in the old days, he fell in effortlessly, and with an immediate expenditure of imagination and foresight, with whatever his friend had in mind.

"I don't know. Do you think that, these days, it would even be possible? I should so like to try. Just to see if I could."

"Well, in that case I don't suppose the Lord Chamberlain would wear what you wrote. But there are always the theater clubs. You wouldn't find it easy to defeat them. I hardly like to tell you this, but *Giggle*'s not a bit nauseating, by contemporary standards."

"It isn't? That makes things even more difficult. But I think I might try." Tom paused. "I will try."

He heard a clamor at the end of the line.

"One of the girls has got out—O.K., Zena, half a tick!"

"Got out where?" Tom asked, not without anxiety.

"Just got out. They do get out, like wild beasts. Oh, she does look so sweet! I wish you could see her. . . . Grrr! Go back to your bed, you little stinker, or I'll . . . Look, I've got to go now. I'll write you a letter. A considered one."

"If you please."

4

DOROTHY CONTEMPLATES GIVING
A PUBLIC READING, FROM WHICH
SHE IS DISSUADED, AND PRINGLE
MILTON VISITS A HAIRDRESSER.

Though it was commonly believed that Cosmo
never opened a book, this was untrue. He was a passionate reader with positive tastes who could easily get
through a dozen advance copies in a week: but what he
liked best was novels about mad people, and through
sheer personal enthusiasm had managed to sell thirty
copies of one of these the previous Christmas. He also
enjoyed books about drug addiction, but kept this to
himself, since he had a clientele wholly uninterested
in the subject.

It was a cloudy morning, cool for the first time in a
fortnight, and Cork Street was unstriped by the great
bands of incandescent shadow that might, on a bright
day, have been sprayed over it by Rothko. Dorothy,
having just finished her Anti-Verse play, which was a
work entirely in monosyllables, was in the flaming temper that always took her when she had completed an
act of creation. Her neck patched with red like stains of
cranberry juice she was berating her husband because
only one of her volumes of children's verse had been
sold—and that one to Breckenridge, who hoped that
by buying it he might induce her to forgive his debts as
he, at any rate, always forgave his debtors.

"Why do you say you can't sell them when you know you can? It only needs push."

"Well, Dotty, I have pushed, but it didn't answer."

"The lot who come in here are just miserable shell-backs, years behind the times. Your job is to educate them."

"It's not, my dear. It's to sell books."

"Suppose I gave a reading, one afternoon? Wouldn't that bring people in?"

This inspiration for the moment appeased her.

Opening her book, she recited from it, in a gay, motherly voice:

> Au pair!
> *Apples and pears!*
> *In the garden and up the stairs,*
>   *O PAIRS!*
>   *Pears and prayers!*
> *Womb of pears and womb of prayers,*
>   *Shares—*
>   Cares!

She added didactically, "You see, Cosmo, it may look like mere light-hearted punning, but in fact it is technically intricate to a degree. You have to look at it on two levels—"

"I don't think we can have a reading, Dotty. And don't you feel that, for children, this particular poem is a little suggestive?"

She looked as if she were about to burst, which, for a woman so small and thin, was quite a feat.

"Of course it is suggestive! Isn't it our job, as parents, to *suggest?* That is how we bring our children into the light of adult comprehension. Not by preaching, no! Not by the statement. They resent statements. But by suggestion."

"There was a phrase in the war," Cosmo said wearily, " 'Up them apples and pears.' "

"Don't you see, that is just what I intended? Precisely that overtone? Why shouldn't I give a reading?"

He marveled, not for the first time, that eight or nine years ago Dorothy had had something of a success with a verse play called *Joyful Matrix*. She had fooled some of the people some of the time. But he knew those happy days were now over.

"Because nobody will come."

"I say they will come!"

"We are not going to make the experiment, my dear."

She sat down heavily and burst into tears. He looked at her with something like clinical interest. These bouts of depression were new.

"You give me nothing, nothing. You refuse me another child—"

"Oh, come. It is surely rather late in the day—"

"You refused me when it wasn't at all late in the day! You've left me empty, empty, empty. And, furthermore, you won't try to sell my book."

"Shut up," said Cosmo, "someone's coming in."

A new customer appeared, opened six or seven books at the penultimate page, gave a sphinx's smile and went out again.

"Dotty," Cosmo said not too confidently, when they were alone again, "don't you think it ought to be 'womb of pears and womb of prayers, *share, care?*' "

"Certainly not! What do you know about it? Each of them, singly, 'shares' and 'cares.' "

"You wouldn't have done it just for the rhyme?"

"You toad," said Dorothy, blurting out into new weeping.

She had some reason to weep. He was, in fact, cruel to her when the fancy took him. He was not a good husband. Yet it is fair to say that he might have been a better one if Dorothy had talked about motherhood less and practiced it more. In addition to his other idiosyncrasies, he rather liked his sons and thought she should never have sent away, at so tender an age, Wilfred and Percival. They were both terrified of school and were guaranteed to sob bitterly, or even to be sick, at Victoria Station, when the school train was about to leave, and parents, strung up to false jollity by grief, relief, or a combination of both, were gathering strength to flap their arms wildly in farewell. But she had said— "I have my work. I have to work in solitude. Do you suppose they would ever respect me or themselves, if I had allowed them to inhibit that work? As they grow older, they will understand."

Cosmo particularly liked Percival, a pale little boy who seemed to be fond of his father, and would cling round his neck with etiolated arms, like hyacinth roots in water, when the time for departure came. Percival had doe's eyes and hair fair as Devonshire cream.

"Oh, come," said Cosmo, "that sounds severe."

Miss Few, his chief assistant, came from the back room.

"Mr. Hines, are we ordering only a hundred of *Custom and Costume*? We ordered a hundred and fifty of his last, and got rid of most of them."

She was forty-one, a tidy, dust-colored woman, tall, flat-breasted, who had been living contentedly in sin for fifteen years, and was as happy as the day is long. Nobody had ever seen her lover; nobody had even begun to envisage what he saw in her. They had achieved a nirvana of peaceful adjustment, incomprehensible to anybody else, which was so much to the good for both of them.

"Yes, of course order the same. Books only make a living for us if they sell in large numbers. You know that as well as I do."

"That's what I thought."

"Then what's the trouble?"

"I expect," she said, "that I got muddled. I've seen four travelers this morning and the telephone's been braying like a jackass. So the same, then?"

"The same. The logistics of this business," Cosmo said thoughtfully, "are very subtle."

"You're telling me," said Miss Few, before he could tell it all to her again.

"We might always get a bit of discount for the few copies we don't manage to sell."

"Right," she said, and vanished with an efficient and encouraging whisk of the tail into the back room.

"*I* told her not to order more than a hundred!" Dorothy stormed. "There is no need for her to come pestering you. I understand the ordering perfectly well."

"Oh, she's quite right. She always is."

"And I?" cried Dorothy, "and I?" She was at her most dangerous. If she had been in a more or less placid frame of mind, she would have said, "What about me, then?"

Fortunately, Duncan came bouncing in from over the way, eyes like forget-me-nots which have suddenly remembered everything.

"I've found her! I've found her! I'm going to put her all among plastic gnomes in a flower-bed, head only, that beautiful head among all those hideosities. Her neck's too short, so I shall bury her up to the chin."

"Bury whom?" Cosmo enquired.

"Pringle, of course! God, I had to work hard with her. Would you ever credit that she doesn't want to be a new face?"

"And what a ghastly face!" Dorothy exclaimed, in her near-scream. "Oh, yes, and don't you think I've forgotten what you called me the other day. If you can't be polite, don't come in here at all!"

Duncan ignored her; he was dreaming of other things. She shook herself violently, like a dog coming out of water, and went away. She let the door bang upon their idiocies. They were silent for a moment, until they heard her smash something.

"She is a sweetie," said Duncan, relaxing.

"Who, Dorothy?" Cosmo had relaxed too, and was smiling.

"Dorothy, of course. That goes without saying. But I meant Pringle."

"I ordered six copies of her book. We have to look to the future, we never know. But nobody has bought one."

"Damn her book! All she's got to do in this life is to exhibit her head. She's so stupid, too," Duncan added in a gauzy manner, "which is of course no end of a help. By the by, if you really haven't sold her books—"

"I have not."

"—I'll buy one. I have to keep on the right side of her. I shall talk to her about it while I'm posing her. Quick, give it to me. She's due in half an hour."

"You will be able to read it in that time?"

"Of course I shall. Well enough to pass muster. Oh, my God!"

Duncan was staring out of the window, horror-struck.

"My God, she's early! It's not that, though. Look at her!"

Pringle had been to the hairdresser; otherwise she looked as she had ever done.

She was teetering outside the building in which Duncan's studio was, as if uncertain whether to enter, or to run away. Her dusty hair bulged upward, and was fixed in a cone as if by glue: a great deal of hair that could not have belonged to her had been added.

"Dear Lord, and I won't have time to tear it down and wash it. She's ruined herself. Doesn't she understand that only Czechs still wear beehives?" He was at the door, shouting across the road in a manner quite wrong for Cork Street.

"Miss Milton! Pringle, come here! Pringle, what the hell have you done to yourself?"

Her blush was something almost independent of her face, a flowery burning in which her features were semi-obliterated. Stalking into the bookshop, she clasped her hands so tightly that her knucklebones gleamed.

"What do you mean? I'm here, aren't I? And you know quite well I didn't want to come."

"Pringle," Duncan said, his eyes wet, "why couldn't you leave well alone? We can do nothing today, absolutely nothing, and I'd got everything lined up. Oh, Pringle, Pringle, your hair!"

"I was only trying to please you! I didn't want things to be all on your side, especially as I wasn't pleased at all. You talked me into it."

"How long would it take to wash it out?"

"I think it's fab! And it cost me fifteen shillings."

"I said, how long would it take?"

"I'm not going to wash it out. I never wanted to pose for you. Oh, you've got my book!"

"I am simply carrying it around with me," he said, the lachrymosity induced by weak tear-ducts not undermining his cunning, "because I can't put it down. I've got to page 73. I wanted to talk to you about it."

She rallied faintly. "I don't want to talk about it. Only to people who understand."

"What I liked," said Duncan eagerly, "wasn't so much what you actually said, but what you didn't. That was electrifying!"

"What didn't I say that you liked?"

"Well, it was really your whole philosophy. You couldn't actually spell that out, could you?"

Pringle, maddeningly, and with a lack of cooperation, said she wished he would try.

"Look, sweetie, you go to the hairdresser along the street—I'll pay—and have all that washed out, and I swear I'll explain it all to you while you're drying."

"One can't hear anybody explain anything while one's drying."

"All right, then! You come along with it wet. It'll look better when it's wet. Much better."

"I won't go till I know what you saw in my book that I didn't put in."

"Well, there was the way you made us feel about the brother—"

"There wasn't a brother."

"Surely that," said Duncan, "*is the whole point?*" Nonplused, she stared at him.

"If you'll forgive me," said Cosmo, "we're approaching the busiest hour of our day—"

"Of course you are. Come on, Pringle, shampoo and no set. Quick, march!"

He bore her out before she could resist. Cosmo saw them going along the street, colliding with each other as people do when one has too firm a grip on his companion.

Trade looked up. In half an hour, he sold an Audubon bird book, a Mitford and a Powell, a Swedish dictionary and a novel called *In the Pads*, which was a favorite of his. (This last was sold under considerable sales-resistance to a young man of no great resolution who wanted a silver-wedding present for his mother.)

Dorothy did not emerge again until it was time for them to shut up shop. She had broken two heavy glass ashtrays: but both were cheap ones.

5

TREATS OF A HOUSEHOLD WHEREIN TOM
HARIOT IS PERFECTLY UNDERSTOOD, AND
OF HIS FIRST MEETING WITH MISS MILTON.
AN IMPORTANT CHAPTER IN OUR HISTORY.

Tom Hariot thanked his friend for the considered
letter and said he thought he had taken the main
points. "All the same, I'd like to talk it over with you."

Harold said the whole project seemed a waste of
time, but that if Tom would like to come over to
Highgate for a meal, they might between them develop
some ideas.

"It is so inconsiderate of you to live in Highgate. To
your friends who are central, I mean. I hate it on the
tube."

"The air is fresh up here," Harold replied, "I feel fit
all the time. We all exercise every morning before an
open window."

"All six of you?"

"Certainly."

"Then that would mean at least two open windows,
or the front row would block the air off."

"The children aren't so tall as that."

Tom went off to King's, glad that he had never felt
the necessity either to marry or to be particularly
healthy. Normally a conscientious teacher, he felt his
thoughts straying all that morning. It is said that one
cannot touch pitch and remain undefiled; but Tom, despite some ideas that had come to him unbidden, had

not felt the touch of defilement as yet. Cool, objective, he let his fancy play around the unspeakable, and was made uneasy only by an idea that his natural imagination wasn't unspeakable enough by half. He relied on Harold to make up this deficiency.

The Boultons lived, amid a tangle of children's toys, odd slippers, cats, rubber ducks and plastic chamber-pots, in an extremely fine house left to Zena by her father. "You can't possibly," she said, kicking something of vaguely disreputable appearance under the sofa, "have children and kittens *and* be smart. Do you know, there are so-called animal experts who recommend removing the cat's claws so that he *can't* tear the furniture? Good grief! Removing the poor brute's natural means of defense! Anyone who puts furniture before cats and children shouldn't be allowed to have either. Nor any furniture, come to that."

In all this clutter she remained a chic little woman, in feature not unlike George Richmond's drawing (the flattered one) of Charlotte Brontë, never a hair out of place, who rode life as easily as a young American mother. She never raised her voice to anybody, and never seemed tired at the end of the day. Vivacity she left to her husband. She herself was simply calm and nice.

After dinner, she said she was going to leave them to their dirty talk, since she had a dress to finish for one of the girls. "Also, I might inhibit you; that is, if Harold had some ideas which were simply too obscene. You might not like to air them in mixed company."

"Anyone who could shock Zena," Harold said, gazing after her, "should win some sort of enormous prize, like the Nobel. It is not that she doesn't understand things. She just lets them float around her, like the rings of

Saturn. I don't suppose Saturn notices his rings, do you? Now, then, to work. Protagonist: m. or f.?"

"Oh, m., I think," Tom said earnestly, "but of course not a hero. A reeking skunk."

"Of course."

"And not normal."

"That goes without saying," Harold said, a trifle reproachfully.

"But all the abnormals seem so normal these days. I mean, there isn't much left that's new. Havelock Ellis had a patient who fell in love with an undertaker at her father's funeral, and had to have the funeral ambiance whenever she made love. But that's tame, don't you think? Kid's stuff?"

Harold pondered. "There will be other people, of course? I mean, it won't be pre-Aeschylus?"

"Not unless we want to be boring *in toto*. But then, perhaps we do?"

"People seem to love being bored these days. It is something I simply cannot understand."

"We might have a dirty protagonist," said Tom simply, "with a dirty chorus, have the whole thing last twenty minutes and then play it through twice more, only with the words backwards."

"Hasn't something like that been done before—? Jimmy! Go back to bed at once!"

A little boy in an old-fashioned nightshirt, smelling sweetly of soap and Zena's scent, raced into the room screaming with glee, ran up and down with the speed of a mongoose and flung himself onto his father's chest.

"Ag-ag-ag-ag-daddy, silly old daddy!"

Harold picked him up, smacked him with moderation, put him outside the door and bolted it.

"We had to have bolts put on. Otherwise there

could be no conversation. You would think it might stop them having a happy childhood, but it doesn't. Now then. Where were we?"

Tom poured himself a drink. "I thought, the dominant m., interested in two other m.'s—"

"One of them black?"

"Isn't that," Tom said respectfully, as to a master with whom it is necessary to disagree, "out of date? Mind you, you're the authority."

"You may be right. Drugs? No, I hardly think that's necessary. Old hat, too. People doddering around after a fix, so dreary."

"And two females."

"One," said Harold, "is only twelve years old. The other?"

"I haven't got round to that."

Both of them seemed to be stuck.

They were, in fact, so stuck that the conversation drifted into other channels, till Zena came in with a plate of cheese tarts. "I've just made them. Eat them while they're hot. All going well?" She drifted out again, and they ate.

"She knows I love them," said Harold, "and she knows I belch. Ah—wait a minute! Do you remember my brother?"

"He was in the Far East somewhere, wasn't he?"

"He was a District Commissioner in Fiji. He used to try cases, as part of the job. There was a man and a goose."

For the first time, a faint color came into Tom's cheeks, perhaps as the result of excitement. It could hardly be called color: yet it made Tom look just a little fitter than usual. "I see."

"There would be something rather beautiful about

it, don't you think? The flutter of perfect whiteness—
Chinoiserie, almost—" Here, Harold looked just a little
soppy.

"In reported speech," said Tom.

"Not a bit of it! Right on the stage."

"But surely no one would ever allow—"

"Listen. Concentrate. Isn't that just the point?" A silence fell. Then the door heaved under the onslaught
of children. The windows rattled.

"Will you two get the hell out of it? Go to your
mother. Go to bed. If I have to come out to you—"

At last the susurration of retreat.

"I do smack them so that it hurts, sometimes," said
Harold. "It is necessary."

"A goose," said Tom. "Of course, sub-plots as well."

"First things first. Would his attitude towards the
goose be normal? Now, just suppose . . ."

Here Tom began to look healthier than ever. "Oh,
for Pete's sake—"

"You don't want the thing actually produced, do
you? I do wish you'd keep your eye on the ball. Still, I
shall have to think about that one further. I'll drop you
a line."

"I do wish you would. Will there be a ritual
murder?"

"Of the goose? Oh yes, but it will be a real one too.
You see, we could do that on the stage. I mean, it isn't
like human beings; I know actors need jobs, but you
wouldn't get a queue halfway down Wardour Street for
the privilege of playing a real victim. Not even for one
night of glory. Now, there are plenty of geese at Smith-
field, or somewhere of that order. Think of it! Blood
spurting all over the front row of the stalls—people
don't mind it at big fights, do they?"

Tom said firmly, "Look here, Harold. It would be damned cruel, and I like birds. I won't stand for that."

"Have you still not understood," Harold cried, his eyes sparkling, "that all this is never going to happen? That it isn't meant to? Old boy, you're being inconceivably obtuse."

"I do tend to forget. Sorry."

Tom pondered. Then he said, with some deference, "I suppose it couldn't be a drugged goose? A goose with a fix?"

Harold gave the matter thought. He said, in due time, like a Civil Servant announcing that something is entirely impossible, "No. I want to ruminate over my original idea."

Zena returned to spend the rest of the evening with them.

"All O.K. upstairs?" her husband asked.

"O.K. now. I did find Philip on the roof."

"That's all right. We've got netting right round it."

"It's only that he needs his sleep. Have you two finished being obscene?"

"For the moment, yes. There are points outstanding."

They spoke of her things until it was time for Tom to go.

The next day, when he had returned from King's and was putting his key in the lock, the door of the studio opened, and Duncan himself ushered out a young girl.

"Darling Pringle, you have been absolutely too wonderful, especially considering the fact that you don't like it one little bit. I am infinitely obliged to you, more than I can say. I'll get in touch."

The door closed. The girl glanced at it, then stamped her foot three times, like a toddler who has discovered the charm of stamping to relieve its overburdened feelings. She had not noticed Tom, who should have gone into his chambers but was halted by fascination.

He said, in his nervous way, "Are you upset?"

She peered at him first, then saw him.

"Who are you?"

"The next-door neighbor."

"Of *that* man's?"

He saw to his surprise that her neck was extremely dirty, but that this was not the cultivated dirt of advanced youth: she seemed, literally, to be smeared with mold.

"Forgive me. None of my business. But I do hate people being upset. I am sure poor old Duncan can't have upset you. He does like young women, but he always asks, and if they say no, then he never does."

"You don't understand! I am an author."

This seemed to him so odd a designation that he almost said, "Author of what?" as if she had meant, "the Universe": but his wits were sharper than that.

"It is quite customary for Duncan to photograph writers. He takes their photographs for nothing and then, if they're a success, he has them to sell to the papers. See? And he will give you a free one."

"But he doesn't photograph me as an author!"

"Sorry?"

"He photographs me as a face. Why am I talking to you, anyway? You know nothing about it."

"Of course I don't," said Tom, with all his reassuring limpness, "but I could learn. Do let me give you a drink. I will leave the door open all the time, if you like —all the doors."

She hesitated.

"Please do."

So she came in and accepted a sherry, which she drank standing just inside the hallway.

"You know him?" she asked suspiciously.

"I've known him for years."

"Is he on the straight?"

For some reason, he was shocked. "Entirely straight."

Shadows darkened behind her eyes, and she spoke with a touch of fear. "He has a whole ton of earth there, in a box. He got me into it, and put plastic gnomes all round me. He did it before, only then it didn't come right. And there's nowhere to wash properly."

Tom assured her that all this could only imply Duncan's aesthetic seriousness.

"But he hasn't read my book! He may pretend he has, but he hasn't. He keeps on talking about the brother, and there's nobody in it with a brother."

"Do introduce yourself. I'm Tom Hariot. I will read your book."

"Pringle Milton."

"I like that. But what has your book got to do with Duncan?"

She burst out, little pieces of mold falling from her neck as she did so, "I wouldn't mind, if he were photographing me *as* an author! One needs publicity, I see that. But he says I'm just a new face."

The bottleglass eyes widened as the pupils narrowed. Tom was hypnotized by them. He had not yet looked at her properly, but now he did so.

"A very nice new face."

"It might be better if he didn't drink! Do you think he could be cured?"

"Duncan is a hard drinker, not an alcoholic."

"You can't help pitying him, can you?" she asked unexpectedly. "He could be fab if he pulled himself together!"

Tom assured her, as well as he might, that Duncan was in no need of pity. He was most successful in his profession. He had never been known, in business hours, to behave himself unseemly.

At this she relaxed a little, and he observed with tenderness that she was slightly knock-kneed, as a child may be before it has learned the art of true balance. Her figure, though inclined to stockiness (the sweater may perhaps have been deceptive) would fine down during the next three years, and by the age of twenty she would have lost her desire to conform with what she took to be nonconformity. All would go well with her, the darling.

He was so startled by this last word, which had floated improbably into his mind, that he thanked her quickly for coming and hoped they might meet again.

"My book's called *The Sick Ones*, if you want to know," said Miss Milton, sounding shy.

"I shall buy it at once. Tomorrow."

"Make the man order it at that shop opposite, then. I do wish you would. That is, if you really mean to buy it at all. It costs eighteen shillings!"

"I will raise a mortgage," Tom assured her, shook her hand, put her outside and closed the door that had been open all the time.

Within a minute, there was a knock on it. He admitted her again.

She said hurriedly, "Look, you know him, you know if it's all right. The last three times, it was in a box of earth. Now he wants to do me as Millais's *Ophelia*, only he says he may have to get permission from the Marylebone Public Baths. Do you think that's all right?"

"I'm sure it is, but be sure not to catch cold, as she did. That is your sole risk. Anyway, you couldn't possibly be in danger at the Baths. There are all sorts of attendants in white ducks."

Now she had really gone, he pushed her out of his mind. He had work to do. He sat down at his typewriter, confronting the blank page, the red and black ribbon. It was necessary to put something down, no matter what. Were stage directions necessary nowadays? Weren't they the director's job? If so, it confronted him with the necessity of writing a line of dialogue. This, since no general scheme for the play, no definite characters, even, had been conceived, presented a difficulty which seemed insuperable. For a long time he sat with hanging head. Then an inspiration came to him, bright as the moon reflected suddenly in a midnight pond, and he set down the title—in caps, heavily underlined.

Afterwards, well-satisfied, he went out to dinner and to a cinema, and slept dreamlessly.

The morning's mail brought him a postcard from Harold.

"No. Its beak would be too hard."

6

CONTAINING AN ACCOUNT OF DOROTHY'S EXCITABIL-
ITY, THE REASON WHEREFORE, HER VIEWS UPON
THE SUBJECT OF BEING ANTI, AND THROWING
A NEW, PERHAPS NOT ALTOGETHER REASSURING,
LIGHT UPON HER HUSBAND, MR. COSMO HINES.

Dorothy was expansive, euphoria for the moment
overcoming her now habitual, and deepening, depression. She took her seat in the bookshop with the air,
both modest and righteous, of an M.P. who has just
overturned a majority of five thousand. She was polite
to Miss Few, who did not in the least care whether she
was or not, and decent to Pringle Milton who, between
spells of resentful posing for Duncan, had become an
habituée.

September had brought a nasty dampness to London, a dampness with an undercurrent of threat. It was
not cold now, but it was going to be: and Pringle was
glad of a roof over her head. She had, of course, her
own roof; with another girl, she shared a one-room flat
in Earl's Court: but she had almost exhausted the advance on her novel, and though she had a small allowance from her family and was now paid a fee by Duncan per sitting, these things did not enable her to live
in any sort of comfort. She was glad to be warm and
dry, and to accept from Miss Few, who had taken a
fancy to her, a surreptitious sandwich now and then.
Miss Few's fancy had gone so far as to persuade Cosmo
to let her order three more copies of Pringle's book, and

47

she herself had even contrived to sell one of them. Meanwhile, Pringle kept an eagle-eyed watch on the ones remaining, elated to heaven when a customer picked one up, dashed to the depths when he put it down again. Which invariably he did.

Dorothy had a reason for her new-found vigor. Yesterday she had finished typing her Anti-Verse play and had sent it by special messenger to the Director of the Royal Shakespeare Company. She was already casting it in her head, designing the sets. Now, seated beside the center table with Cosmo at her back, she held a little court, distributing her attentions between Pringle, Duncan, Breckenridge and a nameless young man with very narrow trousers and very long hair, as she might have distributed Maundy money to old-age pensioners.

"The question is, shall I appear in it myself? In *Joyful Matrix* I was projected onto a cinema screen, but that wouldn't do this time."

"You loomed, Dotty," said Duncan, "you simply loomed. You were unforgettable."

For the time being, they were more or less friendly again. Dorothy, like a good many bad-tempered people, was quick to forgive affronts, so that she could start giving and receiving them again. Also, she feared any diminishment of what she thought of as her Circle.

"Missed it," said Breckenridge regretfully, "I was in Aden."

"But—!" Dorothy's arm rose, and with it a monumental forefinger reminiscent of Brompton Cemetery —"Anti-Verse is a new form. It must be spoken with precision. And surely I, as the originator, am the one to do that?"

"It sounds m'hav'lous," said Pringle. "I do hope people won't suddenly turn Anti-Anti, though. I've often felt they might start to—you know what people are. It would be an awful shame for you."

Duncan looked at her, his eyes glowing, and seemed about to speak; but he did not.

Dorothy, struck with terror by the thought presented to her, took refuge in shouting. "You don't know what you're talking about, so don't talk!" Then she tried to pretend that this had been said in fun. "You mustn't be so naughty," she added, "trying to pull my leg."

"One never knows with trends," Pringle muttered obstinately. "I often think the trend had just changed when my book came out." Another idea struck her. "Perhaps it's going to be square to be Anti soon."

Duncan looked like the recipient of some golden annunciation. "Oh, Dotty! Suppose she's right? —It wouldn't affect *your* play, of course, but just suppose! And supposing I've been wrong all this time?"

"About what, may we ask?" said Cosmo, his mad eyes veiled.

"Why, about Pringle! Suppose earth-boxes and Ophelia are out?"

"I am not interested in—" Dorothy began.

"No, no, no, no. Do let me go on, just for the moment. Let me think aloud."

He yelled out, his body jerking though his feet did not leave the floor, "But that's it! *I'm* falling behind. I've got to find something new for you, sweetie—" he pinched Pringle's bottom "—and I will!"

"If you do that again, Mr. Moss, I'll never sit for you one more time."

"Duncan," said Dorothy, "do not be disgusting. And do not talk your shop in my shop."

"But look, you must see the point—I haven't sold one of her yet, and there's nothing wrong with the *face* so there must be something wrong with me. We've got to revive an image, I believe, perhaps something people have forgotten."

"J'know," said Breckenridge, who was quite quick in the uptake, "when I was a child I used to be fascinated by cats in mugs. Cat could just get inside, j'see? Nice little fluffy face, front paws too, sometimes." He could not know that by this speech he was to determine Pringle's whole life.

"By God," Duncan exclaimed, staring at him, "by God!" He looked at Pringle with the analytic awe of discovery.

"If you think I'm going in any tatty old mug—"

"With a little pink ribbon round your neck—"

She began to back away. He caught her wrist. "Oh, Pringle!" She took a smack at him. "Pringle, there's a wonderful chap who makes theater props, he's worked for me before—"

Dorothy was angry. This was her court, not his. "Look, Cosmo and I love you all, that goes without saying, and we adore the shop to be a Center, but we can't have it turned into a beargarden."

The young man with long hair said, in a high voice, "We're going to be Anti for ages. Why not, when life is?"

"Is Anti-what?" Breckenridge asked, in a spirit of genuine enquiry.

"Is Anti-Life."

"I see."

"That is true," Dorothy breathed, all her attention upon the newcomer, "it is entirely true. Forgive me, but do you write yourself?"

"No, I act."

"Oh, what can we see you in?" She clasped her hands.

There was a moment's pause. "Well, actually I'm in a musical show." He mentioned a cretinous one, which had already run for two years. "Not my line, but it's a stop-gap. One has to pay the rent."

"I saw that," said Breckenridge, with interest. "Which w'you?"

"Actually, I was one of the dancers."

"You dance!" Dorothy half rose from her seat. "In my play, there is a character who dances the Five Cruelties of Man. I wonder, just possibly, if you—"

Breckenridge asked which they were. He always enjoyed himself in Cork Street. The young man palpitated.

"Yes, you could!" Dorothy peered at him, narrowing her eyes to slits. "You're just the type. Write down your name for me, will you? And when we're casting—"

"I should be madly grateful, Miss Merlin."

"You should say, my dear," said Cosmo, " 'if we're casting.' You mustn't raise false hopes."

"Of course they'll be casting," Duncan said, "won't they, Dotty? And we'll all be there on the first night, clapping like crazy. Come on, Pringle, we've work to do. I want to measure you."

"Oh, Editha!" Miss Few ran out of the back room. "You've forgotten something."

"Thanks a lot." Pringle's hand closed on a packet of sandwiches, neatly parceled and cellotaped so as to look like a book. "Thanks ever so."

"What are the Five Cruelties of Man?" Breckenridge asked again, but got nobody's attention.

"Who is Editha, may we ask?" Dorothy demanded.

"I am," said Pringle defiantly, "and now you know why I won't have it on my novels."

"I can't blame you. Did you say novels? I thought there was only one—"

"On any novel I'm going to write."

"Come on, come on," Duncan said, and led her away.

The actor, seeing that the court was about to break up but not wishing yet to be turned away, bought a book he could not afford. "Miss Merlin, here's my card and I do hope you won't forget me."

"I never," she assured him heavily, "forget anybody. I shall be in touch with you. But do not expect too much. I might not feel you were right for the part, when the time came. I cannot guarantee that I should."

"No, no, of course you couldn't."

"You yourself might not *feel* it."

"It sounds just like Me." The actor was cautious, not wishing to overplay the hand which, poor chap, he fancied he held.

She gave him her quince-smile; it puckered and yellowed her, and did not make her look quite so gracious as she supposed. "Well, we shall see, shan't we? *Au revoir!*"

He was forced to leave. After chatting for a moment Breckenridge went too, plunging out after some friend he had spotted through the window.

"My dear," said Cosmo, "I do wish you would not count all your chickens so long before they are hatched. You're not fair to yourself. I've told you so before."

Her elation disappeared. Yes, she told him, that was just his way, wasn't it? To destroy her confidence? And why did he want to destroy it? Because he hated her fame, he wanted her only in the background, a tradesman like himself. She explained that her mother had always had a horror of marrying into trade—not because she was a snob, not that at all—but because trade stultified the entire personality. "You'd ruin me if you could. Oh, don't think I don't know! I remember you sniggering to yourself in Bruges that night, when that horrible man Skipton insulted me. *Don't* think I didn't see you, because I did!"

Miss Few brought them tea and biscuits. She caused a diversion by telling them that one of the packers had had a hemorrhage in the basement, but that she had tidied him up and the doctor was on the way.

"You are very good to us," said Cosmo, with the simplicity of a dear old parson receiving a parcel of groceries from a parishioner.

"Harmless and necessary," she replied.

"These people shouldn't come to work if they aren't feeling well," said Dorothy, "it's hard on all of us!"

"I'm sure he feels that," Miss Few said on her way out.

A small run of custom diverted Cosmo's attention for a while. When they were alone again he asked Dorothy when she was going to see her doctor.

"That man! I'm not. I didn't like him. His name is Hubble."

"There is no point in you making another change. Not unless you pick some back-street swindler who doesn't mind that shopping-list of yours."

"I don't want a doctor."

"In that case," Cosmo said, "I have done all I can."

"So that's all you care about me!"

"Yes," he said, bending over and looking straight into her face, his nose no more than three inches from her own, "that is all I care."

She stared at him, shocked. She fumbled with her fingertips round the edge of the chair as if afraid she might fall off it.

Cosmo smiled in silence. Then he put out a teasing finger and tickled her just below the ear, very gently.

"Oh, you are a damned fool," Dorothy said, relaxing. "Why do you say that's all you care for me when you *know* it's not?"

7

IN WHICH PRINGLE FINDS FAME AND BE-
LIEVES HERSELF RUINED, RAISES HER
HAND TO DUNCAN MOSS AND MAKES A
CONFESSION OF LOVE FOR A STRANGER.

Duncan stood enraptured. Pringle stood almost crying with rage. He had, upon information received, whipped her down in a cab to the Victoria and Albert Museum: on a billboard over the way, the paste still damp upon it, was the first public showing of his photograph, enormously blown up into a poster advertising milk. It was very simple. In the middle of an expanse of whiteness, which could have been curds and whey, or cirrus clouds, floated a great silver mug, out of which projected the cat-like head of Pringle. All was in monochrome except for the icing-pink ribbon tied around her neck and made into a smart bow under her left ear. However desperate she may have felt when the photograph was taken, however sunken in shame, here she did not look desperate at all. She looked like a small, calm, exquisite cat who had just finished licking its whiskers and was proposing to fall, after one single blink at a passing bird, into cream-fed sleep. The huge eyes, ferned about with pale, thick lashes, were wide open, pupils contracted, irises luminous. Duncan had managed to give, to the fine hair chopped short and uneven, a suggestion of delicate furriness, as if it had been a kitten's. The whole effect was ridiculous, touching, a little disquieting and curiously beautiful. He had wanted to give just an overtone of Max Ernst, and he had done it.

"God," he cried, "God!"

She turned on him. "Everyone will see it! Everyone will know!"

"That's the point, my pet."

"I can never hold up my head again."

"Oh yes, you will, dozens of times," said Duncan, his mind not upon her.

"I shall never be taken seriously as a writer, never!"

"Come, come. You're going to be taken seriously as a Face."

A little knot of people had collected, to stare up at the hoarding. There were smiles, giggles, murmurs of admiration.

"If I wrote *War and Peace* tomorrow, I'd get no respect! You've ruined me. I don't know why I ever let you do it!"

"I'm sure they'd respect anyone who wrote *War and Peace*. Of course they would. Don't fret."

"Suppose people had seen Tolstoy in a mug?" Pringle cried. She was not a very humorous girl.

"Times have changed. Nobody now would think anything of it. Faces are the thing."

"Not if Tolstoy had been plastered all over Russia in a mug!"

"Do stop carrying on about Tolstoy, pet. I want to drink it in. It's my masterpiece. God!"

She saw a 74 bus and ran for it, leaving him standing there. He did not even notice that she had gone. "I assure you," he murmured, to the space she had occupied, "that there's no need for you to worry. You write a really good book and no one will care about the mug.

If Tolstoy could have got away with it, as we agreed, so can you— Oh, you're not there. Sorry."

When he had stared his fill, he went into a pub and drank three double whiskies in a row, drank to the opening rose of the future. Then he drank two pints of beer.

It was a glorious October day, the leaves clattering together like pieces of eight against a sky of exhilarating blue. He walked for a while, as far as the terraced pavement opposite Harrods, which was said to be the site of one of the plague-pits. Above these forgotten graves the tall, smart women darted like swallows, in and out of the shops, and back and forth across the road. Harrods itself, that strange baroque pile, had caught from the sun the color which suited it best, glowing in orange and burnt sienna where no shadows fell, and burning slow violet where they did.

Duncan was swaying a little, but not much. He was very happy. Further on, he caught sight of yet another Pringle poster and he began to sing quietly to himself.

> Kitty, my love, will you marry me,
> Kitty, my love, will you go? O
> Kitty, my love, will you marry me?
> Either say yes or say no. . . .

Such a jolly, innocent, pure little song, pure as his photograph minus the Ernst overtones, pure as the sky, jolly and pure as life itself was going to be from now on. "Kitty, my love, will you marry me—" Not that he was going to marry Pringle. But, by God, thousands of people were going to want to do just that. He had made the girl, bless her.

It was characteristic of Duncan that he gave not a single thought to her present ingratitude, nor would he think a jot the worse of her if she went on being un-grateful. He was happy for himself and happy for her.

He hailed a taxi. He meant to go round to Earl's Court and see what he could do about putting her under contract.

She was not in. She was walking the streets in distraction, the rumblings of her stomach unheeded. The collar of her white mackintosh was pulled up as far as it would go to conceal the lower part of her face. In tartan stockings (Royal Stewart) and buckled shoes, she tramped on, flinching in something like terror whenever a new Pringle flashed into sight, complacent above the silly pink bow. Hardly knowing what she did, she went into a bookshop and wandered round the shelves, impelled by habit to look for a copy of her book. In a corner she saw one, gathering dust, and she picked it up as if it were an amulet which might give her comfort, or a baby stolen by some childless one from a luckier woman's perambulator.

An assistant, a girl, came to her. Could she help?

"No," Pringle whispered, "no, thank you."

Then:

"Oh, oh, oh! Oh please, may I have your autograph? Wait till I get a bit of paper!"

Pringle's head shot out from the mackintosh like the head of a tortoise from its shell. Her heart began to thump.

"Of course," she said. "I'll be thrilled! Did you like my book?"

"Book?"

Pringle patted it. "This book."

"What book?"

"You don't know who I am!" Pringle cried. "Then why do you want—?"

"I do know, of course I know. You're the cat-girl, I recognized you at once! Please may I have your autograph?"

Pringle gave her one horrified glare, then raced out of the shop.

The assistant stared after her. She muttered, "Do you *mind*? You stuck-up little bitch. . . ."

So, like an escaped prisoner who can find shelter nowhere but at home, while knowing that at home the sagacious police will be waiting for him, Pringle returned to her flat and there, of course, she found Duncan, propped boozily against the doorpost.

He had taken the precaution of bringing a bottle of whiskey with him, and when he had persuaded her, by dint of something like violence, to admit him into her terrible room, decorated with "sick" birthday cards and reproductions of Picasso from one of the Sunday color supplements, he made her drink with him. She would not, however, agree to anything contractual, but, weakened by misery and unaccustomed liquor on an empty stomach, began in a maudlin way to chide him for his bad habits.

"I wouldn't so much care what you did to me, how you ruined my life, if only you'd pull yourself together. You could be so sweet, if only you wouldn't soak. Do try for me—please try for me. Don't do it!" She had him on the edge of the bed, which pretended to be a divan, and tried to cradle him in her arms. "Oh, Duncan, you're an important man, everyone knows about you, and just look at you!"

"It's a dear, dear girl," he replied slushily, "but it mustn't be a great big bore. I'm too old to change my ways."

"You're not old!" Pringle released him so suddenly

59

from her embrace that he fell over backwards and hit his head on the wall. "Sometimes you look just like a little boy. A sweet, silly little boy. Why have you got to be a bad little boy too?"

"You hurt my head."

"No, I didn't."

"How do you know?"

"You did it yourself because you drink too much."

"If you really want to know," Duncan said, the blow having sobered him, "you're only behaving like this because you're tight yourself. Not that the fact fills me with moral indignation. Come on, Pringle, snap out of it. I want to make an arrangement with you so that we both profit—"

"I won't make any arrangement. I never want to see you again."

She began to hit at him feebly.

"You stop that, or I'll photograph you in a pot next time!"

Pringle slapped his face. Hard.

At that moment the door opened, and Miss Few came in. This was not so surprising, since she lived with her lover in a very pleasant flat two squares away, and on her afternoon off would not infrequently visit Pringle, bearing a meat pie, a cake, a tin of fruit.

"What has Mr. Moss being doing to you, Editha? —Good-afternoon," she said to Duncan politely.

"Nothing. Not in that way."

"Oh, didn't I? She was being such a little beast that I said if she didn't stop I'd photograph her in a—"

Pringle raised her hand again and he rubbed his cheek in a surly way, though he was not really hurt. He was too well-cushioned by flesh to bruise easily.

"In that case," Miss Few continued, "you seem to be behaving in a very uncontrolled manner."

Pringle hung her head. She mumbled, "You've seen those things. You know what he's done to me."

"What things?"

"Those milk posters."

Miss Few had not noticed them. A busy-minded woman, she was usually unconscious of her own surroundings in their physical aspect, which was why she had endured so many years of Dorothy. On being told that Duncan had wrecked Pringle's literary career and ruined her whole life, she merely remarked that this career hardly existed as yet, and that life was long. She turned to Duncan, who was swaying again.

"Mr. Moss, you seem to be sleepy. If I were you, I'd go home and have a good nap."

He thought it best to agree with her. He had had a wonderful triumph and wanted to think about it quietly, sucking at the idea as if it were a great, sweet gob-stopper.

When he had gone, Miss Few said, "I don't think he was making love to you."

"Certainly not. And if he tried, I wouldn't have it. I don't feel like that about him at all."

"Who do you feel like that about?"

"Somebody you don't know. A man I only met for a few minutes. And now he'll despise me, everyone will. I can never hold up my head again."

"These are chicken patties, Editha, and they're still warm. Please to eat them."

"Thank you, Mildred."

8

TOM GIVES A LITTLE PARTY,
AT WHICH THE CONVERSATION
IS OF A PHILOSOPHIC NATURE.

Tom Hariot, waiting on the tube platform for his homeward train, and finding himself confronted by an enormous representation of Pringle in her mug, caught himself thinking, Ah, there she is, the darling, and decided to ask her in for a drink. Still, because *l'amour courtois* was in his make-up but not *l'amour* of any more trenchant variety, he decided to ask Cosmo, Dorothy and Duncan too. He had finished Act II of his play and he needed to celebrate. He fixed this modest roistering for the Wednesday of that week, left a note for the Hineses at the bookshop and for Duncan and his model at the studio. As an afterthought, he invited Harold and Zena, though he knew that only Harold was likely to come.

What he did not realize was that in the past three weeks Pringle had become famous, and that if she had not been shy enough (and haughty enough) to detest the manner of her fame, she would have been in the process of becoming rich. She was so sought after as a model that Duncan was only just managing to keep a grip on her, and could do so merely because she preferred to live on what he paid her, while she grimly wrote away with signal rapidity at a new novel, rather than enter further into a world which, she believed, not only despised her brains but made fun of her face.

She had been offered three film tests, by directors planning stories about abortion in Newcastle, miscegenation in Liverpool and lesbianism in Salford. Manufacturers of cosmetics, chocolates, laxatives, hot drinks at bedtime, were prepared to overwhelm her with bounties. She had a growing fan-mail, most of it from old gentlemen and schoolgirls, and replied conscientiously with stiff little notes like those children write under compulsion on Boxing Day. She hated to use the public transport, since people stared, muttered, and finally cried—"The milk girl!" and, since she did not believe in taxis, preferred to walk from Earl's Court to Cork Street rather than expose herself to the humiliation of the one, or the corruption of the other. All she cared about was the novel: and when a newspaper which had got wind of it headed its gossip column with "Intellectual Milk Girl," she cried all night.

The book was called *The Cruel Ones*, and was about deprived boys, motherless, who had failed the Eleven Plus, were earning from twelve to fifteen pounds a week, and were protesting against life in general by beating up elderly persons. Such young men Pringle had never met, but she believed in them as she did not believe in lords, taxis or God. It was an article of faith with her that people who behaved in a beastly manner, with a total lack of feeling except for themselves (for themselves they inevitably felt with crooning passion), only needed loving: and she never considered the fact that the loving person would be as likely to be left in the gutter with a kick in the groin as anybody else. More likely, perhaps, since this would be more fun.

One change only had come over her, and that as a result of Duncan's pressure. She was no longer wearing the furry sweater, the tartan skirt and stockings. Cunningly, he had suggested to her that if she altered her mode of dress, she would be less likely to be recognized. (The fact that only her face was recognizable had somehow escaped her, since she was a nice girl but obtuse.) He had decided upon a new style for her, and had persuaded her to adopt it. She was to have a special image, and was on no account to depart from it. So now she wore straight dresses, rather long, either of black or mulberry, with high necks, long sleeves and no ornaments of any kind. She wore nylon stockings and flat black shoes with crossed elastic, like those popular at infant dancing-classes forty years ago.

Tom, opening the door to her, automatically thought —Ah, there she is, the darling! and noted a great improvement.

"Here she is, the darling!" Duncan cried, like a jovial Frankenstein presenting his monster.

She looked at Tom and gasped.

"I'm afraid there are quite a lot of stairs," he said apologetically, "and awfully steep ones. Do come on in."

Harold, who was there already, greeted Pringle out of the delicacy of his heart. "I did enjoy your book," he said, "my wife and I kept snatching it away from each other." He had not been told about her hatred of her new fame: he simply assumed that anyone who wrote novels would rather be praised for these than for personal appearance, unless they were really successful novelists, in which case the converse would certainly be true.

"Oh, thanks," said Pringle, looking piteously grateful, "I'm so glad. I'm working on another." She had adopted the American usage "working on," as if writing a novel were something like hacking out chunks of Portland stone. It was a phrase calculated to bring the novelist awestricken respect, the kind of respect one might give to Sisyphus or to Atlas himself.

She accepted a glass vaguely, and Tom led her to an armchair, putting a little table at her side, a cushion at her back, a stool at her feet.

"This is fab," she said.

"No," said Duncan, "no, Pringle sweetie, not any more."

She said resentfully, "You know what I mean."

"We ought to drink to work in progress!" cried Harold, with a Pickwickian sparkle.

"So we shall," said Tom, "but we are also going to drink to the completion of Act II. My Act II."

Tottering excitedly across to his desk, he picked up the typescript and waved it at them. Harold cheered.

"It is almost inconceivably nasty," Tom said simply, "and Act III will be worse. Also, it is quite a neat job of work."

He did not quite realize what he was saying, for the corruption of literary pride had touched him. It should not have been neat at all: it should have been totally incoherent. But this, to the credit of his intellect, he was later to perceive and to remedy.

Duncan, of course, knew about the project and had explained it to Pringle, who was bewildered. Her gaze did not leave Tom's gentle lips.

"Have you got all the important words in?" Harold asked.

"Well, there are really only four major ones. It is a great mistake to assume that the English language is peculiarly rich in obscenity. There is, of course, a good deal of infantile scatology, and it is not without interest that the largest *single* grouping of words refers to the buttocks. But that is a somewhat nursery outlook, don't you think?"

Insensibly, he had fallen into his lecture-room manner, which was modest, easy and precise.

"Still," said Harold, "you have done your best? To be compendious, I mean."

"I have done my best."

"I just don't understand," said Pringle. "Duncan says you don't want your play to go on."

"I am making it impossible for it to go on."

"Oh. Then why—?"

She is a darling, he thought, and so very dense.

"I am attempting to prove that there is always a line that can be drawn, and will be drawn: I shall leave it to others to prove just where it shall be drawn."

Dorothy and Cosmo came in, Cosmo affable, Dorothy greeting everyone with an air of impatient contempt. She was carrying a stone of rage in her soul, since her own play had, that very morning, been rejected by the Royal Shakespeare Company.

"No, I *don't* know Mr. Boulton," she snapped, by her emphasis giving the impression that she never intended to, if she could help it. "Duncan, you might bring my ledger back! I've asked you again and again. Pringle, your feet are in the way. Please remove them."

Tom made a comfortable ensconcement of Dorothy, who refused anything to drink. "No thanks. I don't feel like it."

"And I," said Cosmo, "feel like a beautiful, long, clear, foaming lager."

"I'm so sorry, I'm afraid I haven't got—"

"Why don't you look, Cosmo?" Dorothy demanded.

"All you do is embarrass people. It only needs a little care, a little forethought—"

His stony gaze rested upon her face; precisely, upon the bridge of her nose. It is said to be dangerous to look a dog between the eyes, but Cosmo's method silenced his wife. "That was mere hyperbole," he told Tom, "gin will do splendidly."

"No," said Duncan, squatting at her side, "you can't deceive me. Darling Dotty is cross. Aren't you cross, Dotty? Tell us what it is."

"I am not cross. I am just a little sickened by human stupidity." Relaxing, she permitted herself a deep sigh and the half of a sweet smile. "But let it go. I prefer not to talk about it."

"Dorothy's play," said Cosmo, with a single demoniac gleam, "has not been preferred. That is, it has not found favor in the eyes of the Royal Shakespeare Company."

"Terribly sorry," said Harold. "But things can be very chancy there, or so I am told." He had been told nothing of the sort. He was just trying to be kind.

"My dear Mr. Boulton," Dorothy said, swinging gently round upon him, "I'm afraid you don't understand at all. That they should reject my play, as such, is a matter of no moment. But I am angry because I can see where their policy is leading!"

"I'm sure you are, Dotty." Duncan patted her knee.

"It is not on my own account that I am angry!"

"I'm sure it's not. Nobody even thought so for a minute."

"I am angry because *they are losing the spirit of innovation.*"

"I said it was going to be Anti to be Anti," Pringle murmured, meaning no harm.

"It is not that at all!" Dorothy flared at her. "Anyway, how on earth should you know?"

Pringle mistook this for a prelude to the mention of mugs.

"Well, I am a writer! People forget that!"

Dorothy's eyes glowed. She had not intended to attack Pringle, but now her intention had changed. Dorothy, though ridiculous to the eyes of many, was not ridiculous to herself. She had believed in her play, and was wounded to the heart. She was an animal in pain, and ridiculous animals are no less capable of suffering than animals with the proper amount of *gravitas*. "Well, we're invited to forget it, aren't we? On every boarding in London."

Pringle burst into tears.

Tom said, as host, "Pringle, please stop. And Dorothy, that was a sore spot, though you couldn't have known it. You are much too nice for that. Please have a drink now, because you'd feel better if you did, and Pringle, you are showing too great an excess of sensibility."

This struck everyone silent, as he had meant that it should. "As a matter of fact," he said, "when Cosmo and Dorothy came in, we were talking about my play. Do indulge me by letting us go on."

Pringle looked at him with the damp-seaweed eyes of adoration. "Sorry," she said.

"My God," Duncan whispered to Harold, "I think we all feel disciplined, don't we?"

"The old boy is like that," Harold whispered in reply. "He is consistently underestimated."

"What play?" said Dorothy, smoldering. "Oh, your experimental one. Duncan told me. If you want to know, I think it's all a waste of time. And furthermore, it looks like an attack on total literary freedom."

"You are a clever sweetie, you know," said Duncan, "because that's precisely what it is."

Dorothy reared up, lifting herself, by the force of tantrums, at least a quarter of an inch from the seat of her chair.

"You are supporting censorship? Don't you realize that so long as there is any censorship whatsoever, of any kind, of anything, art can never be really *true?*"

Tom sat on the arm of Pringle's chair, causing her to quiver.

"Dorothy, you would not ask me whether I supported the sun or moon, because they are simply there. I neither support nor withhold support from censorship of the arts; that would be a waste of time, because it is there. That is the point I am making."

"It is a point, you know," Cosmo said, pouring himself another gin.

"I don't see it. Do you see it, Duncan? Don't pretend you do when you know you don't!"

Duncan sat at Pringle's feet and leaned an arm across her knee. The men, quite unconsciously, were bestowing upon her that appearance of an object of admiration to which fame had given her due, and she did not notice. At least, she did not notice Duncan. Dorothy, herself accustomed to the goddess-position, was angrier than ever. Harold, perceiving this, quickly went to sit at her feet, but she pushed at him and said he was crowding her in.

"Let me explain," said Tom. "For years past, people have been arguing from a false position. They are arguing for the total abolition of censorship. That makes no

sense, since it is impossible for it to be abolished totally. The real question to be asked is this: On what
line of rear guard shall censorship halt?"

Dorothy screamed out, long before the party had
reached screaming-point, and thus giving her usual impression of isolation from her fellows, that there was no
need for it to halt and no need for it to exist.

"Come now," said Tom, "I shall give you an example. We have seen the breaking of wind on the stage—
symbolized, of course, since it is probably beyond the
powers of any actor, however devoted, to achieve real-
ism in this respect. We have seen people being, or pretending to be, sick. I dare say it would be acceptable if
they really were sick, if their backs were to the audience
or the light wasn't too bright. It is obvious that we have
ritual murders on the stage because, as I once explained
to Harold here, even the most ambitious of actors
would scarcely clamor for the role of victim. So far, so
good."

"I don't see what's good," said Dorothy. "All that
has nothing to do with censorship. It's just what *people*
will refuse to do."

Duncan scrambled over and hugged her. "Darling
Dotty, always right on the ball. I knew you would
be."

"No," said Tom, "all that has not. But I *think* you
are never going to see a real"—here his color deepened
a little and did not appear to fade again—"er, act of
copulation on the stage."

Dorothy, remembering a certain "spectacle" at which
she and Cosmo and Duncan had assisted in Belgium,
some years ago, forgot herself sufficiently to say she
hoped not.

"You hope not?" Tom could never have been described as pouncing, but he did seem to alight on her with the firmness of a bird upon a bough.

"I didn't mean that. I only meant, there ought to be *no* censorship. People can always stay away."

"People so often do, Mrs. Hines," said Harold, "which is why the theater is not in too good a shape. But, of course, they often stay away because they are bored silly."

"Only the stupid are ever bored," said Dorothy majestically.

"Dotty," said Duncan, "you're so wrong. You'd be surprised how often I am."

She hushed him with a wave of the hand.

"It is terrible," said Harold, "to be faced with the alternative either of being bored silly, or of having to pretend to be shocked." He took from his pocket a clipping from one of the Sunday papers and read it to them. " 'An epic farce about test-tubes, the fear of illness and the castration complex—epic in Brecht's sense, meaning that the human being is an object of enquiry instead of being taken for granted . . . a giant lunge in the right direction.' " He added, apologetically, "I didn't see it, I'm afraid. I expect it was excellent. But the description deterred me."

Dorothy said that everyone was off the point, nobody was talking sense, her question still hadn't been answered.

"I'm not sure I know which question." Tom smiled at her, and Pringle fondly moped at the back of his long, narrow head. "But if you will allow me to be crude, I will make one, to me cardinal, point, just for the sake of example. You are never going to see the act of defecation upon a public stage. I do not mean horses. That has happened."

"Don't be foul!" said Dorothy, and he begged her pardon.

"But do you think it could ever be permitted?" He was persistent.

"At a small theater, in Hamburg," she retorted, "I believe there was a quite stupefying set, with an enormous violet toilet-bowl—"

"Genteel," said Cosmo, "my dear, you are too genteel."

"—reaching right up into the flies, and the idea was that there were pitiful little men (dwarfed by life, was the idea) trying all the time to climb it, and falling back, and back—"

"I was not speaking of symbolic representation," said Tom. "I meant precisely what I said. Can you, any of you, foresee a censorship that would allow it, or a state of things whereby there was no censorship and it would be allowed?"

There was silence, since nobody could.

Pringle said, "You would have to rely on people's good taste."

They turned to her, all but Dorothy delighted that she should have had a contribution to make.

"Is there the faintest evidence," said Harold, "that one could? The capacity for old nonsense of people in the arts seems to me quite limitless. And most of them, while devoted to the Absurd, have long failed to recognize absurdity, with a small 'a,' when they see it."

Dorothy rose. "Well, good people, I'm going home. I don't think anything profitable is coming from all this, and I've had a hard day." She sighed, and looked down her little length as from the heights of Helicon. The men jumped up. "I don't understand what you're getting at, but I must say it seems desperately reactionary. And time-wasting."

"But it is his own time, isn't it, my dear?" Cosmo took her arm gently. "Thank you so much, Tom. It has been a pleasant evening."

"I say," Dorothy shouted back over her shoulder as she was halfway through the door, "you *are* going to let me read it?"

When she had gone, Tom refilled glasses.

"So you see."

"Dotty's not quite such an old sweetie as she used to be," Duncan observed. "It is such a pity. What do we see?"

"You see the hopelessness," said Tom, "of me trying to convince anyone of anything. I am not reactionary. I do not wish to tighten the censorship, or to do anything about it at all. It is not merely a necessity, it does and must exist in some shape or form, like the sun and moon. It is of no importance who exercises it, the Lord Chamberlain or anyone else. For myself, I should favor a Court of Appeal. But remember: such courts don't only exist to lift the foot up, but also to put it down. No. I only want people to think about where the line that must be drawn is to be drawn. It is so much more productive a line of thought than the present one." He hesitated, then went on: "I might give you the example of the four-minute mile. Now somebody has done it in less time. Somebody will do it in less time still. But nobody is ever going to run the mile in no minutes at all: so we shall be bound to find a stopping-place, and that for good and all."

"I'm longing to see your play, at all events," Duncan said. "But now I'm going to take Pringle for a light meal at Claridge's, where no one will recognize her, or if they did, would never dream of showing it."

"I don't want to go to Claridge's. I don't believe—"

"You will believe in it when you get there."

She looked wistfully at Tom, hoping he might offer to come also, but he did not. When they had gone, he and Harold went in the blue of the evening to the pub on the corner of Stafford Street.

"That girl is staggering," Harold said, "and she's in love with you."

"Is she? I don't think so. I say, ring me up when you've read it."

"The goose is there?"

"Certainly."

"And all the words?"

"Most of them. They look very tedious on paper. They seem so unoriginal by this time."

"It's cruel, isn't it?"

"Revoltingly."

"And Absurd?"

"I can't beat the masters at that. But I've tried. How are the children?"

"Ah," said Harold lovingly, "you may well ask. One of them put the sleeve of my best shirt, with a cucumber in it, through the wringer. Most ingenious."

"I could put that in the play, do you think?"

"As Cruelty, or Absurdity?"

"What about putting a shirt with a human arm in it through a wringer?"

"You might try, though it's a little Jacobean. I'm glad the children are of some use in the world."

"One of my characters gets his finger stuck in his ear and can't pull it out."

Harold said it all sounded most promising. "By the by, what is your title?"

"Oh, that came easily. A *Potted Shrimp*."

"Do you fancy," Harold said, a touch of reverence in his light tenor voice, "*Potted Shrimp 614*? Numbers are rather the thing."

Tom replied, "No, I don't think so. It is always a mistake to overdo things. Or so I believe."

9

IN WHICH WE LEARN SOMETHING OF
OLD FRIENDS, AND OF THE BALZAC
OF MR. MATTHEW PRYAR, WHO FINDS
HIMSELF IN A DELICATE POSITION.

Despite stabilizers, the ship was rolling heavily,
but Matthew Pryar and his wife Jane, both good sailors,
found comfort in the lounge, listening to the *Pastoral
Symphony*, which was being relayed through the loud
speakers, and which brought into harmony with itself
the suck and swell of the waves. Pale-blue cushions,
veneered wood, heraldic inlays, surrounded them. It
could have been any expensive hotel anywhere, except
for the plunging of the sea beneath them.

Both attended the hour of classical music whenever
they were up in time. They lay back in deep chairs, the
coffee before them sloshing gently in the cups, in
rhythm with the creaking of the ship. On their knees
were books from the library: they were reading Balzac.

Now it is a curious thing that Matthew, having been
saved from a feeble fling at academic life by the inter-
vention of Mrs. Merle, who married him, had suddenly
acquired a wistful longing to be learned after all. He
had always danced lightly round the fringes of literature, publishing in smart periodicals little essays on persons with only a very small output of work; this had
seemed to him a perfectly satisfactory way of proving
himself. Mrs. Merle, however, had been one of the
richest widows in America, and Matthew, though never

poor himself, had felt a little more oppressed by it all than he had ever expected to be. Not that he would have had things otherwise. He was exceedingly happy, and so was she.

He was fifty-seven and looked forty-five: Jane, some years his senior, looked much the same. Her small, diamond-pointed face was scarcely lined, her triangular eyes were still as dazzling, her fair hair only a little more fair, where, with charming effect, she brushed the white into the gold. Her figure was still trim (though this had taken a lot of hard work), her carriage still erect, almost military. Her voice still rang out with the clarity of a bugle over a parade-ground. Balenciaga dressed her for the evenings, Dessès for daytime. She was an amusing, easy-going companion (as for living, she expected her servants to do that for her), undemanding except in one respect, and this had surprised Matthew. She still made him go to bed with her once a week, on the grounds that it was good exercise. It was something of an effort for him, as he had never made love very frequently: but he could not pretend the idea was unsuccessful. Furthermore, she had encouraged him to do quite well.

Yet he wanted to be learned: he wanted to feel himself a solid citizen in the world of the intellect. He had never had the slightest impulse to be so before, but now it was gaining upon him.

"There are many people on board who must be very sick-sick this morning," said Jane comfortably, as "Glad and Grateful Feelings after the Storm" came to an end, and they waited for the opening bars of a Vivaldi oboe concerto. "I'm afraid the thought adds to one's own enjoyment."

An elderly woman nearby, who had stuck it out this

far, rose hastily and scuttled for sanctuary. Matthew rose to assist her from the lounge and place her in more professional hands.

"That was horrid of me, Matt-Matt," Jane said, when he skidded back to his chair.

He smiled at her fondly and picked up *La Rabouilleuse*, which he had been reading.

"How would you translate that?" she asked him. "The preface said it couldn't be done."

"I'd call it *The Troubler of the Waters*."

"How nice, and how appropriate for the day."

At that moment the ship shuddered and lurched, and a steward carrying a tray foundered with a crash of glass.

"Oops!" he said, self-rebuking, "there goes my reputation. Bit choppy today, Mr. Pryar."

"I shall win the ship's auction tonight," said Jane. "I think we shall make precisely one and a quarter seamiles by midnight, at this rate. You've slowed down again in the last half-hour."

"Oh, come, come, never say die!" The steward swept up such glass as he could and lurched away again.

The Vivaldi had begun, but they went on talking.

"Balzac is a very great man," Matthew said. "He writes so well about people who would be just like you and me if we were worse people. His only mistake is to think that all people know how wicked they are."

"He is rather chilly," said Jane, always willing to encourage her husband in his fancies. "Did you see that horrible bit in *Le Cabinet des Antiques*?" Both religiously used the French titles, though neither of them was really up to reading Balzac with facility except in English. "The bit about Diane and Victurnien—'They went through their romance in advance? His marriages are all quite dreadful. Except for that girl Ursule somebody."

"I shall prate about him in England. It will be good for my old friends to hear some prating about a writer who really needs working at. Most people shy at his surface, Jane, because though it is often wonderful, it is quite as often silly, and they don't see that underneath, it goes deep as this—Jane, I have to say it—this really rather unpleasant sea. It makes great *cathédrale engloutie* boomings about the truth."

Jane repeated Pilate's perfectly sensible question.

"Oh, the truth is that the world is a great working ant-hill," Matthew said seriously, with a wave of the hand, "not a great disorganized mess. That is not to say, of course, that it is a nice ant-hill. I would never say anything of the kind."

"I think I should have left you at Cobb. You would have changed the face of the campus. You are not going to be sick, are you?"

"Certainly not. And I didn't want Cobb, I wanted you. By the way, they still haven't got an inn."

It had been Matthew's aim to induce the college to build one.

"I never supposed they would have. And since I gave them my money for no other purpose, it must be simply swelling up in the bank like a sort of boil. How dull!"

"Balzac," said Matthew, reverting to his first train of thought, "isn't a writer's writer. He is read by the people he writes about. Not that that is an original reflection, but when I talk to my old friends I shall pretend it is."

"Matt-Matt," Jane said slowly, "you seem to have these old friends much on your mind. May I ask who they are?"

He flushed. He had some news to break to her which he fancied she might not like. It was her pleasure, when they went together to Europe, to leave the fixing of accommodation to him, and she usually managed to look child-like and dewy with pleasure at whatever arrangements he achieved. This time she had suggested that they might take a service flat in London for the month they were to be there, and he had met her wishes. But he had as yet given her no details and Jane, who loved surprises, had not asked him for any.

"Oh—any old friends. You know how it is."

"You are not, by any chance—perhaps feeling much water has flown under the bridges—suggesting that I meet Miss Merlin?"

"Look, Jane—"

The ship went down with a huge lurch, appeared to spin at the bottom of the vortex, then slowly heaved itself back into position.

"—you know perfectly well that I have never forced anyone on you. And Dorothy is awful."

"But you have gone a bright pink, just like one of those nice geraniums we planted round the squash-court last year. So I know you are guilty about something."

Matthew called the returning steward, and asked for two large Scotches.

"I will have Bitter Lemon," said Jane, "as I'm in no need of stimulation, so that will be one large Scotch. Now then, Matt, out with it."

At the sound of her military rasp, his heart sank.

"Well, Jane, I have got a terribly nice apartment for

us. I got it through ———." He mentioned a rich friend of theirs, who lived between London and Florida. He described its glories.

Jane's eyes, bright as her own aquamarines, sprayed a minatory light upon him. "It sounds perfect. Where is the snag?"

"There isn't a snag. Only—"

"Out with it."

"It's in Cork Street."

"Good God," said Jane, "great God! Right on top of that dreadful crowd of yours—"

"We needn't see them. We can just slink by."

She looked quite angry. "Matt, when did you ever know me to slink?"

"It's such a terrific apartment," he murmured. "Jane, I am not sure I shall want very much in the way of lunch. After all, I had an enormous breakfast—"

"You will eat," she cried, stentorian above the oboes and the waves, "a perfectly normal meal, and if it upsets you, it will not be because the sea is rough but because you have a bad conscience. I shall not pity you at all."

"Perhaps we can cancel the flat. We could go to the Connaught."

"We will not cancel anything. If you have made our bed we shall lie on it, even if it is in the middle of a nest of vipers."

"You'll like Tom Hariot," said Matthew, "he's not one of that crowd. And Duncan's not too bad."

"If you mean that stout boy Moss, he took an absurdly *kitsch* photograph of me once. I refused to use it."

"Oh, dear."

"I shall bear it all," said Jane, "but do not ask me to

entertain Miss Merlin. I may have to meet her, since we shall be cheek by jowl—what a repellent thought—in the same street. And," she added thoughtfully, "I have to say, in justice to you, that she might be something of an experience."

He looked at her gratefully. The concerto came to an end. There was no sound now but the creaking of the ship, the muted roar of the tumultuous sea, the snoring of an old manufacturer of vermicelli fast asleep behind a newspaper two days old.

"Read your nice book-book," said Jane.

10

DOROTHY GETS HER OWN WAY, AND
ENTRAPS AN OLD ACQUAINTANCE.

Cosmo would never have yielded to his wife's demands that she should give a poetry-reading in Cork
Street, but for two things. The first was the pressure of
her disappointment after the rejection of her play by
the Royal Shakespeare Company, which had increased
her capacity for nagging by a hundred per cent. The
second was this. A fortnight ago, she had gone to a
publisher's party and, after drinking two half-glasses of
sherry, had blacked out completely in the middle of the
floor. This had given rise to the rumor, which prolifer-
ated through the literary world like convolvulus in an
untended garden, that she had become an alcoholic.
The London literary world is no kinder and no crueler
than other literary worlds in other capital cities: but it
is remarkably homogeneous, and any good piece of gossip, however implausible, can make the rounds completely in a matter of forty-eight hours

When the rumor got back to Dorothy, by way of another woman poet who hated the sight of her and who
telephoned in tones of sisterly compassion to assure her
that she, personally, never believed a word of it, her
rage was so alarming that Cosmo really thought she
might go off her head. Therefore, when she insisted
that only a public reading would prove the absurdity of
the slander to the world, he was forced to succumb.

He felt the humiliation acutely. Such readings, he

felt, were all very well for bookshops in Hampstead or Chelsea, or in nice little towns in the stockbroker belt, but they could only make Cork Street ridiculous. He did induce her to announce hers for 6:30 P.M., an hour after the shop closed, but could not deter her from fixing a horrible typed notice in his window. She also sent out fifty invitations, one to every notable stage director in London, and others to literary persons of eminence who, as he knew in advance, would all reply with old-world courtesy, saying no.

Cosmo had a dreadful ten days while the replies came in. Looking back in later years, he even believed that he had never had a worse: yet, of course, Dorothy had set up a good many standards of comparison in her time. A very distinguished poet, known for a spirit of kindness like a permanent benediction, did accept, and so, to Cosmo's surprise, did two of the directors: this at least was a comfort. But as the no's came in, so Dorothy grew increasingly frantic, sending out more invitations to literary figures of—she considered—the second rank: then to the third: and finally, an admission of defeat, to her friends. She next became obsessed by the idea of buying what appeared to be, in her mind, a conspicuously non-alcoholic dress, and she badgered Cosmo, Miss Few, even the packers, for advice.

Miss Few put an end to the debate by saying, in that tone so conclusive that it carries instant authority, a tone known only to nannies and really efficient mothers, "Mole-colored silk jersey."

"Why not velvet?" Dorothy demanded.

"Velvet always has overtones of the *louche*. It is a most suspect material."

So the shop was quiet again while Dorothy went in

search of her dress, which was what Miss Few had intended. The latter knew just how hard that mole-colored jersey would be to find, if not impossible. Still, by a blind chance, Dorothy did find something of the sort and, when she suggested that she should wear her amber beads with it, nearly quarreled with Miss Few.

"I don't think that would do at all, Mrs. Hines. Amber bears a certain alcoholic connotation. It is often worn by tipsy old ladies who live with parrots in the back rooms of Lewisham and hold *séances* on Thursdays."

Cosmo, the only person in the shop, perhaps the only person in the world, except her lover, who suspected Miss Few of a sense of humor, grinned behind his hand.

"Look here," said Dorothy, "I know what suits me and you don't! I don't know what you think you're up to, telling me—"

"Amber suits you admirably, Mrs. Hines. But I would not suggest it for this occasion. Perhaps a small brooch. Jet."

Then there was the business of the programme. Dorothy had planned an hour's reading. She would begin with a selection from *Light Thoughts*, old and new, including two as yet unpublished—"That should be a draw," she said, with her occasional strange innocence —and then she would read the last act of her Anti-Verse play. If there were any time left, she would read the famous "Should Seven in the womb be laid" from her early success, *Joyful Matrix*. "People will expect it of me."

"I am sure they will," said Miss Few. "It is like Paul Robeson always having to sing " 'Old Man River.' "

Dorothy's eyes bulged and, for one bedazing moment, seemed to rotate. "I cannot see what that has to do with it! I am not a musical-comedy star!"

"Well, nor is he, really."

"Of course I shall recite 'Should Seven!'" cried Dorothy, using the familiar shortening in the way American publishers are accustomed to clip titles, speaking of Mr. Salinger's book as *Catcher* and Mr. Golding's as *Flies*.

"Of course."

"Well, then, why are you looking so doubtful about it?"

"It does seem to be my natural look," said Miss Few, "or so people tell me. It is perhaps the set of my features."

It was decided to hold the meeting in the back room, Miss Few's office, on a Tuesday evening towards the end of October.

It was a wet night. Rain tumbled heavy and unceasing from the plum-colored, dropsical skies and poured in great gulps and splashings from the waste-pipes and gutterings. It glittered and seethed around the lamps, roistered along towards the drains, made a Niagara of solid crystal from the edge of Cosmo's shop-blind to the pavement.

Dorothy, refusing to appear downhearted by this (though her stomach muscles had tightened with apprehension), was busy setting the scene. On Miss Few's desk, which she had pushed almost to the back wall so that there was only a small space in which the poet could stand, she had set an enormous vase of lilacs and red roses, forced, and appallingly expensive. She had ranged thirty hired chairs in three rows of ten. "The late-comers will have to stand where they can find space," she said lightly. "I dare say they will think it's all in a good cause."

She kept running to the window to see if anyone were reading the notice: she was expecting quite a crowd of strangers. Indeed, some people were reading it, having nothing much else to do while taking shelter from the downpour. She looked better than she had done for some time past, excited, almost radiant.

"I should take it easy, old girl," Cosmo observed. "Don't get overwrought. The balloon doesn't go up for over an hour yet."

Because of the weather there were few customers, so her hope of trapping any of these for the reading had faded: but Breckenridge walked in just before closing-time, to pay his bill (which he always did in the end), and with his customary amiability said he'd stay for a bit, though he was due at his club by seven-fifteen.

The first sign of life was a telegram from the eminent and kind poet, regretting that he would be unable to come after all. "BROKE LEG BELFRY ST. MARY WOOLNOTH." Since he was incapable of disimulation, this was the truth: even Dorothy, despite her bitter disappointment, dared not denounce him.

Then Duncan came in with Pringle, Duncan obviously a little the worse for drink, but invincibly gay. "If only you *wouldn't*," Pringle was heard to mutter, as she steered him to a seat. "Sometimes I could kill you."

"Dotty, Dotty!" Duncan cried. "This is just like old times. I always said you were a clever old sweetie, didn't I? Pringle, didn't I always say it? Cosmo, you know I always said Cosmo was a clever old sweetie, I mean, Dotty was, though of course you are too."

"Oh, do be quiet!" said Pringle despairingly

She took off her drenching mackintosh and, looking

wonderful after her own fashion, sat down at his side, keeping a grip on his arm so that he should not sway.

"Y'needn't worry, Miss Milton," Breckenridge said comfortingly, "he'll get no worse. He never does. He'll steadily improve."

Tom came in. Pringle stole a glance at him, gave him a quick smile.

"Tom!" Duncan roared. "Isn't this like old times? Didn't I always say sweetie was a clever old Dotty? You know I did. Don't you dare tell me I didn't," he added pugnaciously, with an effect of squaring up.

"Keep him quiet," Dorothy hissed to Tom, "people will be pouring in, in a moment."

Already the room was beginning to smell of steaming rubber.

"This is jolly," said Breckenridge, purely to give pleasure and to establish a happy atmosphere.

Miss Few came quietly in and sat in the second row, so as to swell the audience. It needed swelling badly.

Harold Boulton and Zena arrived next, and were greeted graciously by Dorothy. "So nice of you, on such a terrible evening. So brave!"

"Oh come, come," said Harold, "we couldn't let the weather deter us, not from anything so exciting as this."

"It makes it all the cosier indoors," said Zena.

The half-hour was up. There was an audience of eight, including Miss Few and Cosmo; he, for this evening, proposed to retire into anonymity.

"We'll give them just ten minutes," Dorothy said, starting to sound only a little desperate. "Taxis are going to be held up in all this."

The next entrant cheered her. It was one of the stage

directors, who would soon be operating in Liverpool. Even though he had to apologize for the unavoidable absence of the other one, her heart rose at the sight of him

Then a complete stranger came in, hung his mackintosh over a chair and went to sit by himself.

"Good-evening!" Dorothy cried. "Or perhaps not such a good evening? But so charming of you. Do let me introduce myself. I am Dorothy Merlin."

"Couldn't be anyone else, could it?" he replied in a Midlands accent crossed with cockney. "My name's Poplett."

He was in his middle twenties, small, spare, going bald, bullet-headed, flat-nosed, flat-eyed, thin-lipped, with a markedly contumacious look. He might have been a conventicler, or perhaps one of Cotton Mather's up-and-coming youngsters, or even (though they had tended to look more vivacious) a fact-finder for the late Joseph McCarthy. His drooping cheeks were strangely babyish, as Queen Victoria's were, and she was austere enough, so far as anybody could guarantee.

"Now, come, Mr. Poplett, let me introduce you to some other people."

By this time the others, tired of sitting, had risen and were chatting together. It looked less like a reading than a cocktail-party, though there was nothing to drink. Cosmo was beginning to feel he might have to produce some sherry, and this he would hate to do.

Poplett turned his unsmiling gaze upon them all, then permitted it to rest on Dorothy.

"What do you do?" she enquired.

"I'm a satirist."

"Ho!" cried Duncan. "And where do you Sat?" Overcome by his own joke, he gave a great lurch and was heaved back into the true by Pringle.

Poplett stared at Duncan. He mentioned a club in W.1. "That's where I *Sat*, if you want to know."

"It must be fun," said Harold. "Anyway, great fun for you."

"I don't know that you'd call it fun. It's a social duty."

"Would you say you were Left or Right?"

"We're all Left," said Poplett, lifting one side of his mouth and displaying a remarkable eye-tooth.

"But are you? You don't like hanging and you don't like Apartheid," Harold said reasonably. "Only sillies do. Isn't that rather primitive stuff, though?"

Zena gently touched a hand to his thigh. She rarely heard, from her husband, an undertone of asperity and she meant to check this before it went too far.

"I told you what we were."

"But what do you attack—in general, I mean?"

"Anybody. Anything. Just as it comes up."

"But you do have a basic point of view?" Harold persisted.

"He has thousands of points of view!" Duncan exclaimed. "Like Swift. And *he* was a clever old sweetie too, Dotty. You know I always said he was."

"Swift did not have thousands of points of view," Tom intervened, in the odd, stern way that came to him occasionally, and Pringle's eyes adored him. "He knew what he was after."

"Well," said Dorothy, with the lightest of her light laughs, "I do hope you haven't come to satirize me!"

"Answer that one a bit later," Poplett replied, disconcertingly. He sat down again.

"Do tell us something about your career," Cosmo

murmured, in the hope of rapid appeasement, for Dorothy was looking much less radiant.

"My dad was a trade union organizer. I went to Grammar School."

"Then—?"

"I read English at Cambridge. Nearly all of us did," said Poplett, with the air of one whose credentials can never henceforth be assailed.

"I think he's a beashly man," said Duncan suddenly, "beashly, beashly. He's come to make fun of Dotty. Pringle, he is beashly. Turn him out!"

"Sit down," she said, "and shut up."

"All sit down," said Cosmo, above a mounting noise of excitement. Poplett had risen. He had clenched his fists and was swinging them.

"Put them down," said Zena, "please do. You look much nicer when they are down, and I am sure you are much nicer."

"My wife, Dorothy Merlin, is about to begin her reading. I—"

At that moment, the door opened. Two damp girls in specialized four-inch heels teetered in, and with foreign-sounding titters sat down at the back.

"Cosmo," said Dorothy, "people are still arriving. Perhaps another ten minutes—"

He said no, and there was something in the way he said it that hushed not only her, but all of them.

Except Duncan. "Beashly man, Pringle, knocks everyone who does an honest job of work. Who does he set himself up to be? I say he's smug, Dotty says he's smug, Cosmo says—"

"If you don't shut up, I shall never sit for you again!"

She said this with an authority equal only to Miss Few's. Intimidated, he sat down.

Harold, Breckenridge and Zena began to clap Dorothy, who was standing behind the table, a swollen look on her face.

The girls at the back gave brief, mad giggles, then fell silent. One of them took a stick of something from her bag and began to lengthen her eyelashes.

"I was proposing," said Dorothy, collecting herself, "to begin this little reading by some *Light Thoughts*—you will not miss the reference to Young's *Night Thoughts*—old and new. But I think they are more suitable for encore pieces, don't you?" (Head on one side.) Having no response to this query, which had been considered rhetorical—"I do. So before my play-reading, I shall *say* to you—'say,' mark you, never 'recite'—a poem of mine which is, if I may dare so put it, moderately well known." She drew a deep breath, touched fingertips together. " 'Should Seven.' "

Hearty applause from Tom, Harold, Zena, Cosmo and Pringle. Duncan shouted "Huzza!" and Pringle clamped her hand down upon his knee. No sign of life from the satirist, or from the stage director. The girls clapped belatedly.

Dorothy's swollen look was succeeded by her pure one. No one so pure as she looked could, she knew, be suspected of alcoholism. Her mouth formed a perfect O. Her voice came from her chest.

> Should Seven in the womb be laid,
>> O cord of peace,
>> O seven-raveled cord—
> Pulsing in womb of dew, youth dew, due maid,
>> And now dew-mother, cease
>>> The sword—

She paused, and her voice dropped to an incredibly
breathy depth—

The Word.

Refreshed, she lit up her eyes and began again on a
fluting note

> *The Word and Cord—*
> *For seven? Seven? Truly? Flesh and grass*
>   *Pass*
> Toute casse, toute lasse . . .

And so forth.

It might seem inconceivable today that anyone could
have written poetry of this sort, and been heard at all:
but a few Dorothys had done so, and Dorothy Merlin
could not credit that the whole thing sounded now not
merely ridiculous but archaic. She went steadily on, losing Breckenridge and the two girls halfway through,
but was unaware that she had done so. When she sat
down at last, she bowed her head in humility to the
melody of applause heard and unheard. (Actually, she
heard more of the latter.) Cosmo breathed a sigh of relief, and sweat trickled down the back of his collar. He
stole a sidelong glance at the satirist, half of whose upper lip was rolled back, but who otherwise displayed no
sign of emotion. Cosmo glanced at him again: this time
half the lip fell back into place, giving Poplett the air of
a surly rabbit who wants to resemble one of the nice
rabbits of Beatrix Potter.

Then came the play-reading. It has been established
already that the work was written entirely in monosyllables, but not that there were never more than five of
them to any one speech. There is no need to go further

into the matter, except to say that the reading took a very long time. The director sat it out, but afterwards he left.

Smiles were glued to the lips of Tom, Harold and Zena. Duncan was drowsy. "Say what you like, she's still terrific. Not such an old sweetie as she used to be, but she gets you. She gets you."

Dorothy leaped to her feet. She had a different personality now, teasing and lightsome. Without announcement she broke out, in a voice calculated to bring a tinkling to all the bells of St. Clement's, St. Martin's, Shoreditch—

> Au pair!
> *Apples and pears!*
> *In the garden and up the stairs—*

She stopped dead: her jaw fell. She was staring over the heads of the audience, out through the door, through the shop and through the window. Beyond this, an elegant figure, glossy in the lamplight, was paying off a taxi.

"Matthew!" she yelled, and bolted for the street.

Scuttled out upon by so Nibelungen a figure from his past, he looked faint. He would never have stopped a cab in Cork Street until he thought the shop had closed, and the Hineses had retreated to Kensington: Dorothy's reading had flushed him from coverts. He had been living further up the street for a month, but had successfully managed to remain unseen, except by Breckenridge, whom he had sworn to silence, and by Tom Hariot who would never have betrayed him to anybody, least of all to Dorothy. Jane had been going about freely, but then, she was not known by sight to Cosmo or to his wife, and Matthew had envied her liberty. He had begun to feel that the service flat, though admirably appointed, had been a mistake. It had been a bore always to drop off in Sackville Street and skulk in shadow the rest of the way

"Matthew, how wonderful!" She darted at him again, this time barging against one of the struts of the blind so that she drenched both of them with water. "Do come in! I'm giving a reading, but it's almost finished."

"Dorothy, this is quite miraculous, but I'm afraid I can't. My wife's waiting—"

"Oh, how is your Jane?"

He flinched at this.

"I'm dying to meet her. You must both come to us in Kensington and have a modest little dinner. Not the sort of thing you're used to nowadays, I'm sure, but I do make a rather special sort of shish-kebab—"

"We'd love to, sometime, but I can't stop now, I honestly can't—"

"Now, now, now! I always let bygones be bygones, but you do owe me something, you know."

"Dorothy," Matthew said, not without a touch of firmness, "you've made yourself very wet. And me too."

"What does that matter? I'll soon dry off."

"So we must hope."

"You did promise to finish that book on me, and then you gave it up and started on that loathly man Skipton."

"But I didn't, Dorothy. I gave that up too. I am studying Balzac."

"How dreary! Just what you would do."

"Have you ever read any?" Matthew said, as incensed as so mild a man could be by this slur upon his hero.

"All I need to have read. Anyway, why should you

slave away on people not a living soul cares about?"

"Some of the French do."

"Nobody bothers about the French, except for the *Nouveau Roman*. You might as well write about Landseer."

"Now Dorothy, if you knew about painting, you'd realize that even Landseer had his points. It wasn't all dogs and lions, whatever you may think."

He wished he could resist the temptation to argue with her.

"Oh, damn Landseer. Come along, you simply must come in!"

"Dorothy, I can't. I—"

At that moment the audience, tired of waiting, began to leave. They gathered round Dorothy on the pavement, all protesting that they had enjoyed themselves enormously.

"We've met before," Tom murmured, when she attempted to introduce him to Matthew.

"Matt!" Duncan cried, and caught him in a Russian embrace, planting a huge damp whiskeyfied kiss on each cheek. "Marvelous, marvelous! How long have you been over? Where are you living? I say, there was a beashly man came to Dorothy's reading, he goes round shneering and shneering and I'm sure he's going to shneer at poor Dotty—"

A passing taxi, skidding in the wet, came too close to the gutter and threw up delicate bubbles of mud.

The satirist, having made no farewell, was slouching off through the rain, which had now moderated. Dorothy ran after him and clung to his arm. "Mr. Poplett!" Her face was roguish. "Don't you dare to satirize me, or I shall be terribly cross!"

He said, "No."

"No?" She gaped at him.

"Public's got to have a recognition symbol. I thought we might be able to send you up, but they'd never get it. Luck's on your side, isn't it?"

He gave her a cold leer, and went away.

When she returned to the shop, Matthew had vanished, Duncan was putting Pringle into a cab (insisting meanwhile at the top of his voice that Swift was a good old sweetie, with a thousand, a million, a billion viewpoints) and Tom, Harold and Zena were exchanging rapid good-byes. Soon, she and Cosmo were alone.

She gave him her half-smile. "I think it was a success, don't you?"

"Blazing," said Cosmo politely, the twin Irrawaddys of blood coiling across the azure of his eyes.

"Michael Whatsisname seemed absolutely riveted by the play. And after all, it could easily get a transfer from Liverpool to the West End, couldn't it?"

"Nothing easier, m'dear."

Dorothy began to cry.

"What's that for? Oh, I see. Overwrought. Well, I told you so. I knew where all this would lead."

11

WHEREIN JANE PRYAR TAKES A
HAND WITH PRINGLE AND FOR
FIVE MINUTES IS MADE VERY SAD.

Next day there was a soft, toffee-colored fog, disastrous to bronchitics, but delightful to people whose lungs were as roseate, as untainted, as Jane's. Sitting up in a great gilded bed, wearing about the upper part of her body a jacket as frail, infantile, angelic, as candy-floss, she regarded Matthew soberly.

"You haven't committed me, I hope?"

"No, Jane."

"You haven't told her she may call?"

"Certainly not."

"I don't mind you inviting Tom Hariot. I knew his father."

"That would be nice."

"But I don't think I want that man Moss."

"There you are quite wrong. Duncan is not without his attractions. He is shallow and silly, but quite harmless."

She lit her first cigarette of the day: she would smoke one more before bedtime, to accompany a very adulterated nightcap. The curtains were drawn back to reveal the lovely furriness of the fog: she was sentimental about Sherlock Holmes. For her, Cork Street at this moment was alive with hansom-cabs and four-wheelers.

"Matt-Matt."

"What now?"

She caught his tone. "You are not entirely complaisant this morning. What are you keeping back?"

"Well, I met a *rabouilleuse*."

"Who? That milk girl?"

"Jane," said Matthew, "you are full of the most extraordinary surprises. How the devil did you know?"

"I got back just before you did. Out of the cab-window I saw a knot of seething persons, with you among them. And I saw the girl, too. I am madly observant, Matt, as you should know by now. My cab was responsible for the mud upon your trousers."

"And I saw that young woman," he said, not emphatically, since there was no need to convince her of his interest in anyone but herself, "for precisely half a minute. Nevertheless, Jane, she is really something."

"Not clever, though?"

"I shouldn't expect so, would you?"

"At a glance, I should not. You may allow Tom Hariot to bring her, if you like. That is, if he knows her."

"Everyone in Cork Street knows everyone else. Of course, she may find the invitation peculiar."

"She will not. When I ask people, they do not think, they come."

Jane slid down into the bed, rucking up the bed-jacket around her like the frill around the neck of Dog Toby. The room pulsated with warmth, with a pink, dulcet comfort: it was not unlike, Matthew thought in a strange flash of disloyalty which was to be the last he ever had, one of Dorothy's idealized wombs. Well, in such a womb he was prepared to bring up his fists to his chin, his knees to his chest, and be happy. He could feel the charming foetus-creases about his wrists, below his abdomen, around his ankles.

"They may come in for a drink this evening at six," she said.

Matthew telephoned Duncan, who left a sitter in a position of exquisite discomfort while he indulged in a long chat. "Can't I come too?"

"We'd rather have you to ourselves," Matthew replied. "It would be so much more amusing."

"All right, I'll tell Pring. But I say, don't get a frightful shock when you see her. You know she hates being a Face? Well, she does." He explained the circumstances of her misery. "And the latest thing is that she creeps around wearing a wig. She looks awful. Just before we went into the shop last night—my God, that reading! You were well out of it—I whipped it off and stuck it in my pocket. Every time I felt for a cigarette, I got the idea that a dog had slunk in and died there. It was horrible. Also, I wasn't quite at my best. Do you want me to tell Tom about this evening?"

"Don't worry, I'll telephone him myself."

"Poor child," said Jane, when informed about Pringle, "perhaps I can take her in hand."

It was true that the wig, so loathed by Duncan, had made Pringle's life a little easier. It was a very unrealistic one, of black nylon, but it so efficiently disguised her that she feared the public transport no longer. People stared at her still, but only because she looked terrible.

She arrived wearing it, ten minutes early.

"Oh, how nice!" said Matthew. "Awfully good of you to come. Would you like to take"—he had her coat in his hand— "er—anything else off?"

Pringle went red. In silence she handed him what he thought of as a shocking bad hat, and he put it on the table in the hall.

In the longish mulberry frock, the crisscrossed slippers, she appeared before Jane and she drew a sharp breath. Jane, whose taste in clothes was naturally conservative, could get herself up like the fairy queen when she chose and tonight she had chosen to do so. "People expect it of me. If I've got all that money, then I should have something to show for it, shouldn't I?"

She was wearing jersey and tights of gold lamé, and on top of this a long mandarin coat of black and gold. On her shoulder was a brooch of black pearls and yellow sapphires; her wrists jangled with emeralds, her delicate bony fingers were loaded with more emeralds, more sapphires, more pearls. She contrived not to look flashy, but only spectacular; and also, perfectly right.

Pringle, who didn't believe in riches, was forced to suspend disbelief.

"You are lovely," said Jane, and she meant it, though with reservations.

"Well, you too. I mean, if you don't mind—"

"They tell me you are a writer. I have ordered your book. The moment it arrives I will read it, and when I have done so, which should take me about two and a half hours, I will write to you."

"Oh, thanks!" said Pringle, still dazed.

She accepted a drink, and Matthew made it a stiff one.

"They tell me," Jane said, having been well primed, "that you don't like being a celebrity."

"Not that sort," said Pringle, her head hanging. "People stare."

"I have been stared at all my life, and for less worthy reasons."

"I hate it."

"You will come to enjoy it. I promise you." She turned on Pringle her hypnotic stare, like that of a drill-sergeant conveying to an ill-dressed ranker, before he starts to roar at him, precisely the explosive darkness that is in his mind. "Also, you are not being altogether kind to poor Mr. Moss, who has done so much for you."

"Done so much for himself," Pringle mumbled. She was trying to fight back.

"It is often impossible to do something for one person without automatically benefiting oneself, and vice versa. I assure you that you are going to adore all this later on. So why not begin now?"

Pringle burst out, "Because the people I do like think it's pretty ghastly. They don't say so, but I know they do."

"Who," Jane asked, "were you thinking about in particular?"

Tom was announced. Unlike Pringle, he did not gasp at Jane. He had met Janes before. He greeted her warmly.

"I knew your father," she said. "He used to come to Redrock, when Calvin and I were living there."

He saw Pringle. "Hullo! I'm so sorry I couldn't pick you up. I was kept late at work."

"Hullo," she said. She raised her splendid eyes and seemed to see, not him, but a Catherine wheel of light, as about the head of a John the Baptist by Gustave Moreau. Jane, looking at her, saw love, timorous but resplendent, lighting the girl from within by a violent electrical disturbance that sent a shudder through her body. This was the classic love, in all its silence and tenacity, which Jane herself had never really known, though she had been perfectly happy without it. She realized that whatever she wished to do with Pringle, she could only do through Tom Hariot.

To Pringle's momentary transfiguration, Tom appeared to be blind. He again expressed his pleasure at meeting Jane, made so mild a joke about the reading that it could scarcely have offended even Dorothy, and said how glad he was to see Matthew after so many years.

"Rumors did reach us about your academic prowess, you know."

"I was so hoping they hadn't," said Matthew. "What are you doing these days?"

"He's writing a play," Pringle replied. "He says it's going to be unplayable, he says it's only for fun, but I bet it's fa— . . . wonderful."

"Then I hope he will let me see it," said Jane.

"As a matter of fact, I've just finished it. But I don't think I ought to let you see it, Mrs. Pryar; that is, unless Matthew approves. My father would have said that it wasn't fit for the eyes of a lady."

Jane laughed outright. "Mr. Hariot, you said that as if you really meant it."

"I'm by no means sure that I don't."

"How very, very nice of you!"

"I don't believe in ladies," said Pringle, "I think that's only for squares."

"Nevertheless," said Jane, "I will get my hands on that play by hook or by crook."

"I seem to derive the idea from Duncan," Matthew said to Tom, "that you don't care for the tenor of English contemporary life."

"It would be uppish of me to put it that way, wouldn't it?" Tom's brown eyes were sincere and innocent. "However, I do find some aspects of it scruffy.

Most popular art seems designed as a text-book for the fumbling young. It seems very selfish to want more for adult persons."

"It is the fumbling young who have the paying-power."

"As you say," Tom replied courteously. "But it does seem a shame. Most of what we're offered is infantile messiness, which seems to me not only explicable but positively desirable, for infants. At some time or other, we must all make mud-pies. No. What worries me is when adults feel compelled to join in and clap hands. They remind me of bright young things in the Twenties who used to dress up as babies and coo in perambulators. It is so very degrading, as all dressing-up must be."

Jane, like an attentive student, questioned him about all this and Tom, feeling in his element, expounded. All the while Pringle said nothing. She sat upright, sipping at her drink, her shoes neatly paralleled like shoes outside a hotel bedroom. Time passed, and she did not realize its flight.

When she reluctantly said she thought she ought to be going, Tom went downstairs to put her in a taxi for which, despite her protests, he paid in advance. When it had turned the corner of the street, the red light dwindling in the fog, he went back to Matthew's flat. A note had been slipped into his hand.

"Now come and have another drink," said Jane. "I'm sorry I was so conspiratorial, Tom—may I?—but I wanted to talk to you about that strange-looking child. She is rather like one of my dogs, only so much prettier. In fact, one can't take one's eyes off her, which, of course, one can with dogs or life would be insupportable. Matthew and I both think she must be encouraged to enjoy her fame, if that is what we may call it. She is simply wasting her youth. She could be having a marvelous time, if only she would stop being so silly."

"She's left that dreadful wig in the hall," said Matthew.

"Well, that may be a hopeful sign. Tom, I am quite old enough to be your mother—"

"That I find impossible to believe."

"Nonsense, you can count. And since I am old enough to be your mother, I can allow myself to be impertinent. Only you can do anything with poor Pringle. Because she is in love with you."

"People keep on saying that," said Tom mildly, "but I can't see the faintest sign of it."

"You aren't in love with her, and never will be?"

"Jane," said Matthew, "this isn't even your affair, though everything does seem to be."

"Be quiet, Matt-Matt. I asked an important question."

"She is a darling," said Tom, "but no."

Jane sighed, and her face was momentarily dulled by age. The large tragedies of life she had always met boldly, even lightly, as if they could be slapped out of the way by an act of will. The small ones invariably upset her. By Pringle's inevitable small tragedy she was saddened to the heart.

"I see. Thank you, and forgive me."

"I'm sure you're wrong about her, if you honestly don't mind me saying so."

"We shall see. But I do want you to talk to her. Do stop her running round in disguise. Tell her it's idiotic, or cowardly, or whatever you please. But *you* tell her. Take her out to dinner and tell her. Will you?"

He hesitated. "I'll try."

"Good man. And you'll show me your play?"

"I shall show Matthew first," Tom said stubbornly, "then it will be up to him."

"I do hope he's going to be permissive with me, then," said Jane, with a soft, pussified smile, "because it is not at all the right occasion for him to be masterful."

When he had gone, her sadness for a moment returned. "You mustn't become too wrapped up in your Balzac, Matt, or let him lead you astray. That girl is no more a *rabouilleuse* than I am—she is too simple to be, and I am too clever. It is no sort of life for a woman, troubling waters all the time. She is simply very attractive and very nice. But Tom, now: he's a *rabouilleur*, if there is such a thing, and he will always cause trouble because he is completely unaware of it. It's a great pity he can't settle down."

"That's past praying for," said Matthew, with the self-satisfied contentment of one who has himself settled down exceptionally well.

12

A PLAY IS READ, AND TOM TRANSPORTS
PRINGLE TO THE SEVENTH HEAVEN.

Harold shut the typescript. He looked straight at
Tom. His eyes were wide and candid, holding but one
emotion.

"It is superb!"

"What do you mean?" Tom demanded, aghast.

"I mean, old boy, that it is just as repulsive as you
said it would be. It is quite filthy and quite unactable.
Not even a San Francisco fringe theater would touch
this one."

"Thank God! For one terrible second I thought you
actually liked it."

"Of course I don't like it; that is, not in a general
sense. But as a total achievement of intention, I like it
more than words can say. I didn't know you had it in
you."

"Nor did I. I find it distressing."

"I say, you're looking very healthy these days. Better
color. Have you been taking exercise?"

"Not a bit of it."

Harold laid a reverential hand upon the play. "There
is not a single kind of nastiness in which you have been
deficient. It is all there. It is the works."

"Do you think it's callous enough? There are no
softer emotions?"

"Not that I can detect. Could I have missed anything?"

It was nearly midnight. They were sitting in Tom's flat, and Harold had been reading for the best part of two hours.

"Let's have another drink. To its total failure!"

"Absolute and total failure."

"Now what," Tom said, "do we do next?"

"We submit it to an *avant-garde* management."

"It shall be done, though I'm not sure quite how to start. By the by, I don't think I can go to the lengths of putting my own name on it."

"Come, come," said Harold, "that's skulking."

"I don't think so. I don't mind people knowing it's me—that is, managements. But I shall put 'by Tom Grutch.'"

"Spelled how?"

"G-r-u-t-c-h. I think it has the right ring. Any management seeing that on the title page should know what sort of play it's likely to be. If questions are asked, I shall say my full name is Thomas Grutch Hariot. By the way—" Tom looked almost shy "—do tell me the bits you like best." He was artist enough to be unable to resist this.

"Well, I liked the beginning, with the chap coming downstage and yelling out his one word."

"Not too much like *Ubu Roi?*"

"Well, yes, but it's a different word. And the whole point of an *avant-garde* is to be *derrière* by about thirty years, so that its present generation of admirers are all too young to know it isn't new. It would be an awful sell for them if they found out that most of it wasn't. How many copies did you take?"

"Three. I'll send one off, keep one for myself, and try the third on an available dog. In fact, I think I shall let a lot of people read it."

"Well," Harold said, "I must get back to Zena. This has been an historic evening."

"And I must put in half an hour on Chomsky's *Syntactic Structures* before I go to bed. I have to remind myself, and my students, that despite all appearances life is real *and* earnest. Chomsky is way out, and will stretch their minds for them."

As it happened, it was Jane who was the first, after Harold, to read *A Potted Shrimp*. They had already outstayed their intention; she had a great deal of business to do in London and Matthew a certain amount of catching-up with old school friends who would have been of small interest to her. He spent the weekend in Somerset, and it was on the Saturday of his absence that Tom's packet arrived.

Matthew and Jane always opened each other's correspondence. They had no secrets, and if she happened to be elsewhere when anything important turned up, she liked him to telephone and tell her about it.

The play took her an hour and a quarter to read, less than she had expected: but sheer horror spurred her on. She stared at it in dismay through her reading-glasses, which she never wore in public, and when she had finished found herself looking into space, murmuring, "My God, a goose," and "Good God, 'put the boot in!'"

When Matthew returned she cried to him, "Have you the slightest idea what your friend Tom Hariot is really like?"

"Of course I have. The nicest of fellows."

"Then how *could* he have written this?"

"It's bad, is it?"

"It is appalling."

"Not technically so?"

"I suppose not. In fact, it's pretty slick; that is, if you don't mind it meaning nothing whatsoever. But it is nauseating beyond the dreams of man."

"Bless him," said Matthew, "then he really has brought it off. What a good chap he is!"

"It is certainly not fit for the eyes of a lady. Or for the eyes of anyone else."

Matthew, when he had read it, agreed. "Well, dear Jane, he will certainly succeed in his objective. No stage in the world would give house-room to this." He kissed her.

"I do not think," said Jane, "that I want to be kissed, for the moment. Not until I have had a bath. Your Tom has turned me against all human contact."

"I do like the old man's soliloquy in the loo. You must admit it's ingenious. And I adore the gas-inspector; you know, the one called Babybaby."

"Do not talk to me about the gas-inspector. I would rather forget him. I suppose all the characters are criminals?" she added.

"All of them."

"I thought as much."

"George Saintsbury is good on that." Matthew found a book and a place in it. He read: " 'I must confess, though it may sink me very low in some eyes, that I have never been able fully to appreciate the attraction of crime and criminals, fictitious or real. Certain pleasant and profitable things, no doubt, retain their pleasure and their profit, to some extent, when they are done in the manner which is technically called criminal; but they seem to me to acquire no additional interest by being so. As the criminal of fact is, in the vast majority of cases, an exceedingly commonplace and dull person—' "

"I wonder how true that is," she mused. "One is never going to know."

" '—commonplace and dull person, the criminal of fiction seems to me only, or usually, to escape these curses by being absolutely improbable or unreal. But I know this is a terrible heresy.' Written round about the turn of the century," he added.

"Don't read to me," Jane said with sudden pettishness, "even if it is hoss sense. You know I hate being read to." (Normally, she loved it.) I am still crawling with distaste, and it makes me feel as if my underwear was dirty."

"Your reaction is quite splendid, Jane, as you are always quite splendid. Tom will be so pleased."

When she returned, trailing white candlewick, from her bath, she was calm again. "I do not think the 'boot' should have been 'put in' to the goose as well. There are societies for the protection of animals."

"But that's where he's been so superb!"

"Or into the old father. Though I suppose that would be more acceptable, these days."

"Clever old Tom," said Matthew. "You see, absolutely none of it is."

Tom, who called for his typescript next day, was congratulated cordially by Matthew, with a concealed shudder by Jane. He took it next to Duncan, who said, "I can't wait. I'll drop in tomorrow night and tell you what I think."

"Not tomorrow. I'm taking Pringle out to dinner."

"Well, have a wonderful time!" Duncan's blue eyes widened until the coppery lashes seemed to form a circle about each as precise as Giotto's O.

"You needn't be arch. I am doing it on your account only. Jane Pryar says I might persuade her to stop all this flinching and lurking. I shall take her to the Black Parrot, where it is quiet, and then, if I have the slightest effect upon her, to one of those places called *discothèques*, where she will make an instant sensation. It will be rather like pushing a nervous swimmer off the deep end, but even that has been known to work."

Pringle came racing down the steps and into the taxi, the door of which Tom was holding for her, as if pursued by bloodhounds

On the way to Soho she sat, or rather huddled, in a corner, as if afraid to touch Tom by so much as the contact of a skirt against a trouser-leg. In the swordplay of the lights, however, her face looked serene, immobile. Duncan had taken away her thickly lined mackintosh, and had had made for her (at his own expense) a straight, well-cut and otherwise featureless coat of mulberry wool. She had two coats: a mulberry one to wear with black, a black one to wear with mulberry. He had also insisted that she buy some very dark stockings, to make her legs look thinner.

Tom, sensing her nervousness, kept his length and legginess well away from her. He was beginning to believe, under pressure of propaganda, that she had a fondness for him, but was disposed to shrug this off. She was not yet eighteen: she would be fond of a good many people before she settled down

It would have upset him to know that this was the most wonderful evening of her life. Her range of literary reference was far from wide, though she had read Salinger (good), Hemingway (good), and the *Kama Sutra* (boring). Therefore, the words running round in her mind were from infancy, from Robert Louis Stevenson, about the glory shining behind her eyes and the stars going round in her head, or something to that effect. And then:

> *The pail by the wall*
> *Would be half-full of water and stars*

What pail? She could not have said. But somehow the whole thing was right, and fit for her. Her head was filled with stars and with all the irrelevancies of love. She was conscious for the first time of drawing breath. In—out—in—out. . . . She felt a beautiful fretfulness, as if she were a tree tentatively flowering after the withdrawal of the last snows.

She was the least vain of girls: she had never thought herself pretty, which indeed she was not. The fact that almost any young man whose standards were not stuffy would be delighted to be seen in her company had never dawned on her. She was obsessed by the fear of being laughed at. Though she had lived for over a year in the scruffier quarters of Earl's Court (her parents were dead and her aunt was nowadays fashionably acquiescent, though she had not always been so), she had remained fastidious. She was not particularly gifted with common sense: yet she had never seen the point of putting an end to her virginity with the assistance of a young man for whom she did not care. It struck her as a painful business (from what she had read) with nothing to show for it afterwards but a deluded glance into the mirror to see if she had changed—which, as she knew, she would not have done.

So she lay, or rather, hunched herself up into a corner of the taxi, all Danaë to the stars, and the stars showed no signs of falling.

Her heart was high. If Tom were not interested in her, why had he asked her out?

"What have you been doing today?" he asked her conversationally.

She scowled. "Nothing much."

She could have told him that she had been posing for Duncan, stuffed into an outsize basket half filled with flowers, the hated ribbon round her neck, another ribbon tied in a big flashy bow round the handle. She had been forced to do this, less by Duncan than by her own conscience. He was now paying her a generous retaining fee, so she owed him something.

"If I were you," said Tom, "I should be having a glorious time by now."

He was pleased to see her smile, however slightly.

"You'd look a proper Charley in a mug."

"I should have no popular appeal, I'm afraid. But you have." He was tactful. "How's the book going?"

"So-so. I'm always being interrupted."

"Has it got a title yet?"

"I told you. Or if it wasn't you, it was somebody else. *The Cruel Ones*."

"About people you know?"

"People I see around."

"But do you find it enough just to see people?"

No answer. The taxi drew up at the restaurant. It was a quiet, expensive, discreet place, yet when Tom's companion was observed, he himself was treated with a deference to which he was quite unaccustomed. Carefully, he had booked a table in an alcove, and was gratified to observe Pringle's relief at the sight of it

At dinner—he was interested to see that she ate like a horse—he tried to draw her out about her novel. Everything went splendidly when she could be induced to talk, but whenever he talked, her gaze shimmered between his eyes and his lips so that after a while he would have liked to put a bag over his head.

Not until coffee came did he start to work on her. He told her how worried all her friends were that she seemed determined to withdraw herself from the public view. "You see, people think you have a wonderful face, and it hardly seems generous to deny them the sight of it. Also, it doesn't seem fair when thousands of girls would give their ears for your no— . . . your fame."

"You were going to say notoriety," said Pringle with a flash of anger.

"No I wasn't."

"Then what was the 'no—' for?"

"Notability," said Tom promptly. "I changed it because it seemed far too weak a word. As I said, thousands of girls would sell their souls for your position. Is it fair to them not to enjoy it?"

"You remind me a bit of my aunt. When I was little and didn't want to eat my cabbage, she used to tell me that hungry boys and girls all over the world would be grateful for it. All I longed for was to be able to give it them. I used to ask her how it helped them if I put the beastly stuff down my throat. It didn't make it more available to other people than if it went into the dustbin, did it?"

"No, of course not. In fact, less." (Though he sensed a fallacy somewhere.) "I am sorry to be like your aunt. All the same, Pringle dear, I do want you to have a nice time. Won't you try? For my sake?"

She was struck dumb. Love was all over her, in her eyes, on her lips, in the tension of her small, square hands. Tom felt like a cad.

"Well, will you?"

"Only if you say so. But it's going to be awful."

Her forefinger went out to flicker round the red silk pleats of the table-lamp.

"Do stand up straight. Show yourself. When you walk into a room, think—'Here I am! How nice for them all!'" He put a hand on hers. "Will you have a shot at it? For me?"

At that moment a plump shadow fell across the table.

"Look here, I simply had to drop in! I was passing anyway, and I knew, because you told me—"

"Hullo, Duncan," Pringle said, and her shoulders drooped. Tom thought, Damn him.

"Mind if I sit down for a minute? —No, waiter, nothing for me. Or perhaps a small Scotch. With water. I say, Tom, I've finished it! It is totally repellent. It makes one want to throw up. But—look here—don't you think it's actually *got something*?"

"What the devil do you mean?"

"Well, it haunts you. Mad as it is, it's sort of *true*. It has got something, I tell you!"

"It has got damn' all," Tom said furiously, "it wasn't meant to have. It is utterly, entirely, sickeningly, without value."

Duncan, bouncing in his chair, brought both fat hands down with a crash onto the cloth.

"No, no, no, no, no! It's awful, as you meant it to be. But there's something more, far more. Something which has happened despite yourself. Here, give it to Pring. Let her read it."

"Duncan," said Tom, "you must drink that Scotch quickly, because we've got to go on somewhere else."

He felt horribly perturbed. Even if Duncan were an

ass, perhaps he, Tom, had taken too little account of the man's asininity.

"Oh, don't let me keep you, I wouldn't for the world." Duncan was huffy.

"You didn't need that drink," Pringle said bossily, "you've had enough already."

"Never you mind what I've had. When you've been to your damned *discothèque*—"

"I am not going to a *discothèque!*" Pringle cried indignantly.

"Matthew said you were."

"No," said Tom, "we are going to a nice old-fashioned night club, where there is a band and a singer."

"Suppose I don't want to?"

"Yes."

She melted, and beamed at him.

"When you've been to your night club, Pring, you take that play home and read it. I tell you, he may not know it, but it has got something!"

He took his departure, leaving the typescript behind.

Tom said earnestly, "He is being unimaginably silly. And I'd hate you to read the stuff. It's only a kind of joke."

"Then it won't do me any harm, will it?" said Pringle. She was not really interested. She was only hoping that after she had endured the dreadful exposure of the night club, he would reward her by kissing her good-night.

She did not know Tom Hariot. Having nothing to offer her, he would have considered such a thing dishonorable to the last degree. Anyway, he was too worried about his own affairs.

13

MRS. PRYAR VISITS A PRISON, AFTER
WHICH HER RESPECT FOR HER HUSBAND'S
OPINIONS IS CONSIDERABLY INCREASED.

Jane, who in America was up to the ears herself
in philanthropic enterprises, had philanthropic friends
in London. One of these, an Austrian baroness who
had married an Englishman and taken up medicine,
asked her if she had ever been to jail. It was her simple
idea of a joke, since she was a very simple woman, so
Jane replied that she had been there neither as in-
patient, nor out-patient.

"I go to see Percy this afternoon. He was once a National Health patient of mine. His family hate him, so
he is lonely. I go and chat to him every week. Perhaps
you would care to come?"

"What has Percy done?"

"Robbery with violence and one murder, but in
liquor. In four years' time they will let him out, I think.
You will find him a courteous fellow, not at all alarming, but not at all clever, though knowing."

So they drove to the prison, a nasty-looking building
surrounded by geranium beds, and were shown into a
neon-lit room not at all unlike a lorry-driver's café, with
separate tables adorned by plastic tops, green, pink and
yellow.

"He may smoke while he is with us, so I shall put the
carton on the table. But he is not allowed to take it
away with him."

The doctor was a tall, Wagnerian woman with a great deal of fair hair and a firm, self-conscious look.

"Also, I shall not introduce you by your true name or when he comes out he may pursue you."

"By that time I shall be on the other side of the Atlantic," said Jane.

"Ah! That proves you do not know Percy. He is very resourceful." She seemed proud of him. "Once he brought to me a bread-knife and made silly gestures. I had to take it away."

All round them was an air of sociable misery. The tables were nearly all occupied by prisoners entertaining their families. Most of them looked decent-looking men, and so far as Jane could see, only one could have been classified by Lombroso as a criminal type, since his face had a mongoloid quality and half of one of his ears was missing. But even he, with a good suit and haircut, might have passed for a left-handed connection of a brutal-looking earl Jane knew quite well, who had an enormous place in Scotland. She was interested to see how very disagreeable and ill-dressed many of the women visitors seemed. It was not that their clothes were particularly cheap—she saw some quite expensive ones—but they were worn badly: sagging hemlines, slips showing, twisted stocking-seams, rims of dirt round jumper necks. Several of the younger women had dyed and piled coiffures doubtfully clean, with feelers of hair loose at their napes. She wondered whether they had become like that because their men were in prison, or whether the men were in prison because the women were like that. One particularly noble-looking prisoner of middle age was muttering with palpably deep anxiety to a grubby young daughter, obviously resentful, and as obviously unfit to live without parental control.

Jane, wearing her quietest grey suit and no hat, felt distressfully different. She always felt different from most people: but normally the feeling was pleasurable. This was not. She was ashamed of looking decent, ashamed of the moment lying ahead when she could get up and go out into the public streets. She would have liked to take all the prisoners with her, to set them free.

"I know," said Dr. Ames, "you are thinking 'there but for the grace of God—' "

"I was."

"Which is foolishness. Grace or no grace, it is not the way you would have gone, Jane, though if you had been very poor you might have done many things not so desirable as those you do now. But we must not pretend to ourselves that we are all potential criminals, since that is a sentimentality and is quite useless in any therapeutic sense."

Percy came slouching in, a tall, red-haired man in his early fifties, wearing something which resembled grey battle-dress.

"Ah, my friend," said Dr. Ames. "And how is it with you, Percy? Now, this is *my* friend, Mrs. Green."

Percy bowed, and sat down. He stretched out a hand to Dr. Ames's cigarettes.

He had sharp, refined features and very flat eyes, which seemed to have no convexity whatsoever. His stare was direct and disconcerting.

"You a trick-cyclist?" he asked Jane.

"Oh, no. Most certainly not."

"You another doc, then?"

"I'm just Dr. Ames's friend."

"Oh. Well, pleased to meet you anyway." He sounded suspicious.

"And how wags the world, Percy?" said the doctor vivaciously, delighted with her own command of idiom.

"Much as usual."

He had no particular accent. His voice was deficient in tonality.

"Mind you," he said, "they all know me here. I don't have no trouble, you bet."

"Percy has been to Wakefield for a spell," the doctor explained, "but now he is back again."

He turned to Jane, gulping at a cigarette as he spoke.

"Us who's got a long stretch, we get moved about, see? But I like to get back here. I know people, see? And I don't have to make fresh starts."

"What sort of starts?" Jane enquired.

He embarrassed her. She was afraid to appear condescending, yet her experience of the Percies of this world was so limited that she did not know what line to take. She tried to give an impression of interested detachment, but was, even so, afraid she would merely sound like the psychiatrist for whom he had at first taken her. She need not have bothered. He was interested in himself only, and was not given to speculation about other human beings.

"Well, it's like this." He was a patient expositor, working on a pupil from scratch, but by no means contemptuous of ignorance. "You go to a new nick, Mrs. Green, where nobody knows you. So you have to make them respect you, see? That's the first thing."

Jane asked how he managed this. For the first time a refulgent smile spread across his face, transforming it.

"Others have their own methods, I have mine."

"I don't doubt it. But what are yours?"

A trolley was wheeled along; well-stewed tea, soft drinks, biscuits, chocolate bars.

Jane bought tea for the three of them, an assortment of dainties for Percy.

"Thanks a lot." He did not sound pleased and she saw no particular reason why he should be. He ate a Mars bar very rapidly, cleaned his mouth with a spotless handkerchief, then leaned on crossed arms over the table and held Jane's eyes unwinkingly. His own eyes were very curious: in addition to their flatness, they had a light, all-over pigmentation, the tan-colored pupils barely differentiated from the paler tan of the iris.

"You want to know how I do it. Well, see, it's like this. I get sent off to a new nick. I might be a nobody, the way they treat me, and that won't do for me, you bet. So I pick on someone and I put the boot in. I make a proper mess of him, see? And then they shove me in solitary—of course, I always give 'em a bit of a fight first. How long am I there? Four days, five days, maybe a week. I can put up with that O.K., I've got plenty to think about. Then they've got to let me out, and everyone respects me, see? They know me by that time. They know what I'm like, so they don't take no risks."

"Who do you pick on?" Jane enquired, fascinated.

"That don't matter. Anybody. He might be O.K.— that's neither here nor there. What's here and there is me."

Jane felt giddy, but Dr. Ames smiled at him.

"You are a bad boy, though. Very, very bad. I have told you."

"No malice in it," said Percy. "Anyhow, like that I don't get shoved around. You have to look after Number One, in this lark."

He insisted that Jane should bear this in mind, obviously feeling it might come in useful to her someday. She felt a compulsion to thank him, and did.

At the next table, the father was quietly crying. The delinquent-looking daughter was studying her watch, and not attempting to conceal it.

"They'll call him in a tick," said Percy, with an air of satisfaction. He had followed Jane's glance. "They'll call me last. And they won't do that till *I'm* ready, see? They know just how far they can go, the screws."

"Mr.—er—Percy," Jane said in her most military fashion, "far be it from me to interfere in your private business. But couldn't you beat up somebody you actually knew, and had some cause for disliking?"

He gave a weary smile, the smile of a patient teacher obliged to instruct again and again in the fundamentals of his subject. "Lady, it's either him or me. And it has to be me. After all, I get to a new place— see? Where I haven't made no enemies. So it has to be first come, first served. It stands to reason."

He gave a meaningful glance at the trolley.

"No, Percy," said Dr. Ames, "you do not really care for biscuits and chocolates. If you did, I would provide them. But you do not."

"Let me—" Jane began.

"No," said the doctor. "Percy does not expect it. He likes cigarettes much more."

"Better business, too," said Percy, with a flick of his eyes.

"You know you are not allowed to tell that to me. It is your own affair, and I want nothing to do with it."

"Must do something to relieve the monotony."

"You will be in bad trouble, one of these days, and then you will not get out so soon."

"Not an indiktable offense," said Percy. Grinning, he looked round at the prison orderlies and pursed his lips in amiable contempt.

"But you do care about your release."

"I want to see my auntie," he said. "She's getting on, she's not had a good life."

He talked for a long while, extremely boringly, about his aunt, the only living soul in whom he seemed to have the slightest interest. Her trouble was her sinuses. Do what they liked, the doctors couldn't get her straight and she wasn't going to let them mess her about in hospital. "That and her arthritis," said Percy.

"When you do get out," Jane said, feeling her way —this, as had crossed her mind before, was one of the few circles in which she felt at a loss—"are you going to stay out?"

"You're a Yank, aren't you?"

She assented.

"Thought you were. You ever been to Las Vegas?" For the first time he sounded wistful.

"No."

"Cor, fancy living over there and not seeing Las Vegas!"

"I'm an unlucky gambler. Only once in my life have I won anything, and that was in a church raffle—a mauve jumper four times too big for me." She saw that she had lost her audience. He had no interest in anything concerning her. She went on: "But I'm going to ask you something and please don't answer if you don't want to. Are you going to stay out?"

"Well," said Percy, "that depends. Things may crop up, see? You never know. This isn't a bad place, all things considered, always something going on. You see the nobs come in—spies, top sods, all sorts—I've known it worse."

Now Jane was a power in her own world, and was not altogether prepared to be a supernumerary in this one. "My friend Dr. Ames," she said firmly, "mentioned something about a bread-knife."

At this breach of etiquette, the doctor paled. Percy did not.

"Oh, that. You see, it's this way. I go and see doc here. I've got pains in my back, see?—and she says I'm foxing and I happen to have the knife, so I show it her, to make her give me something, see? It's nothing personal. She's got pills, she can give me pills. What's wrong in that?"

"I think I will not ask you here again," Dr. Ames whispered angrily to Jane.

"I think I will not come. —But Percy, if she hadn't disarmed you, what would you have done with the bread-knife?"

This time she had gone too far. Sullenness descended upon him. He pushed some biscuit crumbs round and round on the table top, wetted a finger and made a porridge of them.

"How *is* your aunt?" Dr. Ames said quickly, though he had been telling them quite enough about her.

It was, however, a subject of which he never grew tired. He gave them a prolonged, maudlin character-sketch. Aunty was a good old girl, worth six of the old cow (his wife) and the two tarts (his daughters). He owed more to her than to the rest of the world put together.

"She don't preach at you, see? She's a one, she is, always good for a laugh. I say to her, 'You old bag, don't you ever get out of that mackintosh and put your hair up?' Goes around, see, like some old schoolgirl, with a pigtail dangling down to her behind like a horse's tail, and her touching seventy-five. 'You shut your trap, Perce,' she says, 'you're too clever by half.' We have some rare old times, her and me."

Meanwhile, Jane noticed that all the other prisoners had been "called," and that the other guests had departed. No one seemed in any hurry to call Percy. So she said, "It has been most interesting talking to you. But I'm afraid I must go. I have an appointment."

"See you," he said, without interest.

She left, leaving Dr. Ames to it. She did not go far, since this area was not one in which to expect a cruising taxi, and she was dependent upon her friend for transport. She had to wait, in the doctor's car, for forty-five minutes precisely, during which time she looked up all the fork-studded restaurants in the *Michelin Guide* and became rather hungry. At last the doctor came out.

"I'm sorry. I had another fifteen minutes of Percy, and then half an hour with the Governor."

Jane asked what the Governor had said.

"I am afraid Percy is building up false hopes. It appears that he is not only the tobacco-baron of this jail, but has made nearly forty pounds dealing in spare radio parts. Also, he has twice assaulted a prison officer. The instinct of the Governor is to release him as soon as he can, just to get him off his hands. But he is a man of social conscience, no less. So I think that, in the public interest, he is prepared to endure poor Percy indefinitely."

"Hedwig, who do you suppose supplied those spare parts?"

Over the Brünnhilde cheeks, cushioned and firm, a

blush spread like the blush of an unexpected sunset. "I very much fear I did. He has a transistor radio which I gave him. And I always supposed that the spares were for himself. He was constantly asking for them. I could not think how they so quickly wore out."

It had begun to rain, and the rain had a driven wind behind it. The geraniums twinkled and shivered, making a sudden comprehensive pinkness over all. They were ugly flowers.

"Please," Jane said, "let us be on our way."

On her return, she gazed at her husband thoughtfully. "Matt-Matt, your Mr. Saintsbury is only too accurate. I have met a murderer. He is a very dull person. He is only interested in being respected, and in his aunt. And though he is unsafe with bread-knives, he is entirely unexciting. Doesn't that seem to you the worst of it?"

14

SHOWS THE DIVERS REACTIONS OF
CERTAIN PERSONS TO A WORK OF ART,
AND A GENEROUS SPORTING GESTURE
ON THE PART OF COSMO HINES. TOM
WALKS BY NIGHT IN ST. JAMES'S PARK.

At the dead hour of 9:30 A.M., when few customers
were likely to appear in the shop, Cosmo gave a little
coffee-party for his immediate neighbors. This was held
in the back room, and Miss Few officiated while Dorothy drooped over two chairs in the attitude of Madame
Récamier. She had been feeling tired for the past few
days, and had neglected the accounts.

The party was very little indeed, since only Duncan
and Pringle had accepted. Tom was teaching, Jane
Pryar (although asked by a charming little note in
Dorothy's own hand) claimed to have a cold in the
head, and Matthew had asked if he might leave things
open.

"Well," said Cosmo, settled in a position from
which he could keep a weather-eye on the shop, "I
fancy we have all, by now, read this famous play. What
do we think?"

"He oughtn't to have done it," Pringle said to her
breast-bone, "but—"

"Tom's such an old pet, really, one wonders how he
could have managed such a thing," said Duncan. "Of
course, nobody will touch it with a bargepole. Nevertheless—"

"I," said Cosmo, with his cheerless gleam of a smile, "found the most surprising *lacunae* in my knowledge. There were things that even I, after a long and—I may say—not utterly misspent life, found entirely unfamiliar. All the same—"

"Oh, shut up!" Dorothy shouted, rearing half up and nearly falling off her improvised couch. "To listen to you lot, one would think you were half-witted. 'But'— 'nevertheless'—'all the same'—you make me tired! Can none of you see that it is entirely, unequivocably, a *masterpiece?*"

Duncan protested. Pringle stared at her, but with the air of one who has received a divine revelation. Cosmo's smile did not alter.

"It is precisely as disgusting as he meant it to be," said Miss Few, refreshing Pringle's cup.

"It is a masterpiece, and *I* say so! Do you think I'm immune to common envy? Do you think I can utterly debar from myself the jealousy anyone worth his salt ought to feel when confronted by a master?" Dorothy was panting. "Nothing human is alien to me," she announced. "And let me tell you, I am saying this on the very day of a personal disappointment. That imbecile in Liverpool—"

"There are other managements, my dear," said Cosmo. He raced off to sell something to a huge, gay duchess, was quickly back again.

"On the very day of a bitter personal disappointment, I am objective enough, true enough to myself, to tell you that in its own way, its strictly contemporary way, A *Potted Shrimp* is the equal of *Joyful Matrix!*"

"That could be so," said Miss Few, taking care to keep any hint of dryness out of her voice

"I always said it had something." Duncan had

known Dorothy too long to be entirely free from her influence, though for the past two years he had realized, on the upper level of his consciousness, that she was ridiculous. "I told him so."

"I don't think you should have!" Pringle was anxious. "You know what he thinks of it himself."

Dorothy rose. It was a slow rising, coiling into the vertical like the first wisp of smoke from a fire which has caught properly at the seventeenth attempt. She held the back of a chair for a second, steadied herself, stiffened her back, and proceeded to hold her audience. Since she had quelled the rumors of alcoholism, she had reverted to the colors of her fancy: gentian-violet, blood-orange, arsenic-green. Today, she was in orange.

"Now, my children"—this nursery address always presaged a diatribe—"you are all far too old, and should be far too sophisticated, to imagine that what a writer says he means counts for anything whatsoever! The meaning is outside of his will. He cannot be responsible for what the work means to *us*. 'Don't trust the teller, trust the tale,'" she quoted loftily, from somebody or other

She paused. Scorn darkened her voice

"There was a wonderful book about that long poem by Dylan Thomas, explaining all his symbols in terms of astronomy. I met a silly woman who had known him when he was writing it. Do you know what she had the impertinence to say?"

Nobody did.

"She said that at that time, Dylan only knew one constellation, which was Charles's Wain, because of it being over the new chimney. She *assured* me of it. Cretin! Now, did I doubt her word? Certainly not. But why should she have thought it was relevant?"

"I don't see how he could have used astronomy symbols if he didn't know one star from another," Pringle said, almost cheekily. Since her evening with Tom she had begun to be braver, to be seen in crowds, even to consider the question of screen-tests.

"My poor girl," Dorothy mooed, "you just didn't understand, did you? On the conscious level, he knew nothing about stars. To his unconscious mind, astronomy was an open book. There was nothing he did not know, without knowing it. But never mind Dylan Thomas. I am talking about *A Potted Shrimp*. Whatever Tom Hariot's intention was, he has created a great, *true* work of art. And we are all going to see— because every senior writer's duty is to assist the gifted beginner—that it is put on, without the slightest delay."

"I can't agree altogether," said Miss Few. "Editha, you are looking peaky. Are you getting enough fresh air?"

"Who cares whether you agree?" Dorothy demanded rudely. "You're not an artist."

"True, true. —Editha, you looked better when you were taking those long walks. I'm sorry you've come to believe in taxis."

Pringle gave a lopsided smile.

"You, Duncan! Stand up and be counted!" said Dorothy, half-sternly, half-playfully.

"Well, parts of it would make anybody giggle a bit, wouldn't they?"

His voice was tentative. Plump, ruddy, his Roman hair curling about a bulging forehead, he regarded Dorothy with anxious eyes.

"No serious person would giggle, except when laughter was intended. Pringle? Miss Milton?"

"I suppose it has got some sort of quality," Pringle said weakly, wondering whom she was betraying. "I mean, you can't actually forget it, can you? Though I thought it went a bit far."

"Far?" said Dorothy. "Where is 'far?' Don't you all understand that A *Potted Shrimp* extends the very boundaries of art? After this is performed, *all* roads will be open. Cosmo! Let us have your valuable opinion."

It was years since she had been able to address him in public without suggestion of a sneer, though she was quite unaware of this. Cosmo was not so unaware. He sat down boyishly, straddling a chair, his face to the back of it. One of his buttons flew off. Miss Few mechanically picked it up and put it in her pocket. It was her social pretense that Dorothy would wish to retrieve and replace it, though she knew this would not happen. And so, she kept needles and cotton in a drawer of her desk.

"Well, now, let us see. I think it is an inalienable human right, all too little recognized, to sit on the fence. I may be a trifle old-fashioned in my tastes—"

"Except where his tarts are concerned," Duncan breathed into Pringle's ear.

"—and so, on the fence I shall sit. But this I will tell you, and you, Duncan, may pass it on. I am something of a gambler. You may tell Tom I will bet ten pounds that he doesn't get it put on at all—"

"He'll take that, right enough."

"—against five per cent of the takings, amateur and repertory rights included, for a period of ten years, if he does."

"Cosmo," said Dorothy, "we haven't got money to pour down the drain!"

"My dear, aren't I backing your own faith in this masterpiece?"

"That's right, jeer."

"No, no, I was not jeering. Betting. That's all."

She looked at him suspiciously, then seemed appeased. "All right. I shall take this in hand myself. That party on Thursday, Cosmo—"

"What party? —Oh, that. I thought you weren't going."

"Well, now I am. I'm bound to run into ———."
She mentioned, not one of the Michaels, but a Christopher. "I shall talk to him myself."

"God," said Duncan to Pringle, as he led her back to his studio, "is Tom going to be pleased by all this? Because it is tripe, isn't it?"

She said unhappily, "I only wish I knew."

"Or is it bloody marvelous, after all?"

"I don't know. It made me feel awfully sick."

"But then, we ought to get used to feeling sick, oughtn't we? If we're really adult?"

"I suppose so, but I don't like it. Sometimes I wonder whether we even need to feel sick when we don't."

"The wonderful thing about art in this age," said Duncan plummily, as they went upstairs, "is that it is bringing us face to face with the dark side. It makes us look in upon ourselves without funking it. You know, morbid Falstaffs and all that."

"I hate morbid Falstaffs," said Pringle fretfully, "I want things to be fun."

Had she but known it, this was the cry of the children. Far more people would like to have fun than are prepared to admit it.

"How can it be fun, under the shadow of—?"

"Duncan, you really can be silly sometimes. Don't

you know that bomb of yours is old hat? At least, till someone gets a better one. And you know you don't spend all your waking moments brooding about it, so why pretend you do?"

She was so testy that he looked at her in awe as he put his key in the lock. "All right, don't carry on. Let's have a drink."

"No, you don't, not at this time in the morning. Duncan, you could really be so sweet, if—"

He gave her one of his splashy kisses.

"So could you, if you didn't nag. Do you know, you are the first girl in years I never tried to—"

"And don't you try! Just don't you try!"

She was kept busy that morning since, though by exploiting her reputation she could have bought him up, she was content to spend two mornings a week in the studio as model and receptionist. She had ceased to disbelieve in lords and ladies, for nowadays she saw too many. She didn't give a row of beans for the lot of them.

Sitting over a sandwich at lunchtime, she leafed through one of the daily papers. "Oh, look, Duncan, there's Mrs. Merle! Doesn't she look m'hav'lous?"

It was a picture of some girl's coming-out ball. In the background Matthew could be faintly seen, in his familiar knife-thrower's-target attitude, leaning back against the paneling with a bright flinching smile on his face. In the foreground was Jane, in all her emeralds, chatting to the débutante's father.

(Could Jane have known it, this photograph was being studied with interest by Percy, who always intimidated one of the weaker warders into sharing his morning paper.)

"She looks terrific," said Duncan. "Do you remember the girl? We photographed her last month. She has a face like one of those very insipid pale buns, the ones with a bit of coffee sugar on top."

"I don't believe in debs," said Pringle, "I think it's all daft."

"Just for once, I don't either. But they are very good business. Surely you remember this one, though? She turned up in a sort of beat uniform, and then her mum rushed in and made her change into pink satin and pearls. There was pretty well a stand-up fight."

"So there was."

"She hit her mum with a French loaf she was taking home for supper. They don't live together, you know. I couldn't get up much feeling about it, despite the Fifth Commandment. It seemed to me six to one and half a dozen to the other."

Duncan left a note for Tom, sketching the outlines of the coffee-party and mentioning Cosmo's bet.

Within five minutes of receiving it, Tom was telephoning to Harold.

"My God, it's terrible! They're all deciding they like it! Dorothy Merlin's going to talk to managers about it herself."

"There is one born not every minute, but every second," Harold replied peaceably. Tom heard him call out, in a faraway voice, "Get away, sweetheart, and take your damned marmalade with you!" He added, "They are quite maddening this morning. You are not to worry, old boy. Dorothy can show it to every management in England, but it is quite impossible for that play to see daylight. Of course, you would never permit the alteration of a single word, would you?"

"On no account."

"Fine. You stick to it. Then that's all right."

"But I don't want it shown to managements!"

"Now look," said Harold, "your sorrows are unhinging you. Showing them is the whole point. We want to get it clean into certain turgid heads that there are things they simply cannot do, and in a more or less civilized country can *never* be permitted to do. We are then in a position to squash this ridiculous and time-wasting argument about abolishing all censorship, and get down to the much more fruitful one of where lines may reasonably be drawn. —Damn you, you've got the stuff all over my trousers! Zena, take her away, will you? —Sorry about that, old boy. Of course the play is going to be shown. To everyone. And you are going to take Hines's bet. If you don't want the money, you can send it to charity."

Relieved, Tom went out to walk in the dusk. He strolled down Sackville Street, along Piccadilly, down St. James's Street and into the beautiful park. The birds had gone to bed for the night, but the lights beyond the trees sparkled against the last lime-colored ravelings of sunset. It was mild enough for lovers to be strolling hand in hand, and home-going Civil Servants to slacken pace. As always, London on a fine night gave him joy.

It might be true (in fact, it was) that England could no longer roar and swish her tail as she had done when she was a great world power: yet the capital, especially when you could not see its inhabitants too clearly, still looked like a center of greatness. It was not a young-man city, like New York, a grandfather city, like Rome, a great chic mother-city, like Paris: it was an uncle-city. It had all the force and detachment of a powerful uncle, not emotionally involved as a father might be, but interested enough to care for the family fortunes and lofty enough to put a foot down. It occurred to Tom, as it had many times before, that it was a great pity for the rest of the world that this uncle-city was not boss-city also: the English at the height of their power had done wicked enough things, but rarely had these been squalid things. Stamping round Europe in the nineteenth century, universally detested but never giving a damn, they had impressed upon the world that certainties were perfectly possible, and the ultimate answers by no means dusty. There had been nothing hysterical about the English then, as there was nothing outwardly hysterical about this night-time London now: but the times were changing, and for the worse.

Blackguarded, blackmailed by the cult of youth—the cult, that is, of early school-leavers in dead-end jobs with more purchasing power than any consonant generation in history—the English were beginning to lose their nerve. Cultivated but weakly parents were pretending to be beguiled by a smeary sub-culture because it was a craze with their children. Parsons went forth in search of words more complaisant, more man-pleasing, than "sin." Physicians, confronted with pregnant schoolgirls, were giving uneasy lipservice to phrases such as "early maturation," which could only have meant—had there been any sense in it at all—that the age of puberty, having certainly lowered itself within a hundred years, had lowered itself at almost three times the normal rate since the end of the Second World War. People to whom cruelty was repellent were acquiescing in the ridiculous notion that the more one dwelled on beastliness, the nicer and more liberated one became. Men and women who found self-conscious absurdity boring after the first startling ten minutes, were learning to sit through the stuff patiently, resisting the temptation to leave at the end of the first interval. Kindly people had learned to titter, though with some queasiness in their souls, at little magazines devoted entirely to a callow variety of cruelty and smut. They were, in fact, laughing at nasty children whose ears they would once, without the slightest hesitation, have clipped. Parents were abrogating all moral responsibility out of fear that their sons and their daughters would despise them: and when they trimmed their thoughts and their words to that end, the sons and daughters grew up to despise them much more.

Meanwhile, the streets got steadily dirtier, through lack of litter-baskets, and the shelves of erstwhile selective booksellers made visitors from, say, Russia, first gasp and then relapse into satisfied contempt. And nobody really wished to be despised by the Russians.

I, of course, Tom thought to himself, am a young-old man, or an old-young one. The times are out of joint, so far as I am concerned.

Head on his chest, hands in his pockets, he went with his curious teetering walk into a Whitehall pub, where he had a meal. He thought he had better eat something before he found himself working out the phraseology of a brand-new Commination Service.

15

JANE IS TRAPPED, IN SO FAR AS IT IS
POSSIBLE TO TRAP PERSONS LIKE JANE,
AND MISS FEW DROPS A BOMBSHELL.

Matthew and Jane were waiting at the corner of
Conduit Street for a taxi, and debating whether they
should stay on in England for a few weeks longer still,
since Jane had not yet completed her obligations and
had many friends yet whom it would be pleasant to
visit, when Dorothy came upon them

She had been keeping watch. The moment she saw
them pass the door, she had flung on her coat and
raced after them, only at the last moment achieving the
impression of one who has been sauntering. It was
not a very good impression, since she was hard put to it
to catch her breath, but at least it was convincing to
herself.

"Well, Matthew, fancy seeing you! And this must be
your Jane."

Mrs. Pryar was too well bred to freeze. Instead, she
simply smiled and was silent, which would have had its
effect on anyone but Dorothy.

"Jane," said Matthew, "this is Mrs. Hines—Miss
Merlin. Dorothy, my wife."

"After all these years! We've heard so much about
you."

It was hard luck that taxis were scarce that morning
or they could have escaped.

"How do you do," said Jane.

"Look, I know how busy you both must be, but surely you could fit in just a little dinner with Cosmo and me? It won't be grand, but I do make a rather special shish-kebab. And we will have lichees afterwards. I can give you any evening in the next fortnight."

This detestable trap might have caught a lesser woman, but not Jane Pryar. "I am sure we'd enjoy it," she said, "but we haven't a book with us, so I can't be sure of anything till I get home. I will send you a note."

Dorothy fixed Jane with a peculiar look meant to express dazzled admiration.

"Matthew," she said, in a faintly bullying tone, "I can't blame you. No, really, I can't, and I won't. I can't blame you at all. *Elle est ravissante!*"

Fine words, for Jane, buttered no parsnips. Not even in French, with r's elaborately trilled. All her life she had been told that she was ravishing, but she had the sense to know when she was or wasn't. This morning she was not. She went on smiling.

"Oh, Matt," Dorothy cried, "do you know Tom's marvelous play is probably going to be accepted?" She told him the name of a management, which had strong convictions and was almost entirely lacking in sense. "Of course, it's only in the air now, but I'm sure something will happen. And if it does, it will be *my* doing!"

"Oh Lord, oh no!" said Matthew. If Jane were not ruffled, he was. "This is quite awful."

"No," Dorothy said, with such solemnity that she might have been consecrating a cathedral, "there you are wrong. It is a profound and wonderful play."

"It made me sick-sick," said Jane. She hailed a passing taxi, but it was taken. Meanwhile, spots of rain were falling from what had appeared to be an innocent sky.

"Mrs. Pryar," said Dorothy, "Jane, if I may call you so, since Matthew and I are such very old friends—"

"Please do, Mrs. Hines."

"—don't you think we have to face things? It is surely the spirit of our age. There is nothing we must refuse to face, don't you agree? However cruel, however repulsive, however it makes us *cringe*—"

"A friend of mine," said Jane, "a German woman, spent the best part of the war in Ravensbruck. You would be surprised how little she cares to face. Indeed, I'm inclined to think we're only prepared to face things when we've never had anything to face. I'll write to you."

By some magic she had found a taxi, and she leaped into it, a firm grasp on Matthew's wrist.

"So now I know," she said, as the cab moved away.

"So now you do. But only a very small portion of the reality."

"I am going to be very busy until we leave. So are you. If the worst comes to the worst, we can go to Wiltshire and stay with dear old Betty Hedingham."

"She's in London at present."

"With darling Louisa, then, though the house is desperately cold. Anything is better than your friend Mrs. Hines."

A simple person might have imagined that Dorothy's encounter with Jane Pryar would have been daunting. Not a bit of it. Dorothy felt she had scored a considerable success and went back to tell Cosmo so. She was in the middle of a dithyramb, the subjects concerned being Jane and herself, when Miss Few came out of the inner office.

"If you and Mr. Hines could spare me a private word, I should be grateful."

"Well, out with it," said Dorothy, cross.

"Not in the shop. In my office."

"Of course, if you wish," said Cosmo, with a flash of his distressingly even teeth. "But what is all this mystery about?"

They joined her there. One would have thought Miss Few was the proprietor, since she sat down at once behind her desk and waited for them to seat themselves.

"I am afraid I shall have to ask you to replace me."

Cosmo was thunderstruck. He had underpaid her for years, and realized that even if he found somebody to overpay, she could not be half the use to him that Miss Few had been. She knew the business like the back of her hand.

"This is most disconcerting. Why?"

"Of course you can't go!" Dorothy whined. "Why do you say you're going when you know you can't?"

"Because I am pregnant," said Miss Few briskly.

Silence fell. To occupy this quiet time, Miss Few wrote a note to a delinquent customer.

"You're not married," said Dorothy at last.

"No."

"So you can't—"

"Oh, yes, I can."

"Are you going to be married?"

"I shouldn't think so," Miss Few said equably.

"But it isn't as if you were a girl—"

"No, it is not. I am in my forty-second year. But these things are still possible. In fact, I've proved it. Naturally I shall put everything in order before I leave. I shall be leaving on November thirtieth, so that will give us all plenty of time."

Dorothy said she was surprised she had not been more careful. There was no need for that sort of slip-up in this day and age. Miss Few replied that she had always thought Dorothy believed in motherhood. "Anyway," she added, "there was no slip-up. It was quite intentional."

"But think of that poor child, born with the greatest of disadvantages, with the stigma—"

"My dear," Cosmo said, "I really think this is none of our affair—"

"Oh, there won't be any stigma, or not much. My friend changed his name to mine several years ago. In any case, I am going to settle down."

She looked at her watch. It was her lunch-hour, so she gathered up coat and hat and left them, humming a cheerful tune as she went out.

"It's monstrous!" cried Dorothy. "How anyone could bear to touch her—" She gave a dramatic shudder, as if she were St. Anthony being given a tentative prod by a female demon in a wimple.

"Live and let live. We'd better start advertising."

Though Cosmo sounded serene enough, for he knew that any show of emotion on his part would make Dorothy worse, he felt that the world had given way under his feet. Miss Few knew everything about the business: it was a long time since he had done anything himself but nod and beck at his customers.

"I could kill her," said Dorothy.

16

TOM MEETS AN UP-AND-COMING
STAGE DIRECTOR AND BEHAVES
WITH   SINGULAR   OBSTINACY.
PRINGLE   MILTON   CONTRIVES
TO UPSET HIM AND HERSELF.

The director was very young and abnormally tall.
He had much fair hair, and acne. He wore blue jeans, a
faded green jersey and white plimsolls. His eyes were
small, sharp, and of a blind-looking blue. His name was
Christopher. He had asked Tom to call at his office,
which was a cubbyhole in the attics of a building in the
Haymarket, hung with playbills and photographs of actors. The room had a mouse-like smell which made
Tom's nose twitch. It was not his idea of the smell of
success. Yet Christopher had been surprisingly successful. At any rate, even if he hadn't made much money
for his backers, he had caused a splash or two.

Tom, immaculate, sat as easily as he could upon a
kitchen chair, waiting for the director to conclude what
was obviously an interviewing routine. For quite two
minutes he had sat in silence, sucking at a French cigarette, his hands stuck in his pockets, his face mask-like.
He kept his steady, washed-out gaze upon Tom's forehead. Twice a secretary girl from, presumably, some
other cubbyhole, had come in and laid written mes-
sages in front of him. He had not given them a glance.

Finally he spoke.

"Well, that's a pretty exciting job you've done."

"Thank you."

The director, with clenched fist, hit the copy of the play Dorothy had had to force upon him.

"I might say it is bloody exciting."

"I'm so glad."

"I'm going to do it."

Though he kept a poker-face, he was eagerly awaiting Tom's reaction. In his experience, playwrights confronted with this sort of announcement tended to blush, gasp and topple.

"You can't," said Tom.

"What?" Sangfroid deserted the director. The cigarette fell out of his mouth.

"It would never do, would it? I mean, no sane person would ever let you."

The director retrieved the cigarette and stuck it back in his mouth the wrong way round. He swore furiously, and spat it out again. "Burned my f—— lip."

"I'm so sorry."

The director waited till the pain had abated somewhat.

"Well, we haven't got all day."

"Actually I have," said Tom. "I've no classes on Tuesdays."

"You a schoolteacher?"

"Not precisely. I'm a university lecturer."

"I might have known it."

"Oh, how?" Tom was interested.

"Most of the stuff we get sent in, they can't even spell." The director bristled. "Anyway, I haven't got all day, whatever you've got. Let's get down to business. Now, I'll show this to a few people—Finney might be interested, or Warner, or even Burton—"

"I can't believe they would be. And honestly, you

don't really suppose you can put this play on the stage?"

"Well, of course there would have to be a few changes, just to satisfy the bloody Pilgrim Fathers who run this bloody country."

"There would be no changes," said Tom.

The director said, in a voice that sounded surprisingly genteel, "I beg your pardon?"

"I could not consent to change anything whatsoever."

There was a long pause.

"Now look here, what is it—Hariot—"

"You may call me Grutch. Or Tom, if you'd prefer it. I don't mind in the least."

"Look here, Grutch, you're still a rank amateur. You've got talent—I've said so. Something exciting. But you seem to know damn' all about the theater. Changes are constantly being called for in rehearsal, and we have the author there to see he makes them."

"Thank you," said Tom, "for giving me so much of your time. I'll take that with me."

"The hell you will!"

"Well, I cannot for the life of me see what use it is going to be to you. You see, I propose to authorize no changes whatsoever. Not on any account. Not for any reason."

"For God's sake, that character—what's his name? Oh, Grunt. Grunt could start the play with a different word. The other's all right for later on, but perhaps . . . well, say 'Merde?' "

"*Ubu Roi*," said Tom, "old hat. I thought you were more advanced than that. You must have read Jarry."

Surprisingly enough, the director did not take offense. He lit another cigarette, making it sodden at once, and after a preliminary wince as he put it to his blistered mouth, smoked half of it in silence.

"They might just wear it."

"Who?"

"Lord Chamberlain's office."

"I'm quite sure they would not."

"Never say die. That business with the goose, though—"

"Stays in."

"We could symbolize it—"

"I didn't say that."

"For God's sake, man," cried the director, "do you seriously suppose that we can have a chap trying"—he gulped—"well, *on the stage?*"

"Why, of course not! Now you are beginning to grasp my point."

"I don't grasp your bloody point!"

"I think you will."

The director began to breathe heavily. "Look, Grutch. Tom, if you like. My friends call me Kit."

"So nice."

"We can have a riot with this play. It's not only talented, it's bloody magnificent. How you wrote it I don't know—I suppose you did?"

"Certainly I did."

"You don't somehow look the type. Anyway, how you wrote it I don't know, but here it is. Now, I want you to start in as from tomorrow—I'll even come to your place if you like—working with me. When we've made the necessary changes—"

"I have told you, there are going to be no changes. Not by so much as a comma."

"But in that case, how the devil do you suppose we are to—?"

"Quite. That is what I said before."

Tom rose. "I really am most terribly sorry to have wasted your time. I know you're a busy chap." Resolutely he picked up his typescript.

The director rose too. He was at least six feet seven in height, and he towered over Tom from the peak of his extra five inches.

"You give that back!"

"But it's no use to you, so why should you want it?"

"Man, I can try!"

"You know in advance what the result of trying would be."

"You might be a genius," said the director, "I don't say you're not—but I know damned well that you are a madman. Why do you write plays if you don't want them performed?"

"To prove," Tom said patiently, "that sometime, somewhere, there must be a stopping-point. And when that stopping-point is established it will be final, and carry the whole of sensible public opinion—not that small and noisy body of opinion which has brought silliness to the point of dementia—behind it."

"Please give it back to me."

"No sense in that."

"Let me at least see what I can do!"

"Without changes?"

"Goddamn it, without changes, then!"

"In that case," said Tom, "God rest you merry, and let absolutely nothing you dismay."

Dropping the typescript back on the desk, he tottered lightly down the stairs into the sweet fresh air before he could be obstructed. He fancied he heard the wild, beseeching calls of a voice quite unaccustomed to beseech: but he did not turn his head.

Feeling gloriously that the whole thing was off his hands, he walked along to St. Martin's in the Fields, where he offered up, in his practical and unemotive way, a prayer of thanksgiving, then went into the National Gallery, where he looked at some Flemish primitives with love and intimacy, as if they were dear old friends—martyrs, Marys, Jehovahs and all.

At twelve he telephoned to Pringle, and asked her if by any chance she were free for lunch.

Within half an hour, she presented herself joyously at Brusa's, in St. Martin's Lane, and she was walking like a small empress. Love appeared to have raised her insteps and slimmed her calves. She had abandoned the wig, and her short-chopped, cleanly hair caught fourteen colors from the sunlight.

"How nice your insteps look, Pringle," said Tom involuntarily.

"Oh, do they? I never noticed."

She tucked into gnocchi with even more than her normal appetite, forking the last crumbs around in a delectable mixture of butter and parmesan. Passion reduces the desire for food in many, but it is possible that the most profound passion increases it inordinately. Isn't every meal in love an *agape*?—or so Pringle might have rationalized her behavior, had she known what an *agape* was.

"It is all over," said Tom. "A *Potted Shrimp* is in the hands of an awful man bursting with enthusiasm, who is going to come up against a brick wall. So far as I am concerned, the joke is over."

Pringle said, "I am so afraid of making you angry." She hesitated.

He was touched and flattered. He had never thought of himself as a person likely to cause alarm.

"How on earth could you?"

She burst out: "*I think it is a wonderful play!*"

"No, no, you can't possibly!" He was alarmed now. "It isn't pleasant, exactly."

"That isn't precisely the adjective I should choose for it myself, dear Pringle."

"But one can't forget it. It's so strong! And so brave. So fabulously brave!"

"Please, Pringle."

"But it is."

"Come and feed the pigeons."

It was the off-hour, when office workers have returned to work, and tourists have not yet finished lunch. The pigeons, hungry, settled on Pringle's shoulders and along her arms, and a fat heraldic one disposed itself, like a crest, upon the crown of her head. "Isn't it m'hav'lous?" she shouted.

When she had fed the birds six cans of grain, Tom took her for a walk in the park.

"Pringle," he said.

"What?"

He was delighted to see how impervious she now was to the stares and whispers of passers-by.

"I want you to promise me something."

She looked at him with a beautiful clarity of trust, her eyes wide, without tension, not a tense line in her face.

"Anything in the world."

"No, you mustn't be so sweeping. But you must promise me not to deceive yourself into thinking that you admire that ridiculous, indecent and puerile play. You are, in my eyes, a very nice sort of park in springtime. I don't want to see it all littered with soiled newspapers and used contraceptives."

She flushed, and turned her head away.

"Yes, you thought that was pretty crude of me."

"Only because you're you."

"Nevertheless, you did. So if you can think me crude to say what I did just now, how can you pretend to like a piece of offal like my play?"

"But it has terrific power—"

"Please. You weren't born to sing in chorus. Promise me you will loathe it, and say so. Promise me."

She stopped, and looked at him. Duncan had given her, by now, an "image" of daintiness and distinction. The world was in flower to Pringle, whenever she wanted to open the door of that world more than a crack.

"If you say so."

"I do say so."

He put his arm round her waist and they walked on. She melted against him: she was all softness, like a girl made of swansdown. He took his arm away again, afraid.

"I love you, Tom," she said.

"No, my dear, you don't."

"But I do."

Blue-white sky shone between the last scant trellis of golden leaves. The pelicans were squawking by the water's edge.

"No. Because, darling Pringle, I am no good at that. I am happy only when I am alone and selfish. I am no good to you at all."

"I will make you good to me."

"Don't you realize," he said earnestly, "that you can have pretty well any young man in London to whom you take a fancy? You are what they call a trend-setter. Do you know that shops are selling little frocks called

Pringles, and getting rid of them like hot cakes?"

"Are they? I didn't know. They must be awful."

"If you look over to your right, you will see two Pringles approaching at this very minute. The fact that they look awful and not like you is irrelevant."

"I don't want to look to my right."

"Then if you don't, you needn't. Dear, you are going straight to the top—I don't know what sort of top, but you are. And, you see, I don't care about tops one bit."

They stopped again. Her lower lip trembled like a baby calf's.

"Please, Tom. I won't go anywhere near the top, if only you—"

"Listen, I can't. I shall never be any good to you. Also, I am nearly twice your age. But you are a darling, and I shall think so all my life."

She stiffened, the muscles of her legs protruding. "O.K."

"Good girl."

"Anyway, O.K. for now," she said defiantly. "I shall write books and become famous in quite a different way, and then you won't have to be ashamed of me because you see me all over the place in beastly mugs and baskets. So there!"

"Pringle, I have never been ashamed! You can't think that. Look here, it is not that at all. I—"

But she had spurted away from him, over forbidden grass, and was waving almost dementedly for a taxi. Sadly, he let her go. It occurred to him that he appeared to do everything wrong.

17

IN WHICH WE RECEIVE A BULLETIN
RELATING TO PERCY, AND ARE PRES-
ENT AT A CRISIS IN CORK STREET.

To explain how Percy Cimarosa (that was his
name) effected his jail-break would be not only irrelevant but irresponsible. It might give other people ideas.

As a routine matter, the police waited confidently at
his own home and at the home of his aunt, but he was
too old a hand to go near either. On leaving the jail, he
went to a barber's shop immediately in the rear of it,
where a friend lived, got a change of clothing, dyed his
hair dark-brown and there spent four comfortable days
before he went off again. Television appeals failed to
uncover him. Dr. Ames supposed that he would call
upon her, probably with a knife, so she put a revolver
in the drawer of her desk and awaited him without
emotion; but he did not appear.

Ten days went by.

In Cork Street, a very long way from Percy's hideout,
both in distance and in spirit, Cosmo and Dorothy
were hunting for a successor to Miss Few. She was going placidly about the business of putting things
straight for her supplanter. She had resisted all appeals
that she should stay on for another two months, at the
least.

"My friend is very old-fashioned, I'm afraid," she
told Dorothy, "he doesn't like the idea of me working."

She looked as nearly coy as was possible for a woman of her age, and cast of feature.

It was a Saturday morning early in November. Pringle had come wistfully into the shop in the faint hope of seeing Tom, who had been invisible since the walk in St. James's Park. She was doing less work for Duncan now, more work for purely commercial photographers. This was because he seemed to have fallen in love with her, and could not resist dancing about her with what he took to be an engaging boyishness. He was even making a parade, for her sake, of drinking less, but she noticed that he kept disappearing into the dark room and returning with a fierce whiskey-breath.

"You!" Dorothy called out suddenly, so loudly that Pringle dropped the book she had been holding. "That's an idea!"

"What is?"

"You. You write. You know something about books, I suppose. Why don't you come and lend a hand here? I'd train you myself."

Even to Pringle, who was a very humble young girl, this seemed a wild piece of insolence. Could Dorothy seriously imagine, after all that had happened to her (Breckenridge's youngest brother, who was called Peewee, had offered to marry her last week, on the sole occasion when, in a fit of loneliness and longing for Tom, she had agreed to go out with him), that she was going to work in a bookshop?

Dorothy did.

"Oh, I'm not so mad as I seem," she said, when Pringle did not reply. "We know there's a vogue for you at the moment, but these things don't last forever, do they? And it may be years before you make fourpence out of those books of yours—anyway, it certainly doesn't look like it. So wouldn't it be a sort of insurance to have—well, let's call it a 'trade in your hands,' shall we?"

No answer.

"Well?"

"No thank you," said Pringle. "Thank you very much, though."

Dorothy wagged an admonitory finger. "Now, now, don't be so quick with your answers! We could start you at twelve pounds a week—"

"I make that an hour, sometimes," Pringle said steadily, "and I put it into Post Office Savings."

"Of course, if you don't want to be helped—!"

Dorothy was very angry.

"It was nice of you to think of it."

Cosmo came in. "To think of what?"

"Mrs. Hines very kindly offered me a job," said Pringle, "and though this is a lovely shop, I don't think it would suit me."

Cosmo looked at Dorothy with one of his really terrible smiles, which seemed to be without the smallest kind of meaning.

"Oh, all right," she said furiously, "there was no harm in trying. And there's no need for Pringle to put on airs."

Miss Few came bustling in, a pile of order-books in her arms. "There you are, Mr. Hines! All shipshape. —What's the matter, Editha?"

"Nothing. I'm just going."

"I'll look in on you in a day or so."

"I wish you would. Good-bye."

Pringle walked out, not with a schoolgirl's dash, but

with something not totally unallied to stateliness.

"For God's sake," said Dorothy, "talk about a sweet little swollen head!"

Miss Few took one look at Cosmo and vanished again.

"And now," he said, "come on."

Taking her by the upper arm, he drew her towards a small room which was his own sanctum, calling to Miss Few to keep an eye on the shop for ten minutes

He shut the door softly and completely.

"And now."

"And now what?" Dorothy's eyes glazed. She stuck out her chin.

"Are you totally without foresight? What did you mean by offering a job to that girl and upsetting her into the bargain?"

"Without foresight! It was her future I was thinking of, but all I got was ingratitude and swelled head. Let her be upset, what do we care?"

"Do you realize that that girl may eventually marry Peewee Stanton, or someone like that? And that those people are the customers we entirely depend on?"

"Of course she won't marry Peewee Stanton. She's common."

"I think, my dear," said Cosmo, "that of all the silly women I have ever met, you are unquestionably the silliest."

It would not seem, at first sight, that a remark of this order would be a real crisis in the life of anyone. It might, of course, provoke a pretty stringent quarrel in any family, but one would scarcely expect it to bring a whole lifetime down. Dorothy felt for a chair and sat on it.

Now the domestic relations of the Hineses had not

always been totally amicable: but actual hostilities had not before been declared. It was hard to realize now that in this tight-buttoned man, with the white silk hair and the bloodshot eyes, an avid and cunning businessman, there had once been a young person with sufficient streak of artiness in his soul to believe that a girl-poet with the beginnings (however misguided) of a reputation would be a good person to marry. Like many men who look brutal late in life, Cosmo had once been a disappointed romantic. He was not romantic now. Dorothy, with her mania for motherhood, had used him as a stud animal and then pushed the results out of the way as far as was consonant with her pose as primal mother, Gaea Tellus, and all the rest of it. For a while, he had quite enjoyed her random flutters of success, the company of her literary friends, the elevation of himself (when she felt like elevating him) into a sort of piece-work Maecenas. But since she had flopped, and was quite unlikely to rise again, the last rags of husbandly feeling had fallen away from Cosmo's soul like the last scraps of wallpaper from a bombed site. Her rudeness, which he had once found faintly attractive, since he liked to watch the discomfiture of others, now seemed nothing but a noisy nuisance. It was a long time since he had felt impelled to put the finishing touches to the ruin of the writer Skipton, simply because Skipton had insulted Dorothy in the high style, the grand manner. If Skipton were alive today and having a go at Dorothy, Cosmo would have leaned happily back in the dress-circle, fingers tip to tip, exquisitely non-partisan.

"You can dare—" she began.

"I can dare. I wish you'd stay in Kensington and try to learn how to cook. That filthy shish-kebab is not enough on which to build a reputation. I don't need you in the shop any more. If I can replace Few, I'll get someone who understands figures. When I think of how you egged me into permitting that ludicrous reading—"

"Cosmo," said Dorothy, "I am beginning to think you are mad. I know you aren't drunk. And I know—*I know*—that you love me!"

"Do you, my dear?"

"Well—don't you?"

Bold is the man who can say, just simply, "No." Many men are hard enough not to care about the effect of a "no" upon the recipient: but if the recipient happens to be a wife, they had better care (and they usually do) about the result of a "no" upon themselves. For life has to be trundled through somehow, when two people dislike each other but are too weary, or too afraid, to go through the grimy hodgepodge of separation or divorce.

Cosmo said, "No."

She flared at him, "You know you do! You're trying to punish me, just because you think I made a mistake about that ridiculous girl!"

There was a long silence. Cosmo picked up a Golden Cockerel book and prodded it reverently. He was beginning to think again.

He said at last, "Well, my dear. Love's only a word, isn't it? And 'no' is only a word, too."

It was enough, just about enough, to enable a shared life to be carried on, even if it were henceforth to be carried on in a kind of spiritual bath-chair.

Luckily, business became brisk just then, so it was necessary for them both to supersede Miss Few in the shop, and bow and beck as they always did, as they always would, in the future so far as they could foresee it.

Dorothy had pulled herself together. She was going to forgive Cosmo, forgive and forget. She was even pleased, to some extent, by the thought that she could deal so calmly with such unprecedented happenings. Anyway, she was not going to think about them any more. She was a little afraid of the night, when thinking might become far too easy.

18

"MAKING UP A WOODFIRE WHEN YOU
ARE IN LOVE IS THE MATERIAL EX-
PRESSION OF YOUR SENTIMENTS."
(BALZAC, *Etude de Femme.*) HAROLD
EXEMPLIFIES THIS, UNTIL INTERRUPTED.

The children were in bed, and seemed likely, for
once, to stay there. On the infrequent occasions when
this happened, Zena was apt to think (a) that they
couldn't be well, (b) that they had permanently
changed their ways. Neither thought bore any relation
to the truth. They were simply tired.

Round the heights of Highgate, enormous gales
howled and rumbled like specters graduated from a finishing school for ghosts. Harold, releasing his wife for a
moment from his circling arm, threw another log on
the fire, and a shower of sparks leaped up into a burst
of violent flame.

They were very happy, in one of those intermittences
wherein they looked with astonished delight upon each
other, marveling at the pleasures of their marriage.
Since Harold was by no means sickeningly uxorious, he
did not think about this most of the time: he simply
accepted it, and so did Zena. But there were moments
when he saw her as he had seen her when they first
met, nearly eighteen years ago, and he needed to make
it clear to her just how grateful and astonished he was
that the actual feeling of "being in love" should flash

up, from time to time, even now, as the sparks flashed up into the chimney.

He had never in his life been jealous of her, since, despite her pleasant appearance and personality, she seemed to have small sexual attraction for any man but himself. Perhaps she did not court it. Men liked her and admired her, and she was popular with them; they made no advances, however, and this suited Harold down to the ground. Even a friend of his who was accustomed, when greeting women friends, to thrust a hand down their necks in an unthinking sort of way, as if reaching in a barrel of biscuits, never pawed Zena.

Harold would have been surprised, distressed, and perhaps a little gratified, to know how often she had been jealous of him. His appearance, unlike her own, was thoroughly deceptive; he looked, not perhaps like a rake, but like something which would once have been called a "flirt." He was constancy itself.

"We are very snug and smug tonight," he said to her, "smug like Dickens in his euphoric moods. Let's buy a cricket. I expect you can get them at the Army and Navy Stores."

Rising to put more wood on the fire, he skidded on a blue truck left on the rug by one of the children, and fell over. He swore.

"Do get up," said Zena tartly, "you can't possibly be hurt."

He insisted that he was, so to please him she fetched a plaster and put it over a minuscule graze. "There. Now stop shouting."

"Thank you, pet."

He restored his arm to her waist. "We haven't heard from old Tom recently. What do you suppose is happening?"

"Oh dear!" Zena leaped to her feet. "I forgot to tell you. He's coming round. He rang up this afternoon."

"When's he coming?"

"Any moment now. I'll have to tidy up."

"Damn and blast it."

But Harold did not really mind, and nor did she. Like many devoted people married a long time, both felt instinctively that scenes of demonstrative bliss ought not to go on too long, unless bedtime was immanent. A certain shyness would slip in, expressing itself in the feeling of one or the other of them, or both, that it might be nice to read a book: only who could be the first to suggest this without hurting the other?

So they both bustled around, kicking toys out of the way, emptying ashtrays, fetching ice for drinks

"It was awful of me not to remember," Zena said, "because he sounded in a state. But it was just at the moment when Peter had put his gum-boot in the dishwasher and it all went out of my mind."

The bell rang.

"Only just in time," said Zena, surveying what, by her unexacting standards, was now an orderly room. "I'm sorry, I should have told you."

Harold forgave her.

When Tom came in, he was looking like Hamlet. Since he was not by nature a Hamlet-like man, this alarmed them both. It was perhaps by chance that he was wearing a black suit: but he also wore an air both ominous and baited, and his customary totter seemed more like a limp caused by having one's stockings hanging like gyves around one's ankles.

"Good God!" Harold exclaimed. "What's up?"

"I should like a drink."

Tom did not speak until he had swallowed half a

glassful of whiskey. He sat: they stood looking down upon him, like eminent and anxious doctors in consultation.

"*They are going to put it on,*" he said, "*and I can't stop them.*"

"You mean, the play?"

"What else should I mean? I heard from that damned Christopher this morning. He couldn't raise the money at first, though everyone seemed crazy about the thing. Because, naturally, the Lord Chamberlain's office would have gone mad. He tried it on the Arts Theatre and they said no. But now, God help us all, he's all fixed up to direct it for COBRA!"

"For what?" Zena's question was a little shriek.

"Well may you ask. COBRA. College of British Repertory Art. It's a drama school in Holloway, with its own brand-new theater club. When they put on anything, all the critics flood in. And damned Christopher says they've agreed to do it without changes." He gave a pale smile. "I need hardly tell you that Finney, Burton and Warner were none of them interested in playing Grunt."

"They can't do it without changes," said Zena.

"Well," said Tom, looking down, "I did agree to one only. It will be a property goose."

His feeling for dumb animals had conquered him. So far as he was concerned, there was not going to be a procession of victims through the hands of some avaricious poulterer.

"Also," he added, "how I am going to stop them symbolizing my perfectly practical stage directions in actual performance, I don't know. But it will be foul enough."

"But why did you agree to let them have it at all?

I've read some horrifying stuff in my life, but never anything like yours."

"I am so glad. There is a most sinister tendency growing to admire it. To answer your question by another, Zena, what else could I do? I left the thing with Christopher. I can hardly take it away again now." He drained his glass and held it out at arm's length for refilling.

"When did you hear about this?" she asked him.

"This morning. The man had me hauled out of a class I was taking, just to exult. He seriously imagined that I should be pleased."

"What did you say?"

Tom replied that he had said something courteous and had attempted to hang up. But the director, crazed with enthusiasm, had insisted on detailing his plans. "He's done most of the casting. He's cast Grunt, Roo and Skipper, but not Babybaby. He was so very pleased with himself."

"Whom has he cast?" Harold enquired, interested despite himself in this *marginalia*.

"I can't remember. I'd never heard of any of them."

"I'd know."

"Well, I don't." There was a querulous note in Tom's voice, unfamiliar because it was defensive.

Silence fell. Meanwhile, the fire dropped to pieces, splitting up like a house in a bombing-raid to reveal devastated parlors, bathrooms, lavatories, of purple, rose and cineraria-blue, incandescently burning. It was Tom who, absent-mindedly, made it up.

"The awful thing," he said slowly, still on his haunches over the hearth, "is that it's beginning to scare me. I didn't, as they say, 'know I had it in me.' I wake in the night and wonder what sort of monster I am that I can, in full consciousness, put all that ordure in the way of decent, innocent, harmless people."

"When I engage in jokes," said Harold cheerfully, "I always get carried away by them. People do, you know."

Tom raised his cold, limpid, sherry-colored eyes, and he stared at him. "I want you to promise something. Both of you."

"Of course we will, dear," said Zena.

She was all mother, though not in Dorothy's fashion. He could have put both gum-boots in her dishwasher and she might have smacked him, in a formal fashion, but she would never have raised her voice in rebuke.

"If you ever catch *me* suspecting—even for the fraction of a second—that there is the faintest degree of virtue in that play, I beg you to come down on me like two tons of bricks."

Harold hesitated. "You can't honestly be afraid of that?"

"I don't know. Duncan thinks it has its points. Dorothy thinks it's a masterpiece. As for Pringle—I'm only just holding her in check."

"Matthew Pryar?"

"He and Jane both think it is entirely unspeakable."

Harold hit Tom so warmly on the shoulder that he nearly sent him face-downwards into the fire. "Steady, now! Come on, sit up and have another drink. All is well, the clouds of phantasm have cleared away."

"Why have they cleared away?"

"Because Zena and I think it's unutterable, and so do you, and we always will. With the Pryars, that makes five of us."

Tom drew a deep sigh of relief. "Thank God. Do you know, I have been on the verge of nightmare—"

"Yes, yes, old boy, so you implied, but it's too silly to dwell on."

"I still don't see why you can't take it away." Zena's round face was puzzled.

Tom told her an idea had struck him. Simply as a means of testing how much directors would tolerate, the joke now seemed to be a thin one. After all, everyone knew that they would tolerate anything on earth, given half the chance. Surely the fascinating thing would be to discover how much a first-night audience (which must, presumably, even on statistical grounds, comprise some well-balanced persons) would be prepared to put up with.

"How big an audience?" Zena asked suspiciously.

"It's quite a sizable theater, for what it is. Five hundred."

"Not much of a sample," said Harold, making a face and printing with his forefinger imaginary percentages upon the air.

"Good enough for my restricted purpose." Tom was looking much like Hamlet.

Zena asked when the play was likely to be put on

"God help us, in three weeks' time."

"Oh dear," said Harold, "that means the Pryars will have gone. I was hoping for their moral support."

"One can't have everything."

"But that would have been a something."

"I suppose so. Yes, maybe you're right. But it's past praying for."

"I shall pray for the detention of the Pryars all the same," said Zena. "It seems to me that we are going to need all the moral support we can get. Tom, I expect you are moderately hungry. I have a little tin of pâté and I shall make toast. It is real pâté."

After Tom had eaten, the color (which had been nonexistent before he started work upon his play) returned to his long, thin cheeks.

They began, though tentatively, to discuss the production. All three knew that it was essential for them to keep at a remove from it, that it was permissible to be fascinated, but impermissible to become in the slightest degree emotionally involved. Indeed, Harold and Zena were covertly crossing their fingers.

"The audience will come in," said Tom, "to find the stage empty, apart from a gas-meter and a half-glimpsed urinal at the back."

"Why half-glimpsed?" Harold asked, luminous with suspicion by this time.

Tom blinked. "Could I have been trimming? All right. It shall be fully glimpsed."

"Isn't that making changes?" said Zena.

"I didn't say *I* wouldn't make changes. I merely refused to sanction Christopher's. Anyway, any change I make for the worse must be all to the good."

"And then?" Harold prompted.

"Well, the audience come in to find—"

"Oh Lord," said Zena, "what I'd do for a nice plush curtain! These boring conformist persons have destroyed half the excitement of going to the theater. No shiver of anticipation at a line of light across the stage, low down. No excitement. Just actors trooping sheepishly on. *Nothing* stops them looking sheepish, just for one embarrassing moment. And what a lot of trouble it means at the end, especially if it's Shakespeare!"

"Do you remember, darling," Harold said, "that otherwise wonderful *Lear*, when they had to get rid of the multiple bodies at the end, and there was a rather frail Edgar lugging off a frightfully robust Edmund,

167 ᵷꓷ

who could have given him three stone? I was in row A, and it was all I could do not to offer to help."

"Just like you, pet," Zena said fondly, acknowledging his moral qualities.

"Still you can't have a curtain with *Shrimp*—" said Tom, only too professionally. Their hostile silence checked him. "Sorry. You see, that is the terrible danger. The danger of taking the thing with a straight face."

"It is not that danger, precisely," Zena said with some severity, "it is the danger of calling it *Shrimp*. Do you realize how deeply that could involve you?"

"I do. I beg your pardon. Well—as I was saying: I forget what I was saying. Oh, I know. Curtain's up, anyway, the lights are down. Then Grunt walks on, right down to the footlights—"

"There aren't any."

"I know. Zena, you are humiliating me. He walks to the front of the apron-stage and he cries out—"

"We know what he cries out. It is a tedious cliché-word, particularly depressing because originally it was meant to be onomatopoeic."

"Zena!" Harold looked really shocked.

"Well, so it was."

"Darling, please."

"Anyway, we know all about it. So we will take it as said."

Tom had never seen her in such matronly control. She looked like a perfectly balanced chatelaine who ran the castle perfectly while her lord was fooling around on the crusades.

"Anyway," Tom persevered, "that's what he cries out. I am rather hoping for an immediate hostile demonstration."

"Don't be silly," said Harold, "it is far too early for that, old boy. People would hold their horses; that is, if they had any horses to hold."

"I suppose so. But maybe within the first fifteen minutes—" Suddenly he yawned. "You have both helped me no end." He kissed them, bending from his height like a fishing stork or an anglepoise lamp. "I think now, if you don't mind, that I could do with a good night's sleep."

The gales yelled round him as he waited on the door-step for the summoned taxi.

19

SHOWING HOW JANE AND MATTHEW ARE DE-
TAINED, AND ZENA'S PRAYER IS ANSWERED

There was pretty well nothing Percy did not know
about the Pryars. Through his own observation, he
knew that Matthew invariably went to one of his clubs
for an hour about 6:15 P.M., and at 7:30 sharp returned, perfectly sober, to take his wife out to dinner.
Through enquiry, he knew that Jane had not brought
her maid to London with her, but was employing one
temporarily, an obtuse-looking woman who slept in.
Also, through enquiry, he knew of what their first-floor
apartment consisted: drawing-room, dining-room, two
bedrooms (one with dressing-room attached), kitchen
and two bathrooms. There was gas and electricity. And
through careful study of the silly old press, he knew
that the Pryars were to leave for the United States by
sea on a certain day.

Accordingly, on the day previous to this, at 6:30 P.M
when he had seen Matthew depart, Percy, simply at-
tired as an inspector from the Gas Board, rang the bell.
His attire had to be simple, since it could not be complete: in addition to his only blue suit he wore a peaked
cap with a badge on it, and carried a sheaf of papers
pegged to a wooden board from which a pencil was
dangling.

The maid admitted him, a pert girl, though as he
had suspected, obtuse.

"What, at this hour of night?"

"We've had a leak reported, somewhere along this side of the street. Got to take a dekko everywhere, and don't think I like working overtime. Where's the meter?"

Naturally, she did not know.

Percy mooched round the kitchen, the maid at his heels. He peered into the bathrooms—a most implausible action had she known the first thing about meters, which she did not.

"Who's that?" cried a voice like a silver bugle.

"Gas-man, madam. He thinks we've got a leak."

"Oh. Then tell him to be quick and find it."

Percy enquired what this door led to.

"Broom-cupboard. It might be in there."

"Could be. They stick them in all sorts of places."

He let her precede him into it, then shut the door on them both. Using old, familiar skills, he laid her out with a rabbit punch, caught her as she fell, so that there should be no noise, and coiled her up into a corner.

"Ta a lot!" he said loudly, as he shut her in, and went to call upon Mrs. Pryar.

She was in the bedroom, packing last-minute articles into a small case: her maid had done the rest. She wore a beautiful rose-colored evening dress which made Percy sneer on principle, though he secretly thought she looked a treat.

As he stood in the doorway, two fingers to his cap, she straightened up and turned upon him a gaze of pure aquamarine which would have made a more imaginative man think of a death-ray.

"Why, Percy, what a surprise," said Jane Pryar, by no means put off by hair-dye.

Matthew was astonished, when he returned only

three quarters of an hour later, since a friend of his had failed to keep an appointment, to find his wife, not mixing drinks before going out, but reclining like a sultana in the rosiness of her bed.

"You're early, Matt-Matt! How convenient. Now will you please telephone the police and also a doctor, because I think I have fractured my kneecap. No, don't stand there and argue. I just managed to get into bed, but I cannot get out again to reach the telephone, which is in an absurd position, over there on the desk. Please dial whatever it is, and tell them we have got Mr. Cimarosa."

Relaxed, she was as beautiful as a bunch of moss roses. No one would have thought, to look at her, that she was in considerable pain, since she had no more lines than usual on her triangular face. The only remarkable feature was that she lay there in her underclothes: she had managed to drag off her evening dress, though not to strip and put on a nightgown. Still, many heroes with crosses to show for it had done less well than Jane.

Matthew blanched. "Who?"

"It's Hedwig's Percy."

"Where have we got him?"

"In the bathroom. But I guess, as he is so silent, he has been fool enough to try to escape through the window. I dare say he is on the sill, unable to go forward or back. If he had not been so stupid I should never have been able to switch the key to the outside. I did tell you he was stupid. Now please, Matt, telephone the police, as I told you, and then a doctor. For me. Of course, Percy may need one too. Oh—and let poor Doreen out of the broom-cupboard. I do hope she's not seriously hurt."

The police came very quickly, but not so quickly that, in the space before their arrival, Matthew could not rescue the maid, who was moaning but still healthy, put her on her own bed and rush back to hear the story from his wife.

It seemed that Percy, with menaces, had demanded money and jewelry. Jane had given him four pounds, which was all she had on her, and had then asked him to leave.

"What did you say?"

"I simply said, 'Out!' —Do you know, for a moment, I thought he was going to obey?"

However, he had persisted about the jewels which, she told him, were in the drawer of the dressing-table in the bathroom. But, she had added, there was a combination lock on the case. "Poor Percy, I really do not know how he has managed to get through this rough world. He is so very credulous."

"Oh God," said Matthew, aghast, "was he armed?"

"If you are referring to a bread-knife, yes. He has a one-track mind."

Tactfully she had led Percy to the bathroom and pointed out where the jewel-case was. He had been silly enough, in his cupidity, to let her get behind him. "While he was opening the drawer, I just removed the door-key. Then I backed out."

But he had been a little too quick at this point

"I suppose my dress rustled. Anyway, I was just closing the door when he charged it. Thank God it opens outwards; I always thought it was a ridiculous sort of door, but it does have its uses."

"And then?"

"I pushed as hard as I could, got my knee into it and managed to lock him in. That was how I hurt my knee.

I heard him pummeling and pounding, but I knew he was all right, so I dragged myself into bed, which was as far as I could get. I have been perfectly comfortable, but worried about Doreen. I am so very glad you were back early. I do believe in Providence, don't you?"

When the police arrived they found Percy rigid as a statue on the bathroom sill, as Jane had predicted, funking both a crossing and a drop that would have been child's play to a more athletic man. (It would even have been child's play to Matthew, who had stopped jumping thirty years ago.) They hauled him in, and he seemed quite pleased to be recaptured.

The police were happy to hear that the Pryars felt they must now delay their departure for the United States, because of Jane's injury, since she would certainly be required to give evidence.

By this time the doctor had arrived, and had been ordered in stringent tones to attend to Doreen first. The maid had been very sick and was suffering from shock: nothing else was wrong with her.

Jane had not fractured her kneecap, but had dislocated it. It would have to be set under an anesthetic: meanwhile, she was given an injection and some pink and blue capsules, and went joyfully to sleep.

"Your wife is an altogether remarkable woman," the doctor said, looking coldly at Matthew, as if he felt him undeserving of such a creature.

Matthew agreed. Perhaps he implied agreement, too, with his lack of desserts, for the doctor softened towards him and agreed to drink his whiskey.

Next day was spent by Jane in the London Clinic, and on the following one she returned to the flat, to find herself embowered in carnations, and with a heroine's press.

"How very kind," she murmured, in unconscious reminiscence of Queen Victoria, "how very, very kind. I have never really been praised for my moral qualities before. I do feel, somehow, that Percy has been very kind, too. I don't suppose they'd let me send him some spare radio parts, would they? Oh, these lovely, lovely newspapers!"

She enjoyed herself receiving selected pressmen.

On the third day she was limping around the apartment, as busy as ever, though Doreen was still suffering from nervous prostration and had to be waited upon.

When Dorothy Merlin called, Jane was not pleased to see her. One cannot, however, snub a woman who is carrying a week's takings in lilac and freesia, or not very hard. "So kind," she had to say.

"But how brave!" Dorothy exclaimed. "How splendidly brave! Jane, if I may call you so—"

"Yes, Mrs.—yes, Dorothy. Of course. How very kind."

"We are all so glad we shall have you with us for a little while longer. The whole of Cork Street," Dorothy added grandiloquently.

"Of course, if I liked flying, I could go home more or less as scheduled, but I'd rather have ships, and since, at this time of the year, the sea is quite likely to be rough, a ship is not a place where one can limp in any comfort."

"You'll be here for Tom's wonderful play!"

"Will I?"

"Of course. I shall see to it that he sends you seats for the first night."

"You can't mean that play I read? The shrimp thing?"

Dorothy assured her it was that very one.

"If someone is seriously going to present that most peculiar work, I can promise you that nothing is going to keep me away."

"We shall all go together," said Dorothy, "and form a marvelous little *claque*. Tom's success has quite made me forget my own temporary disappointment. In fact," she confided roguishly, "I may not be so very disappointed after all. I've sent *my* play to COBRA, and if they're too backward to understand, I shall try LBW. Little Balham Workshop," she explained. "It's a new thing, of course, but terribly exciting. I do adore the workshop concept."

"I don't much," Jane said reflectively. "It makes me think of blowlamps and shavings and people breathing hard. I do feel myself that all evidence of work should be out of sight before one gets to the theater. Also, that the actors should have got round to changing their clothes, and not wear tabards on the top half and jeans on the lower."

Dorothy, smiling fondly, said it was probably a question of generation.

"No doubt," said Jane. "But though it seems heretical to say so, it often occurs to me that some generations may be better than others. Come to that, why not?"

20

IN WHICH TOM RELENTS TO-
WARDS PRINGLE, AND TAKES
HER TO A REHEARSAL.

Pringle now made regular appearances in *The Tatler* and *The Queen*, photographed, usually, in the company of Peewee Stanton, though occasionally in Duncan's. Cameramen loved her. In a roomful of toothy fillies, egg-faced and anxious, she stood out in her knock-kneed elegance, cropped hair, little black (or mulberry) dress, cross-strapped dancing shoes. You could spot her a mile away.

Was she at least enjoying herself? Certainly not. Her capacity for enjoyment was, had she but known it, lower than the average: this might have been something to do with her metabolism. Now, she was going through these social antics for a purpose both heroic and pathetic: she wanted to make Tom jealous.

It did not occur to her that he would never have opened either *The Tatler* or *The Queen*. This is not to say that his tastes were particularly austere: he enjoyed non-violent detective stories stuffed with character and atmosphere, and in addition to the *Times* and *Telegraph*, always took one popular paper which he read first. His interest in London "society" was, however, nil, and since he was not a woman and didn't go to the hairdresser, magazines specializing in this field were never made a matter of *faute de mieux*.

So he did not know that she went around with Pee-wee, nor would he have cared if he had known.

He liked Pringle very much, and had it not been for her embarrassing declaration, not only of love but of admiration for the detested play, would have taken her out again. He knew, though, that despite her absurdities she was frail of temperament, easily wounded and, like all people easily wounded, ready at the drop of a hat to court the next wound likely to come her way.

Duncan was still mumbling to her about love, but with less conviction. She was so unlike his usual run of girls that she sapped his confidence. He would even have married her, had she been interested: he had often thought the time was coming when he would have to settle down. Yet he knew that she was not for him, and rather stealthily (as if she cared whether he was stealthy or not) had begun to acquire more Pats, Clares, Paulines and Lisas.

All this Dorothy, from over the way, watched with fury. She had always hated Duncan's young women, and in earlier days, when he was much bound to her, had managed to nip a good many of these romances in the bud. Nobody could have said that she herself entertained a passion for Duncan, but when she saw him bounding out of the shop, breathing animatedly down the neck of yet another Pat, Clare, Pauline or Lisa, her color would darken, her pulse-rate increase.

"He is disgusting," she would say to Cosmo, "he must be over forty. If he isn't careful, it will turn to satyriasis."

"Come, my dear." He smiled inwardly. Satyriasis was a state he himself knew something about.

"Animal!" said Dorothy, not meaning her husband.

They had not yet found a replacement for Miss Few, who had very kindly agreed to stay on for two more weeks. To Dorothy's irritation, she was making herself conspicuous by wearing maternity dresses—which were quite unnecessary, since she was not yet in her third month of pregnancy. If they had been quiet ones, it might not have mattered so much: but she seemed to be glorying in what Dorothy, that emancipated spirit, secretly thought of as her "shame." These dresses were hectically floral, with bulging wrap-over skirts. Cosmo remarked to his wife that if Miss Few could have found one with an over-all design of scarlet A's, she would have jumped at it.

Pringle, as a most unusual privilege, had been allowed to meet Miss Few's lover who, to her astonishment, turned out to be a middle-aged man of strikingly good looks. They were a pair devoted as Harold and Zena Boulton, which was saying a great deal. What Pringle longed to know was what prevented them from getting married: but she was never to be told, and nor was anybody else.

She had patched up her difference with Dorothy, since she hated to abandon the shop as a Tom-watching center—"Why don't you get a pair of field-glasses?" Dorothy had demanded, having divined her intention—and she usually dropped in once a day.

Dorothy, meeting Tom in the street and feeling the impulse to what, in a less serious character, might have been called mischief, and what, in her case, might have been called malice pure and simple, informed him of Pringle's wiles. "I asked her why she didn't buy field-glasses."

"I'm sure you're mistaken," he replied.

"Girls!" Dorothy exclaimed, on a lightsome trill.

He went thoughtfully away. He was regarded by all his friends as amiable, loyal, tough-natured, but rather cold. In fact, he had a warm heart and an aversion to giving pain of any kind.

So he telephoned Pringle and asked her whether she would like to attend a rehearsal with him.

Her immediate silence, followed by a tearing gasp, told him how correct Dorothy had been, and he almost regretted the invitation. Then he thought, Oh, well.

He had only visited the theater once, since rehearsals began, and that was to make sure no changes whatsoever had been made either in his text or his intention. They had not, and he watched the result in baffled disgust. Only once had he intervened, rising thin and lengthy from his stall.

"Please excuse me."

Everything came to a halt. They stared at him.

"I observe that Roo and Babybaby are kicking Grunt in the ribs. I did not say the ribs. I specified the groin."

He was relieved to see, over the faces of one or two of the actors, the spread of a sickly color. He would have thought ill of them had they been enjoying themselves. He slipped away before the coffee-break, waiting to talk neither to them nor to the director.

His arrival with Pringle, a week before the opening, seemed to cheer everyone considerably. They were all so dispirited, and two of them so queasy, that the advent of a famous face was like that of a visiting angel. They all wanted to be introduced to her. As usual, she tripped up to them like a child at her first party, as usual, hung her head and switched her fringe of hair about like a horse troubled by flies. She was beginning to learn, only too surely, what was expected of her.

"Look here, Tom," the director said, "I want to change two words. Only two words."

"No."

"If we don't, it may ruin us. There's a limit to what people will take."

"I'm so glad to hear you say that. It confirms my own optimistic view."

"You've got to let me—"

"I said no," said Tom, adding, "dear boy," a term he had found popular among stage people and which, in the kindness of his heart, he felt might soften the blow. "But *I* was thinking of making a change for your benefit."

"What change?"

"Well, do you think the title is altogether attractive? I was thinking of ———."

He said something so revolting that Christopher stepped backwards and barked his shins against a seat on the aisle. "For Christ's sake! They wouldn't let us advertise it in the tubes!"

"But wouldn't that," Tom said beguilingly, "be all the better?"

"No, it wouldn't! Look here, you said no changes: I said O.K. We agreed no changes. That means, not even yours."

Tom, who had not in any case meant to go through with his latest absurdity, gracefully conceded the point. "All right. Now you can all go ahead. Miss Milton and I will be as still as mice."

He was glad to sit down in the gloom, since he knew he had blushed. He whispered to Pringle, "Lend me your mirror."

He peered into it, and was anxious.

"I don't think your new title was as good as the first," she whispered, her face averted.

"I'm so glad. And you don't think this horror is good any more, do you?"

"Not if you say not." But there was a stubborn note in her voice.

"Look here," the director burst out, "I must have quiet in here! I can't get on with all this wzz-wzz-wzz and fidgeting, and nor can anyone else."

"So sorry," Tom said in his clear, grave voice.

"Right, then! Skipper, go back a bit. Now then, Grunt's on the floor coughing his guts out. You and Babybaby draw back. You pause a minute. Babybaby does his war-dance. Then—cue him, Babybaby."

" 'Why's he dead?' "

" 'Because he's old.' "

" 'And why's he old?' "

" 'Because he's dead.' "

"Let us go and have tea in a shop," said Tom.

"Sh-sh-sh," said Pringle.

It was a nice little theater, designed to have all the qualities of a Boy Scout's pocket-knife: there was nothing it couldn't turn to. It could be arena-stage, theater-in-the-round, Total Theater, any old thing. It could seat about three hundred and fifty in stalls and pit, another hundred and fifty in a functional, if not too cozy, circle. At night, lit up, it looked quite smart in its barren way: with only a few lights on, in the late afternoon, it seemed filled with scruff and dust. There was no orange-peel under the seats, but there might have been.

"Now you've lost it, damn you," said Christopher, giant-like on the stage. There was a rent in the back of his green jersey, which seemed to have acquired large white patches, as if it had rubbed against a whitewashed wall. "Try it again."

" 'Why's he dead?' "

" 'Because he's old.' "

" 'And why's he—' "

"Out," said Tom to Pringle.

They found themselves in the prison-like twilight of Holloway Road. It was a grim area, partly in fact, partly in imagination. Only a stone's throw away, and within a stone's throw of each other, had lived two famous murderers, Crippen, the engaging little dissector (his wife's flesh, in a saucer, passed round the jury for examination), Seddon the mean man, with his reeking lodger upstairs (his little boy sharing Miss Barrow's enseamèd bed) and his cash-box in the parlor. In the murder-haunted crescents, in the squashed terrace houses with plaster flowers above the lintels and mock stained-glass in the blistered doors, pallid lights shone out. Tea-time. Salmon and sauce bottles. The telly's grey and garrulous face. The castellated prison, place of misery, was dominant over the pitch and toss of the hidden hills. Women pottered about in their cells, trying to forget husbands and children, slopped out, pottered the grimy days away. One could have caught the prison-smell in bottles, labeled it *Geôle*, and sold it for seventy shillings a handbag flask in Fortnum and Mason's.

The rain had begun to fall, but so light that it was no more than a polish upon the air, a mere gloss about the neon-lamps. "We'll never get a cab in this part of the world," Tom said, "let's find a bus."

She noticed that he was looking disturbed, and was careful not to speak to him. Suddenly he gripped her arm and began to race her back the way they had come, making such speed with his long stride that she felt like Alice in the grasp of the Red Queen.

"What are you doing? Don't, please don't! I can't keep up—"

They were back at the theater. Still holding Pringle, he plunged down the aisle. He shouted, "Stop it!"

The director halted. So did the actors.

"For pity's sake, stop it! It's enough to make a cat sick."

"Have you gone mad?"

"All of us have. This can't go on."

"Do you realize the money that's gone into it—?"

"I'll make that good. But I implore you to stop it."

The director, with a spring like a leopard's, jumped down into the auditorium.

"You shut up and get out of here. I've had just about enough from you, Grunt, Grutch, whatever you say your name is. Do you think you're going to have all these people thrown out of work, man? Just because you've gone round the bend? This is my show, and my theater, and now you damned well get out and don't come back!"

Tom was quiet. They stared at each other, and the director fell to chewing detritus out from behind his fingernails.

The actor who was playing Grunt, a middle-aged man of some reputation who had been resting all too long, came to the edge of the stage and crouched on his ankles. He said to Tom, "Please. I need this job, such as it is. As to the play, I am in entire agreement with you."

Babybaby began to protest and so did Skipper. Roo muttered, "Load of old codwallop," a phrase Tom was to repeat, with satisfaction, to Matthew and Jane when he met them in Cork Street next day, and which was to entail certain consequences.

"Mind you, I shouldn't have said it if you hadn't said it yourself. It makes my stomach heave."

"Good man," said Tom, with an approving nod.

"All the same, I've had nothing but two TV bits and some advertising work for nine months, and I'm behind with the rent. I cannot afford whiskey, which is the only thing I love. Also, the critics may lap up this deplorable play, and I may eventually find myself back at the Royal Court. So I am forced to join my voice with Christopher's."

Silence again. At last Tom said, "Very well, I shan't come any more. Not till the first night."

"For crying out loud, have you got to come to that?" the director screamed, furious as any man is when his life has just been saved.

"Yes. I think I have. I think I must."

When they were out once more in the rain, which was now falling heavily, Pringle said, "If you don't *mind!*"

"But I do. You have seen how much I mind."

"It's only a phrase. You needn't make a production out of it."

"Why are you so angry?"

"Why are you so selfish? Those poor actors—"

"I do see what you mean. I have made my bed and I must lie on it, verminous though it may be. And I am such a very fastidious man, Pringle. You might not believe it, but it is so."

The last taxi in the world came cruising down the hill, its orange rooflight bringing promise of consolation. Tom got her and himself inside it. She began to cry, her head on his breast. "I'm so sorry, I'm so sorry. Tom, just let me love you. You don't have to give anything in return, I promise."

"I can't stop you, if you must. But I hope you'll soon get tired of it."

"Just *say* I may. It doesn't commit you, does it?"

"If I said you might, it would commit me: yes."

"I'd never be a burden."

"Of course not. But you would make me feel guilty, and I am not guilty of anything whatsoever, or not towards you."

"I know. I think you're perfect."

"That is a ridiculous thing to say. Pringle, I hope we are going to have a nice cheerful tea. I shouldn't have exposed you to all that nonsense this afternoon, and I want to make it up to you. But if you don't stop crying, I will get out of this taxi and take a bus. That is a promise."

She snuffled, blew her nose and sat rigidly up. He saw her little muzzle outlined against the flashing dark and he reached for her hand.

"Good girl."

"I'll try to be."

21

HOW PRINGLE BEARS A HEAVY DISAPPOINTMENT,
AND THE SOCIAL POSITION OF PEEWEE IS EX-
AMINED WITH SOME CARE.

Pringle sat with her literary agent. She was trying
hard not to cry.

Mr. Cropper was a mountainous man, who over-
flowed his chair and wore an air-force moustache. He
had that air of many men who are very fat, of something between the merry and the sinister, with the latter predominating. His room was handsome, the only
handsome room in a tall, sagging building in Maiden
Lane.

"Look here, my dear girl, we've just about scraped
the bottom of the barrel. All right!" He waved his arms
about wildly, though she had not spoken. "We can try
it on ——— or ——— or ———." He mentioned, with
scorn, three minor publishing firms. "But even if any of
'em would wear it, which I beg leave to doubt, they've
no money, no travelers, no sales apparatus of any sort.
Let's face it, you've had it."

"You could send it to ———." Pringle mentioned a
very smart firm indeed.

Mr. Cropper seemed to deflate, as if a great deal of
wind had poured out silently through pinholes from his
multiple tires of flesh. He began to beat at his moustache, while his bulging eyes stared at her coldly. He
might have been trying to put out a brush fire.

"You seriously think they'd give *The Cruel Ones* houseroom? Now be reasonable, darling. You've seen all the other readers' reports. Shocking, eh? And what did your first book sell? *Pre*-cisely eight hundred and twenty-two copies. Does that make you a good publishing risk?"

"I know I can write," said Pringle, looking at her cross-laced shoes.

He rose and went to the window, presenting his huge fat back, his small flat hands clasped behind it. He was attempting to create an atmosphere of defeat, and succeeding admirably.

"All I want to do is write," she said piteously.

He swung round with horrid abruptness. "Maybe. You're not the only pebble on that particular beach. But you won't be much good till you start writing about what you know. All this stuff—" He slapped his fist down on the manuscript. "Drugs. Drink. Queers. What it's like in bed, blow by blow account—do you even know what it's like? I bet half Lombard Street to a China orange you don't."

"Yes I do," Pringle lied, setting her teeth.

"You can't fool me. You do not. And you know nothing about this sort of life in general."

"I live in Earl's Court!"

"That doesn't make you the repository of all human wisdom. No, all you've done in this book is to stick in anything you suppose to be the fashion. 'Cruel Ones,' indeed!" Sometimes he had a curiously aunt-like air. "You don't know what being cruel is. You've got a heart as soft as a chocolate éclair."

"Now *you're* being cruel. You're enjoying yourself. And you know what all this means to me."

He reseated himself. "Here, have a cigarette. Come

on, now, it won't bite you. Listen to me, while I speak in words of one syllable. You might write a book one day—I say, 'might'—but you haven't done so this time, old girl." His endearments were always heterogeneous. "If your publisher doesn't want to take up his option, I can't blame him. He's not in business for his health."

"If people aren't willing to subsidize the young—" she cried out.

"I will subsidize the young. Powder your nose, now, and I'll give you a whacking fat expense-account lunch at Boulestin's."

"Thank you, but I don't want any lunch."

She saw over his shoulder, on a hoarding across the way, her own face peering out of a huge boot. Under her left ear was the pink bow. She shuddered.

"Oh yes, you do. Besides, to be seen with you these days is an honor. You might do something to boost an old man's vanity."

"Not me," said Pringle, "not now you've tried to destroy mine."

He looked at her, unblinking. "I say, whoa! Whoa! This is only for your own good. I've got a soft spot for you. I want to be guide, philosopher and—"

"You don't." She stubbed out the cigarette. Her lashes were grey with the tears that were going to fall when she could get as far as the staircase. "One day they're all going to be sorry."

"They'd be sorry right now, if they published that stuff. Come on, cheer up! What do you say to *Sole Normande?*"

The tears spilled over. He handed her a sheet of clean blotting-paper.

"More effective than a hankie. If you knew how many tears have been shed in this same room!"

"I bet they have," said Pringle, finding the paper as useful as he had suggested.

"They say even Henry James once cried in here. Like a child."

"Oh, rot."

His moustache twitched. He beat at it, perhaps to conceal a grin.

"And Meredith had to be given smelling-salts. He was young then, of course. So you see, there's no need for you to think life's over for you. You come and have some lunch, then buzz off home and start on another masterpiece."

She gathered up her bag. "Mr. Cropper, I have something to tell you. I don't like to do it, but you force me to. I am afraid I must take my business elsewhere."

He said quite distinctly, "Ho," a sound rarely made by human lips.

"What does that mean?"

"Your 'business!' I tell you, you're being a very unkind little girl, trying to break an old man's heart. Do you know what your first book netted *me?* Just under nine pounds, less postage, packaging, sending copies out for translation rights—nil—and all the other overheads. Say I got six quid out of it. Then there's my taxes. You're the cruel one, aren't you?"

"Please post all the work I sent you back to me. I prefer to look after my own affairs."

He rang the bell, giving it a nasty smack. His secretary came in.

"Cora, everything we've got of Miss Milton's back to Miss Milton, please. Pronto. She's given us the sack, a bitter blow from which we may not easily recover."

Pringle waited till the girl had gone. Then she said,

and did not seem pathetic, "That was meant to humiliate me, too, just as everything you've said since I came into this room was meant to. I don't want to see you again, and I don't want any *Sole* anything. Good-bye."

He bounced up to stop her. He was breathing in a sensual manner, or trying to appear as if he were.

"Don't talk like that. Isn't a senior citizen like myself allowed to pull your leg a bit? You'll be all right. You may be George Eliot some day, for all I know. But I can't market *The Cruel Ones*, and I'm not going to try any more. Come on, shake hands."

Always polite, she put her hand in his. He held it tightly, jerked her to him, so that her small breast struck the multiplicity of breasts he appeared to bear above the navel, and gave her a squeeze. "Quite sure about lunch?"

But she had slid out of what was, in truth, a well-meant embrace, since his sadistic instincts were never serious, and indeed, his more mature clients tolerated them as all in the day's work. The trouble with Cropper was that he liked his writers to be neither too big for their boots nor too small for them: if he thought they were either, he made them pay for it. He had once driven an intellectually austere woman writer to take a swing at him, simply by saying, in comment upon her latest novel, "It's a smashing good yarn for the female market, dear"—and this at a time when she could be sure of one middle article in *The Times Literary Supplement* to every three of her books. (She was, in his eyes, much too big for her boots. Pringle was being made to smart because she was too small.) Perhaps he would not have been so mischievous could he have reduced his weight below twenty-two stone. He might pretend to be proud of it, encouraging those stones to jelly and quiver for the amusement of his friends: but it was quite noticeable that the shapelier a writer was, the worse he or she was likely to fare with Cropper.

"Of course," he called after Pringle as an afterthought, watching her head go bobbing down the well of the staircase, "I can't afford to take you to lunch now, can I, not when you've just ruined me?"

After she had gone, he sat rather sadly in his bulbous coils and pushed her manuscript all over his desk with one forefinger. He had only meant to help, he said to himself, and this was what he got for it. Ingratitude. Serpents' teeth. Damn the young. Eating alone in Boulestin's, since he was not going to be deprived totally of a promised treat, he felt depressed.

Pringle went home, cried for half an hour, bathed her swollen face and telephoned a film-studio. She was going at last to submit to a screen-test. At five o'clock Peewee Stanton rang her up, asking her to dine with him, and she submitted to that also. It was her eighteenth birthday.

Now, it is a fact seldom grasped by foreigners that members of the English upper classes called "Peewee," "Toto," "Popsy" or "Tish" are seldom in the least what their nicknames might seem to imply. Foreigners envisage tall, etiolated youths like bolted lettuces, brows high, hair prematurely thinning, chins in determined recession: youths who, though not strictly effeminate, lisp when they speak, drop their r's and are concerned for their sexual potency.

Such foreigners should take a look at Peewee Stanton.

He was twenty-three, of medium height but built like an American fullback. His face was craggy, his round eyes a bright and stormy blue, his forehead low and nubbly under a cropped thatch of butter-colored hair. His nose was Wellingtonian. He had no fear for his potency whatsoever, and his nickname derived only from the fact that, having been born twelve years after his brother Breckenridge, he was at first, naturally, the smaller of the two. He had been at Shrewsbury and then at Cambridge, where he had rowed number six in the university boat. He was as tough as old boots.

He loved Pringle Milton more than life itself, and that is no facile phrase in the circumstances. If somebody had come up with a gun and said, "Either I shall shoot Miss Milton or yourself—in the stomach—" there is no question what Peewee's response would have been. He would have died stoically, making everybody concerned feel ashamed of themselves.

Could he persuade her to marry him, there would be no opposition from his family. He was quite well-off, since Breckenridge's family was not old-fashioned about primogeniture: but he would inherit no title or landed property, so there could be no strong feeling about his heir. Anyway, there were two other robust boys between his eldest brother and himself, and Breckenridge had two boys and a girl of his own. Peewee was as free a man as is possible in a society which entrenches itself in rigidity more and more firmly: despite the fact that, though it has more meaning than French society, it still doesn't mean very much, except, of course, to its own members.

There is something remarkably touching about sunsets, since they are the last brilliance—brighter, often, than noondays—before the decline. Sparks spring up in the technicolored air; there is scarlet and gold and imperial-purple. But night is determined to fall. On the other hand, sunsets can last a surprisingly long time:

enthusiastic gazers have been known to turn away, in sheer boredom, before the last spark has sparked out. Therefore, though the Peewees of this world do not expect much, they do not expect quite so early a debacle as would seem plausible to others. They imagined during the war—or their fathers did—that the debacle might well be on the way. When it did not arrive, they not only plucked up courage but lumped themselves into the saddle and attempted a last-ditch riding-down operation which was to prove unexpectedly successful. After all, it was in this putatively new and egalitarian world that thousands of persons were induced to waste their time deciding, in tones of owl-like solemnity, whether they must forego the word "mirror" for the compound "looking-glass," and whether they must henceforward ridiculously refer to a built-in electric fire with a shelf above it as a "chimneypiece."

An innocent person might have thought that Peewee would have taken his girl to Claridge's, the Berkeley, the Stafford. Not at all. He took her to Jack's Dive, in W.8, a restaurant in a cellar sorely in need of a new damp-course, where garlic-scented food was served by youths and girls dressed as French sailors, bell-bottomed trousers artistically shrunken about their rumps. It was lit by a few low-wattage bulbs and a good many candles. In the quavering light, all faces looked moribund.

Pringle who, in her desperation, had allowed Peewee to ply her with one drink too many before dinner, peered irritably around. She was savoring all the spiritual grittiness that comes after a too-emotional day. "Why do I seem to see a sort of constant parade of horse-chestnuts? I can't get my mind off horse-chestnuts."

"Polished backsides," Peewee said stolidly. "But the food, if a little niffy, and if garlic doesn't worry you, is by no means bad."

It was not, and as she ate, heartily as usual, Pringle's dazedness passed away. She gave him a coherent account of the horrible morning spent with her literary agent.

"If you'd only marry me and stop being silly," said Peewee, "you'd have no need to worry about these oicks. And you could write yourself giddy if you wanted to."

Like Pringle, he enjoyed his food very much and he always would. Finishing his endive-in-ham with parmesan sauce, he did not stay for an answer: nor get one.

"I know I am a writer," Pringle persisted.

"If you say so, I don't doubt it."

At that moment they were exposed to a Guy Fawkes' night of flash-bulbs, and this was the reason:

For some time past, Pringle had been tired of wearing only mulberry and black, and had been badgering Duncan, her pantocrator in matters of dress, for a change. So he had permitted her to order an identical frock, but in white: and, in the fashion of a future-sighting fairy in a story, had begged her never to wear it until some special occasion forced it upon her. Tonight, in an attempt to cheer herself out of a state of rank misery, a state which, she felt, she had no business to inflict upon her escort, she had worn it: and every photographer in London seemed to have found out. PRINGLE WEARS WHITE! She could envisage the headline ploughing its way through the frivolous press. She had a chilling sense of guilt. This was a trivial occasion, not the mysterious climacteric one for which the dress had been prepared. Hysterically, she wondered whether Duncan was likely to turn into a frog as a result of her disobedience. If so, she might have to marry him in order to turn him into a photographer again.

"What on earth are those chaps up to?" Peewee enquired, but not in the tone of one requiring an answer. He had just started on a large steak.

Even Pringle was not entirely immune to human vanity. She saw in a spark of intuition how absurd it would be if the slogan PRINGLE WEARS WHITE were accompanied by a photograph of herself, looking distraught, side by side with an unregarding young man placidly eating his head off. (It will be observed that she had not been altogether unaffected by professionalism.) So she laid her hand upon his forearm. It was enough. He stopped feeding himself, bumped down knife and fork, and stared questioningly into her face. "What's the matter?"

A fresh fusillade of bulbs went off: this time, they should have got an excellent picture.

She relaxed. "Nothing's the matter. Get on with your dinner and pay no attention."

A photographer began to crawl ape-like on his haunches between two rows of tables, holding up his camera to her face. It is not only the Pringles who must become used to this. It occurs frequently to greying American professors, talking about nuclear physics or the causes of the First World War.

"Come on, Miss Milton, smile! Give me a dazzler!"

"No. You've taken quite enough."

Another man popped up from the rear, obtruding himself between her face and Peewee's. "Just one more! Look, suppose you both stand up, so I can get a full length? Make like you were just going to your table—"

"Go away now," Peewee said evenly, "there's a good chap."

"He's only doing his job—" Pringle began.

"He's done his job. They've all done their jobs."

At that moment, a bulb exploded so near to her face that she cried out.

Peewee rose. With a movement rapid enough to deceive the eye, he grasped two photographers by their necks and shook them vigorously. "Now then, out!"

"God, how strong he is!" breathed a naval waiter, putting three fingers to his lips.

There was some bad language.

"No," said Peewee, "not before women. And I said, outside."

He began his march to the door. The cellar was in an uproar: two other photographers came to the assistance of their comrades, but were repelled, in some mysterious fashion, by Peewee's feet and elbows. A third, more professionally alert, stepped neatly out of the way and took a picture of the scene. After that, everything quietened down. Peewee showed all five quite courteously to the door, keeping a physical hold only on two, and put them outside.

"Thank you, sir!" cried the one with the most sensational picture—Pringle was in it, since she had been wringing her hands at Peewee's side—and peace was restored.

"Sorry about all that, Pring."

The naval waiter bent over him, under the pretense of emptying an ashtray.

"But you're superbly strong! How *do* you do it? I'm sure if I did exercises all day I'd never—"

"Runs in the family," said Peewee, "and we'd like coffee." He added to Pringle when they were alone again, "Well, now will you marry me? If you don't you'll only be exposed to this kind of thing morning, noon and night."

"Thank you very much, but I can't."

"Somebody else?"

"Yes."

"Oh, well, perhaps he won't last forever."

"He hasn't even begun. But I shall last forever," she said mournfully.

"He's not in love with you? Fellow must be mad."

"Plenty of people aren't in love with me."

"Then I don't know what people want these days," said Peewee.

The manager came up to apologize for the annoyance to which they had been subjected, and to express gratitude that no cameras had been smashed. However, he was ill put to it to conceal his delight in the publicity bestowed upon his restaurant.

"Only oafs smash cameras," said Peewee, "it's not fair on the poor chaps. Besides, I'd only have to pay for new ones, wouldn't I?"

22

SHOWING, AMONG A VARIETY OF MATTERS
PLEASANT AND UNPLEASANT, THE NIGHT-
THOUGHTS OF COSMO HINES, AND HOW DOROTHY
CAME TO BEGIN ANOTHER IMPORTANT POEM.

Cosmo removed his shoes in the hall and tiptoed
upstairs. He had been to a very amusing club, where he
could watch a lavish Negress in a bubble-bath and enjoy her favors afterwards, if he felt so inclined, for a
further payment of five pounds. Tonight he had felt so
inclined, and though he was tired, his mood was boy-
ish. The hall was in darkness, he would not risk turning
on the lights: but the moonlight was slatted between
gaps in the curtains, and one brilliant ray struck the
bevel of the mirror and made a guiding star.

His progress was very quiet, since he knew the
whereabouts of every crack in the floorboards. He un-
dressed in the bathroom, then sidled into the bedroom
and put on his pajamas. He did not, however, at once
lie down beside his stertorously sleeping wife, but sat
down in an armchair and lit a cigarette. Sound would
always wake her: light and smell, never. He had had
many a peaceful half-hour in that chair, chewing over
the events of the day.

The moon was upon Dorothy's face, which seemed
as small and wrinkled as a pecan nut. Her little plait of
hair, source of the day's *chignon*, stuck out across the
pillow. Her mouth was open. Tomorrow, it would
doubtless be open from morn till night.

The Hineses had made themselves very comfortable in their Kensington house, which was fully centrally heated even in the nest of rooms right at the top where the boys, on the rare occasions they came home at all, were stowed away. Wall-to-wall carpeting was so thick that it moved under the feet: one might have been stepping upon serried ranks of compliant cats. The furniture was mostly Swedish, variegated by what Dorothy regarded as a few interesting "period pieces," and though there were Kandinsky prints in the drawing-room, there were reproductions of Virgins, Flemish and Italian, all over the place upstairs. Dorothy lay in a whopping great four-poster bed, which had cost a small fortune to hang and now cost a fortune to clean. It made her look minute.

Cosmo, in his *omne animal triste* phase, was never unhappy at all, and never repented of the sport, straightway or otherwise. It did, however, turn his mind to fantasy, sometimes quite other than the kind of fantasy he had been attempting to put into practice. Tonight, knowing nothing, of course, of the visit of Tom and Pringle to Holloway Road, he had been thinking about great murderers, yes, about Seddon and Crippen, Armstrong and Palmer.

It was not surprising that, as he passed in his mind from role to role, his eye should light upon Dorothy. If only, he thought, she wasn't there!

She was growing increasingly crotchety and given to complaint. She hardly ever smiled; at least, at him: not that it was a pretty sight when she did so. She had been giving hell to the girl who was to replace Miss Few and Cosmo much doubted whether that girl was going to stick with it long enough to take over.

Lifting the cushion from the chair, he indulged in a little game. He went silently to the bed, still careful of the betraying floorboards, and held it just for a second over the sleeping face. What fun it would be! he thought regretfully, but of course he was only playing.

"*Will* not stand it." The words stole out from her dream, through the sleeping lips.

Cosmo did not dare to sigh till he was back in his chair, for a sigh might awaken her.

He pretended that he was pouring something into his own coffee, then switching cups. Her sugarstuck fingers raised the cup delicately to her mouth. But then, how to conceal it? Forensic laboratories swam before his eyes, like busy little shutters of light, one after the other. No. The string across the stairs, perhaps? Two drawing-pins swiftly removed, a touch-up to the paint? No, again. They would come with their magnifying glasses, Inspector Lestrade would withdraw his finger, staring at the little damp spot of cream upon it. Back to the pillow-idea. Ah—but again the forensic lab. A little threat of cotton, even of fluff, in the respiratory tract?

Naturally—there is no need to labor the matter—Cosmo did not believe a word of all this. He was just enjoying his mental impersonations. He was enjoying them so much that he stubbed out his cigarette too vigorously and sent the ashtray over the edge of the table onto the fender.

Dorothy sat up.

"Cosmo! Is that you?"

"Of course it is, my dear. Who did you think it was, Othello?"

"You're late."

"I went to the midnight film at the Academy."

"Why aren't you in bed?"

"Afraid to disturb you, Dotty. You were sleeping so peacefully, just like a child."

She switched on the bedside lamp. "Well, I'm not now! And I bet I won't get back to sleep for hours."

He apologized.

She asked him the time. He told her, ten minutes to four.

"Well, since you've woken me up you can get me a cup of cocoa."

He did so. When he returned with it, she looked more composed. "Thanks. —No, don't get into bed till I've drunk it. You'll only make me spill it all over the sheets. I say, I don't think much of this! It's got a nasty taste."

"Your imagination, my dear," said Cosmo.

It was pathetic, really: he had put into it the most minuscule pinch of bicarbonate of soda, just to allow himself a few extra minutes of indulgence in his fantasy.

"You know," she said, "I feel better sitting up. I get a pain sometimes, when I lie down."

"Sciatica."

"Not in the chest."

"It's funny stuff, sciatica. You didn't look as though you were in pain. You were like a log."

"I was dreaming I was in pain. No, Cosmo, do *not* light another cigarette. It stinks the room out."

He set cigarette and matches aside.

She said, with sudden chumminess, "Isn't this all rather nice, really? Just you and me, encapsuled in the night?"

"I like 'encapsuled.' "

"We used to be cozy together, didn't we?"

They had never been cozy, but that she did not remember.

"Very, my dear."

"Encapsuled in the night," Dorothy mused. The lamplight, shining through the pink shade, gave a tinge of rosewood to her cheeks. "The two of us. You know, Cosmo, sometimes I feel so alone!"

"Why should you? You've got me."

"I suppose so. But there are times when I do. As though I'm in the middle of a ring of people, really, but the nearest one is a hundred miles away."

"With all your myriad admirers, you can say that?"

"Oh, them. Yes, I know all about them. But this is different."

He studied her, and for a moment was touched to something bearing at least a familial resemblance to pity. She looked so very tiny, as if a giant had crumpled her up into one hand: and she looked afraid. He assured her that she was not alone: no one with a husband and seven sons could be.

"I'm all sweaty," said Dorothy.

"It's the cocoa."

"Encapsuled. Or do you prefer 'enisled?' "

"Encapsuled."

"You know—about my Anti-Verse play. It may have been premature. People just aren't ready for it."

"That may well be true. Dorothy, I think I should like to get into bed. If you'll give me that cup—"

"Not a word from COBRA, or even LBW. Why do they say they're *avant-garde* when they know they're not?" Here the familiar rising whine.

"You were always in advance of everyone else," Cosmo said consolingly.

"I know *that*. But you would think. . . . Oh, well, get in if you must."

He turned out the lamp. They lay in the dark. A strip of moonlight bisected the ceiling, was itself bisected by the reflected headlights from a passing car. In the garden, the trees gave the heave that trees give before dawn, if there is any air about at all.

They took up their usual position, cup and saucer. Cosmo hated it, but Dorothy only felt comfortable that way. She rested like a stick-insect on his plump white knees. The end of her plait somehow got into his mouth and he stuck it impatiently out of the way. She had a peculiar night-smell, like stale biscuit crumbs with a touch of lemon.

"I am going to write a new poem, a poem that is a play, not a play that is a poem."

He began to long for sleep. Northern lights danced behind his lids. He saw a green monkey in a red tree, very clear and bright, and tried to hold it; but the vision slipped away.

"Cosmo, you haven't cleaned your teeth!"

"I assure you I have, my dear."

"If you'd used that beastly electric toothbrush it would have woken me up."

"Just so. That's why I didn't use it."

"But you haven't got another one!"

"Quite. I took one of the electric brushes and used it in the ordinary way."

"Well, I hope you've cleaned your teeth. If you haven't, you'd better get out and do them."

"I did."

"I suppose you're telling the truth." This came from her reluctantly. "How do you like my idea?"

"What idea?"

"For the play."

"I'd rather think about it tomorrow, when I'm fresh."

"I'm going to call it *Encapsuled*. Or *Enisled*."

As a selling-point, this seemed to him to have small appeal. Poor Dorothy! At what stage in her career had she got so hopelessly out of touch with everything?

"Which do you like best?"

"Oh. *Enisled*."

"You said *Encapsuled*, before."

"Listen, Dotty, I must get some sleep. Tomorrow I'll give it real thought."

"I shall speak the prologue, just as I did in *Joyful Matrix*. 'Now we, enisled . . .' Something of that kind."

Cosmo was dreaming of the Negress, beautifully mauve in bubbles of azure and green. She raised amphibious arms for him alone.

"Wake up, will you? I've got a whole line. Listen. 'Now we, enisled, the womb cram: cram the womb.' Cosmo, are you listening?"

"Fine, fine."

The Negress asked him, "Irks care the crop-full bird? Frets doubt the maw-crammed beast?" Cram, cram. Cram the womb. Cram the pillow over Dotty, poor, poor Dotty.

Dotty . . .

Dotty . .

Dotty.

23

DOROTHY ACHIEVES A SOCIAL AMBITION,
AND JANE PRYAR FINDS *le mot juste*.

Jane was pasting up her press-cuttings in an expensive leather-bound book. She had had an infinite number of press-cuttings in her time, relating to her foundations, her trusts, her charity entertainments, her slide-rule position among the world's best-dressed women: but never cuttings commending her for bravery. As a witness against Percy, she had heard mighty eulogies of her courage in shutting him in the bathroom. Kind as always, since "there but for the grace of God" was no cliché with Jane, she had tried to suggest that his bark was worse than his bite and that he had gone there more or less quietly: but her kneecap militated against this Christian approach.

Matthew lay back on the sofa, contentedly humming "Komm, Süsser Tod." All his humming came from his unconscious mind, and meant, in this case, that he was recovering from a hangover. But he would soon be well again, and the sheer exaggeration of this involuntary choice of tune was something of a luxury in itself.

"Four days and home again," Jane said, when she had read through her collection once more. She shut the book with a slap. "Matt, do stop droning. It is quite unnecessary. You know you should never drink port after dinner."

"My dear girl, I could hardly drink it at any other time."

"I think that in future I shall put my foot down on your Commemorations of Benefactors," she said.

"Only three nights to poor Tom's play."

"I know it, Matt. I ran into Duncan Moss in the street this morning. It seems that he has definitely deserted to the enemy."

"What enemy?"

"He has come to the conclusion that Tom's play is wonderful. And so has Cosmo Hines."

Matthew said firmly, diverted from his headache, "No, he hasn't. Not Cosmo. This is pure malice."

"Duncan says he has."

Jane, a puffball in navy-blue wild-silk, every hair giving off its own distinctive spark, left her desk to select jewelry for the evening. She chose sapphires. So simple, so nice.

"Excellent," said Matthew. "I mean, you look excellent. I shan't drink anything tonight."

"A good idea."

"I meant, I shan't drink very much."

"I meant, it would be a splendid idea to drink nothing at all."

She mused over the evening paper, which had just been delivered. "Poor little Pringle again. In white. You know, Matt, I am so sorry for her. She will never get Tom Hariot."

"Damn it, she's barely eighteen. She'll recover."

"That she will marry one day, I have no doubt. But she won't recover. It is rare for young girls not to, but she will not, and it is time for you to get dressed."

He looked at the paper. "That's Peewee Stanton."

"Worth six of his father, and twice the weight."

"Physically?"

"Morally too, I guess. I am sorry for Peewee. I can

only hope he's lucky. Sometimes, Matt, I am sorry for the whole world!"

Though he respected and admired Jane, he often thought that her reflections were somewhat superficial, so he gave her a bemused and loving smile which could have meant anything.

"Your Balzac," she said, a trifle resentfully, "he knew more than you do. There was that book you made me read about a nasty chit called Rosalie who ruined the madly passionate love affair of a man twice her age, and got caught out, and then a boiler burst and ruined her looks. *She* never recovered. And there was someone called Gaston, too, who couldn't have a marquise or whatever it was, so flung himself out of the window as soon as she'd married him off to a really nice girl. Do go and get dressed. We will be late."

While he was luxuriating in the soft water, the soft grey steam, she tapped at the bathroom door and opened it a quarter of an inch.

"Would you recover from me?"

"Look, Jane, I'm not a raw youth."

"But would you?"

"By no means."

When he had dressed and was giving a last flick to his tie, he spoke to her image in the glass.

"You do know where we're going tonight, darling?"

"Certainly I know. To Betty Hedingham's."

Matthew looked nervous. He let his gaze fall away from her reflected one. "Well, we were going somewhere else first."

"You may come out of the corner, Matt, and take off your dunce's cap. Of course I know. You are sacrificing me to the sentimentalities of your past, and I have agreed to be a victim. But at least we have avoided the shish-kebab."

He turned and hugged her. He was so very relieved. Matthew was not one of those men who cling to the past with maudlin fervor, but he could not quite rid himself from some of it. Childhood, yes. Adolescence, yes: the war, yes: but not the gayer times before and after that war. He had never really been able to endure Dorothy, though it had mildly amused him to travel with her entourage. Also, at that intellectually snobbish period of his life, he had persuaded himself that she was a good poet, and had even gone to the lengths of starting a thesis on her work. He had only written down the title, it was true—*Dorothy Merlin, Tentative Steps Towards a Synthesis of Imagery*—still, if that wasn't a beginning, what was? But his eyes had been opened in time, and he had abandoned this project in favor of a slim volume upon Daniel Skipton, which, incidentally, he never completed either. So he felt he owed Dorothy something, and on the previous day, when she had approached him in Cork Street with a desperate plea that he and his Jane (as usual, he winced) should at least drop in at her house for a quick drink, he had feebly agreed to consult his wife on the matter.

When he did consult her, Jane gave him a blue and glittering stare, the kind given by a new-made corporal to a recruit with a button missing and a smear of Blanco on his boots.

"I could tell her we haven't got much time left," he said, with the hint of a question.

"No. Because you have committed us quite sufficiently. It was I who asked you to marry me, Matt, so if you are seriously set upon me paying a call on Dorothy, I shall do it for your sake. Telephone her, and say we will look in for just an hour on our way to Betty's."

She had not referred to the matter again, neither that day nor during the course of this one. Therefore, Matthew imagined that she had forgotten all about it, and he had been dreading to remind her.

Jane hugged him in return. She was a very affectionate woman despite her martial qualities, and she adored Matthew, who seldom gave her any trouble at all. She was not snobbish, though she often posed as a snob in the interests of self-defense, clinging to a small circle of friends so she might resist the encroachments of strangers in search of grants, endowments, lesser charitable contributions or even relief from their personal debts. She had not been well-off before her marriage to Calvin Merle, and had not forgotten how painful it had been to keep up a pose of chic and confidence on the small allowance her father had been able to give her. It was not Dorothy's whine she minded, nor her bad manners: it was her entire *persona*. Also, she had not forgiven Dorothy for calling Matthew a "ponce" on the occasion of his marriage to herself. She knew he wanted to pay this visit no more than she did, knew too how it would embarrass him if she were to dig her toes in.

"I am sure we will have a lovely time!" she cried, all brightness. "Life is often so unexpected."

"This time it will have to be," said Matthew, "if it is to be tolerable."

Dorothy began by playing the fool. She had brought her daily woman back for an hour, simply to open the door and announce them.

"It's Mr. and Mrs. Bryant," the woman said, with a sullen glance at the clock.

Dorothy rose to greet them. In a tubular dress striped with tan and shocking pink, she advanced a few steps and flung out her hand, holding it in mid-air, so that they had to move forward to meet it. Matthew, who knew his Proust (so, alas, did Dorothy who, he felt, should have been prohibited by law from reading it), guessed that she imagined herself advancing as far as the middle of the second drawing-room. Who was she tonight? The Princesse de Parme? Oriane? A Courvoisier? He couldn't remember. Of course there was no second drawing-room, though Cosmo, lurking right against the back wall and advancing several paces behind his wife, seemed to be trying to give that impression.

"My dears, how wonderful of you to spare us a moment of your tremendously busy life! Jane, I don't think you've actually met my husband, though you must have seen him about."

Cosmo, showing a line of teeth, said how much he had hoped that Mrs. Merle would find a moment to look in at his little shop. "It is rather unique in its way," he added.

"Oh, do call her Jane!" Dorothy sang out, with an air of impatience and a pretended scowl. "You know she won't mind."

Cosmo raised his brows enquiringly.

"Do please," said Jane, determined to be good.

"Of course," Dorothy said, as she settled them in rather officious comfort, banging hard but colorful pillows in their backs, "I don't suppose you get much time for reading."

"I read a little," Jane replied. Since there had been no money to send her to college, she had spent most of the later years free from finance, sport and society, trying voraciously to educate herself. So she was not pleased.

When Cosmo had attended to drinks, Dorothy flung herself onto the floor before the fire. She looked up at them roguishly. "Well, now! I have trapped you into my lair at last."

"Such an attractive lair," Jane said, letting her gaze wander away from Dorothy to an inspection of the room.

Cosmo, who sat in what looked like "father's chair," smiled down upon his wife. "Ah, that's all Dorothy's doing. She will tell you I have no visual sense at all."

"Oh, darling!" Dorothy cackled. "You know you've got a marvelous eye. You mustn't try to mislead people." She returned her attention to Jane. "You don't know how strange it is actually to have you here! You've been an absolutely historic figure to us—"

Jane bridled, then, with a sweet smile, controlled herself.

"—hasn't she, Cosmo?"

"Let us rather say, a radiant fantasy from another world."

"How nice of you, Mr. Hines."

"Please call him Cosmo. Why should we all be so formal when we know we're not? Besides, we're Matthew's very oldest friends."

It was not true, but he let it pass.

"Cosmo," said Jane obediently.

"And we're all going to meet at dear Tom Hariot's opening night, aren't we?"

Matthew said he profoundly wished they weren't going.

"My dear," said Dorothy, "you're not still among the Philistines? I thought you'd be past all that."

A permeating smell stole through the house. The daily woman had agreed to put the stew in the oven to reheat just before she left. It must have contained the fashionable superplus of garlic.

Matthew was one of those people with a strong streak of the proselytizer. Whenever he heard of some affectless adolescent who had smashed up a children's playground, some thug who had battered an elderly tobacconist for the sake of fifty cigarettes, he believed that could he have just half an hour with them, he could get to the root of their *malaises* and make them understand perfectly why such activities were socially undesirable. He honestly believed, after all this time, that he could get Dorothy to see reason.

So he laboriously restated how the idea of the play had been born, enumerated every hideous ingredient Tom had deliberately poured into it. "After all, Dotty, you're a wise woman. Lots of people might be taken in, but you oughtn't to be."

This angered her. It was the last thing he should have said.

"What do you mean, taken in? Do you suppose I could be? Do you think I haven't the wit to recognize the magnificent accident when I see it? 'Trust the tale and not the—' "

"Look, I've got to trust Tom."

"Damn Tom! What on earth can he know about it?"

"Firebrand," Cosmo said lovingly to his wife, hoping this jocose complexion could be put upon the matter.

Jane asked her in a gentle voice not to damn poor Tom, who was a very nice young man indeed.

"But you do know that I am something more than a critic?" Dorothy stretched her neck upwards, exposing tendons like those in the leg of a fowl. "It's not to my credit, of course. It's inborn. But I have the touch of the connoisseur. I feel it in my very fibers when a thing is good. And I am never, never wrong. Anyway, Duncan's on our side."

"So he told us."

"Jane," said Dorothy, "I don't suppose you have looked at this play?"

"Yes, I have. At all of it."

"Let us hear your opinion."

Jane said she would rather be excused.

"No excuses!" Below the pretense of facetious scolding, Dorothy sounded violent. "Let Cosmo get you another— No? All right. —We want to hear from you. We need an absolutely non-literary opinion."

Jane pondered this. She crossed her ankles precisely, pressing up the high and delicate insteps. Had Dorothy but known, this was her battle-posture.

"Well, then, let me see. Of course, I can't use the proper terms, not as you can. The technical ones, I mean."

"Never mind the technical ones. People without specialized literary training can often hit on precisely the right phrase. *Le mot juste.*"

"Look, Dotty," Matthew said quickly, "Jane's literary training may not have been specialized, but she's about read the ocean dry."

"Now, there's an example of inexactness! You can't read oceans."

"My dear," said Cosmo, "I think you're getting just a little bit excited, and you know how bad it is for you."

"Be quiet. I want to hear Jane's opinion of the play."

"You are sure you do, Dorothy? Bearing in mind that I am an absolute amateur?"

"Of course I do! For all you know, it might be quite valuable. Just leave it to others to judge."

"For all I know. Yes, well, perhaps it could be. . . . You are *perfectly* sure you want to know my opinion?"

"I've told you so, haven't I?"

"Then I would call it," Jane said thoughtfully, turning round and round on her finger a great cornflower-colored sapphire, "a load of old codwallop."

Dorothy's mouth opened wide and stayed that way. Cosmo's face twitched violently, and he put a hand across his mouth.

Matthew, unable to control himself, gave a great yelp of laughter, and then could not stop. He leaned over the edge of the sofa, hands to his sides.

To Dorothy, this reaction was only too familiar, taking her back to a most disagreeable moment in their common past. She jumped up.

"Stop that! It's just what you would do!"

Not daring to turn her rage on Jane, she turned it on Matthew, forgetting in her simplicity that he and his wife were something more than one flesh. "Do you remember how you *ruined* that evening in Bruges for us all?"

"No, don't." He gasped, hiccuped, and stopped laughing. "Please, Dotty."

"I bet you never told your wife that!"

"It's getting rather late," Jane said, rising. They all rose with her. "Now, Matt, you know how irritable Betty gets if one isn't exactly on the minute."

"Some man," Dorothy continued, as if she were a reluctant prosecution witness tormented by a relentless cross-examination into revealing the bitter truth, "took us to one of those ridiculous, tragic 'spectacles.' Of course, none of us would have gone if we'd known what it was like."

"We must run," said Matthew, "really we must. It's been so nice."

"There was a man and a girl—" Dorothy's voice grew louder—"performing *Leda and the Swan*. You know—*really*. It was repulsive, but it was moving in its very squalor, almost beautiful. And above all, True. Then the girl—er—gave birth to the Gemini, and your Matthew wrecked the whole thing by laughing madly, just like that, just like some silly schoolboy. I've *never* been so furious. It was discourteous, not only to ourselves, but to those human, pathetic, psychically tortured people who took all the trouble to arrange—"

Cosmo had raced out and raced in again, with their coats.

"Let me call you a taxi."

"We've got a car," Jane said. She was feeling so benign that she actually pushed her cheek against Dorothy's. "It's been most stimulating. Thank you so very, very much."

From the corner of her eye, as they went out of the house, she saw the Hineses preparing for battle.

Matthew sat silent as they drove towards Chelsea.

"Penny for them?" Jane asked.

"I ought to have told you. It was all so absurd, honestly. It was Daniel Skipton who let us in for it. He made a rake-off out of things like that. Damn Dotty."

"By all means, damn Dotty. But I knew anyway."

"You knew?'

"Well, Moss is a frightful gossip; I don't think you altogether realize it. He told Betty and Betty told me, ages ago. It was very lucky she did, really, or I should have been wondering why you kept a pink plastic egg under your vests and pants. It is not at all as if you had a child-like sentimentality about Easter."

"Jane, you are a great dear."

"You must have known that before."

"I did. And I adored that wonderful phrase you came out with."

"I hoped you would. Knowing of your great *fou rire* of the past, I was hoping to provoke just that response again, but I hardly dared hope for so much. I wish I had seen *Leda*," she added, a little wistfully.

24

D3 ——— ◄•••►———

WHEREIN TOM IS SUMMONED TO A
MORE OR LESS MOMENTOUS INTERVIEW.

Tom sat with his dozen or so second-year students
around a long scratched table in a room badly in need
of repainting and unlikely to get it. Here, he was in
command. He had never felt himself to be some of the
things he demonstrably was—a personable and relatively rich man, a playwright, by all ordinary standards
a decent person. But he did feel a don, a term not used
in the University of London, but an appropriate word
when applied to himself.

It was a dark day outside, and there was drizzle in
the Strand. London had that strange glamour which
dark days bring to her: windows lit up in all colors from
sugar-pink to corpse-green, from the moment of rising
until bedtime. Strips of reflected light quavered in the
rainsparkled pavements. There was something exciting
about the whole effect: marvelous things might have
been about to happen. They never did.

The lights in the room where Tom was working were
peculiarly nasty, neon strips turning cheeks yellow and
lips purple. They converted to sulphurous yellow or
purplish-black the face-obscuring waterfalls of hair now
affected by most of the girls.

> *Girls with long and lovely hair*
> *Are studying John Stuart Mill* . . .

Tom found himself quoting inwardly, and he wished they were studying John Stuart Mill and not his own subject, in which they seemed to be deeply embroiled and as deeply uncomprehending. He had seven girls, six young men.

"Now, where were we? Ah yes, turn to chapter five, please, 'Words and Meanings.' Some of you seemed to be having a little trouble on Tuesday, but I expect we can clarify things." Clearing his throat, he got up and went to the blackboard. "We had discovered, I think, that the number of cultural meanings (m)," —he wrote a small "m"—"of a word tends to be in direct proportion to the square root of the relative frequency"—a big "F"—"of its occurrence. In fact, here I can show you precisely."

He wrote, in a large hand: "$m \propto \sqrt{F}$"

"You have it on page 73. It was discovered by logarithmic plotting of the average number of different meanings—"

A hand went up, and a voice protested.

"No," Tom said to a youth with Holman Hunt hair falling in caramel ringlets to his shoulders, "you mustn't keep on saying you don't see. Sight is not involved, so I should prefer you to say that you didn't understand. But in fact you do. You are so hypnotized by those words 'I don't see' printed in letters of fire across your consciousness, that you are just repeating them like a parrot. What I am saying to you is perfectly clear, and since you are an able chap, of course you understand me. Please blot out those fiery letters, and think again."

A girl interrupted this time, with the intention of heading him in the direction of more attractive matters.

"Oh, Mr. Hariot! Could I just say something before we go on?"

"Please do."

"Well, it was when we were doing *Puss in Boots*. I wondered about Perrault, when it was *Le Chat Botté*, and whether 'boots' had to do with *bootless* in any way."

"No, Miss Pilgrim. The latter word relates to booty, and not to footwear. And I don't intend to be side-tracked, which is your aim."

Miss Pilgrim, dipping her face between folds of mermaid hair, blushed. Like all the girls, she was half in love with him. It was his bad luck.

"But," he went on, in a burst of generosity, "as it is a perfectly beastly day, and we have struggled with ghastly boots before now—"

An appreciative giggle.

"—let us consider the word 'puss,' instead. It will make a nice change from semantic as opposed to frequency counts, upon which I was going to discourse."

"I'll say, man," the Holman Hunt boy muttered.

Tom, who was really more interested in simple etymology as such, decided to let them all have their way for once in a while.

"The original title says 'cat.' Now why did the translator settle for 'puss?' What is a 'puss?' "

"Vulgarism for 'face,' " said another boy, irradiated by his inspiration. "One used to smack someone in the puss. Now obsolete."

"I fear not. The origin in the Dutch *poes*, and in Irish and Gaelic, *pus*, a cat. Which, I fear, gets us no further."

"Onomatopoeic," said his brightest student, who was called Malinowski.

"In a sense. It is the word of summons which cats appear to comprehend. In England, we say 'Puss-puss.' In Russian, they say 'Kiss-kiss.' Russki-pusski, Angliski-kisski, take your choice."

This was meant to be a joke, and they laughed obediently.

"Has anyone else anything to suggest about the word 'puss?' " Tom asked, meaning to be helpful.

"The French say something like *'minie, minie,'* " said another mermaid, whose hair dripped onto her green sweater like a fountain in the Boulevard St.-Michel on a soaking night, "but that doesn't get us anywhere either."

"I suppose," someone murmured hopefully, "there's no semantic connection between 'puss' and 'pus'—I mean, what comes out of a wound when it's gone bad?"

"No. That's Latin—*pus, puris,* Greek, akin to *pyon.* Our word, as I said, is Dutch or Gaelic."

"Here we go round the mulberry puss," the least pleasing of Tom's students began to drone, *sotto voce.*

Tom's ears were sharp. "If you really think that, Mr. Perkins, you can always scratch from this class and revert to the exclusive study of Jane Austen, George Eliot, Conrad and Lawrence. It should not take quite so much out of you. Besides, I am thinking of starting you on zoosemiotics next term. I can easily get tapes of mynah birds from Indiana." This was in the nature of a threat.

The boy shrugged. "I guess I'll stick around."

"Why 'guess,' Mr. Perkins? No odds are involved."

Here a defeated grumble.

"Let us return to the word 'puss,' " Tom said after a pause, and in a sedative tone of voice. "And when we have briefly returned to it, which is to please you more than me, we shall then get on with our proper work."

The course soon proceeded on formal lines.

The roar of the rain was steady now and oddly delectable, suggesting a steel curtain between the class and the world outside. A lion with dripping fangs and paws akimbo could not have breached it.

Ten minutes of honest labor went by, passing slowly.

A young man came in and whispered in Tom's ear.

"Right. Straightaway." To the class—"Carry on with Whatmough, chapter five. I oughtn't to be long."

He went off to see the Dean, a nice man, not at his ease.

"Oh, Hariot. Sit down. Do smoke."

Tom shook his head. He turned upon his superior the respectful, enquiring force of his mossy brown eyes.

"Extramural this, Hariot. But I hear you have a play coming off."

"Well, sir, coming 'on' is the professional term, though I hope both will apply."

The Dean looked puzzled. Then, being no time-waster, he explained that a nephew of his was connected in a modest way with the production—he was, in fact, the assistant stage manager. "Small beer. But he hopes for better things."

Tom said it was a small world, and stopped talking.

The Dean began to explain further, and he was not happy.

"I'm afraid so," said Tom.

"Of course, I may be hopelessly misinformed. Also, I am out of date. This work of yours may be generally acceptable."

"Again, sir, I hope not."

The Dean failed to comprehend him.

"It is all very complicated," Tom said, and attempted a brief elucidation of his motives, which, however, merely seemed to bemuse the Dean, who reverted to what he had been saying before.

"But if it did not prove generally acceptable, it might —I do hate to say this—prejudice your standing here."

"And so it damned well should," Tom agreed fervently, "if there is any justice in this world."

The Dean said feebly, like one in deep water trying to find some tiny piece of sand to which he might touch a toe, "We have been impressed by your work. And we thought you were happy in it."

"I love it."

"Oh. Then do you not think—?"

"I have thought. I tried to stop the whole thing. But then, you see, there are actors who would be thrown out of work."

"In my younger days," the Dean said thoughtfully, "there was a phrase—'I would rather sweep the streets.'"

"Yes. But you know, when people were given the option, they never did."

Tom, feeling the interview was at an end, got up. The Dean rose too, and put a hand on his arm.

"I should have thought you were a clean-minded man, Hariot."

"So should I. But I find, to my distress, that I simply can't be. Or else, how could I have done what I have?"

"You explained to me, and I do hope I understood you, that it was in a good cause."

"That was my original intention."

The Dean paused. His mild face creased up, like— Tom thought—one of Falstaff's apple-johns.

"I suppose I couldn't help?"

223

"How, sir?" (Tom followed the old polite usages when addressing his seniors.)

"If I attended this performance, what attitude would you prefer me to take? Though I suppose all the seats are sold out."

"I should hope you would express disapprobation. Shall I try to get you a couple of tickets?"

"One," said the Dean, "would be enough. My wife is rather—one would not say prudish. Perhaps a trifle old-fashioned. I suppose, however, there's no hope that this contingency need not arise—"

"Poor bloody actors, sir. Throw them back on the market, and you will find splendid men, who started out full of hope and dreams of *Hamlet,* compelled to moo on television advertising spots, about tinned soup. You would not like that, sir."

"No. But I fancy I could have advertised soup as well as some of the practitioners. Perhaps I am both vain and naïf. Perhaps it demands years of training, at least twenty-five years, as in the Moscow Art Theatre." Astonishingly, the Dean fell into an experimental moo of his own.

> *Warmer for the children,*
> *Warmer for you,*
> *Warm, warm, warm,*
> *Touching those frozen places, warming your very smile,*
> *Warm—warm—warm—*
> *Radiant garden peas, green as emeralds,*
> *With just a soft suggestion of*
> *peach . . . fed . . . ham.*

"It can't be so difficult, one feels."

Tom told the Dean he would certainly be able to sell anything, if he chose.

"In that case, I'd certainly sell soup, rather than do

more questionable things," the Dean replied, his cordiality fading.

"It would bring in far less—"

"Hariot, I can promise nothing. I urge you to think. Much may hang on this."

"Much, sir, does. But I am no longer a free agent."

"Tom," said the Dean, holding the door. (He had never before used an informal style of address.) "Does the state of your unconscious mind ever revolt you?"

"Of course. It is the same for everybody. There is nothing uncommon or exciting about that."

"But do you think it is therapeutic to loose it upon others?"

"It may," said Tom, "be therapeutic for oneself. It isn't for those others. There is no need to be so selfish. To unleash one's nauseous unconscious for the sake of self-indulgence is the action of an invertebrate."

"I see. Yes. Here I am with you."

"But I have posed as an invertebrate. And believe me, I am ready to accept the consequences."

Tom went back to his class with a sorrowful heart. He might not be with them long

25

D3 ━━━◆◆◆━━━

TREATING OF DUNCAN MOSS AND
HIS CONCEPTION OF REVENGE,
AND OF A MEETING BY NIGHT.

Duncan was far from sober. He had had a long
day, photographing young women of tedious appearance with filleted faces who were about to marry, and
when he got rid of the last one, had drunk half a bottle
of whiskey in three quarters of an hour.

Pringle, who had looked in to see him (in the hope
of meeting Tom upon the stairs), sat and preached at
him. She told him, as she had done a hundred times
before, that he could be sweet if he chose, but that as it
was, he was simply ruining his life.

"I'm not," said Duncan, "I've been like this since I
was twenty, and with no further deterioration"—a difficult world—"from that day to this."

He lay back luxuriously on the sofa in his flat attached to the studio, his face damp, the Julius Caesar
hair clinging damply around his plump forehead. "So
pooh. Pooh to you, pooh to your solicitors, pooh to
Dorothy Bloody Merlin and all."

"Why Dorothy?" Pringle asked, her interest en-
snared.

He thought blearily, and with pride in himself, that
she was looking very different these days, far more confident, even—though this he hardly dared hope for—
even a little vain. He still controlled her style of dress-
ing and, since the incident of the white dress, was al-

lowing her to wear only white or dark green: there were thousands of girls prancing around in mulberry and black Pringles by now, thus debasing this particular image. Also he believed he had taken out of her mouth horrible words like "fab" and "m'hav'lous."

"Don't sit there smiling to yourself in a silly way," she said, "it makes me feel left out."

"You know you couldn't be. You know you are a pet. You know that if only you—"

"I said, why Dorothy?"

His mood changed. He became ferocious.

"Why not? Isn't that motherly monster one of the most appalling—"

"Oh, I know that. But why is she particularly appalling today?"

"Pring."

"Yes?"

"You are to have a drink with me."

"You know I don't like whiskey. I hate the smell."

"Don't be a prig." He slopped some into a glass. "Go on."

She sipped a little, to oblige him. "All right. Now tell me."

Duncan blazed with suspicion. "Why do you want me to tell you? Perhaps you already know?" He seemed to puff up, like an adder.

"Of course not. Don't be stupid. Why should I know?"

His always incipient paranoia flared. "Suppose *you* told her about Lucy?"

"I've never heard of Lucy. And please don't give yourself anything more to drink. Who's Lucy?"

"A girl. A beautiful, beautiful girl, so bread-headed—"

227 &d

"What?"

"So bread-headed, but so nice. Peewee's cousin; you must know."

"Oh, Peewee."

"Now there's one you'd snap up, if you had any sense—"

"Well, I shan't. Go on about Lucy."

She was not really interested. She had left the door into the hallway just a little ajar, so that she might possibly detect Tom's foot upon the stairs. She had not detected it.

It appeared, through the general slush of Duncan's information, a slush interrupted by sudden bursts of suspicious anger, that he had been taking Lucy Stanton around a good deal. He was walking along Cork Street with her only that morning, on the way to a sandwich lunch at a place in Conduit Street, when Dorothy had rushed out of the shop like a tarantula from its lair and started to upbraid him about some fancied discourtesy to herself. (Two days ago, he had deliberately crossed over the road to avoid her, or so she insisted.)

"Did you?" asked Pringle.

"Well, of course! Everyone does. But there was no need to make a song and dance about it. It's common practice—she ought to know that."

Though Lucy had tactfully withdrawn a few paces, she was nevertheless within earshot. Dorothy had raved about ingratitude, dropping old friends for new—"The lot," said Duncan darkly. "And the point is, it was done on purpose. She's always wanted to spoil things for me, and of course, if I got serious about Lucy, it would mean a positive *vault* for me into a social avatar—"

Pringle nodded, to intimate that, being a writer, she understood big words.

"—in which Dotty wouldn't even be allowed through the tradesmen's entrance. Not even past the dustbins." He sat up, swiveled round, and brought his face to within an inch of Pringle's. "You're quite sure you didn't tell her?"

"If you're going to be so ridiculous, I shall go straight home."

"Oh, well," he brooded. "Anyway, I'm having my revenge."

"What revenge?"

Opening the curtains, he looked across the street to where a light still glimmered between the shutters of Cosmo's shop.

"She's in there."

"Somebody is. But how do you know it's Dorothy?"

"Because dear old Few, though she said she'd stay on for a bit, won't do any more overtime."

A perceptible change came over Duncan. He had become a different person in his heart. What person? He developed a scowl and a crouch. With a sweep of his hand, he plastered the hair down on his forehead. His eyes bulged. A rapist? (No.) A member of the I.R.A.? (No.) A burglar?

Cork Street, on this mild, dry night, for the early rain had ceased long since, looked as little frequented as the High Street of any small East Anglian town after night has closed down and the world is left to the germination of sugar-beet. A few cruising taxis, with tangerines on their heads. The clicking and clopping of a few pair of feet. In the gutter, a long silvery cat snaking through the lamplight and shadow. Whose cat? Duncan breathed deeply. Bill Sikes's cat. But no, he had a dog. Well, the cat should be a dog, then. Bill Sikes's dog. "God," said Duncan to Pringle, "I can be a dangerous man when I choose!"

She gave him a look of infinite patience.

It may have been too much for him. Springing up, he started to call for a newspaper, much in the fashion that Richard III might have called for a horse.

"You have been sitting on one," said Pringle, picking it up between fastidious fingers, "and it looks horrible. It is all crumpled and hot."

Duncan seized upon it and rolled it into a kind of megaphone. Putting it to his lips, he bellowed: "Death is approaching!"

"What's that in aid of?" she enquired, having retained much of the slang of the past.

"Your doom comes on swift feet!" Duncan boomed, his eyes glistening with the success of his improvement on the original slogan.

"On swift feet comes your doom! —Does that sound better?"

"It sounds daft to me."

"Ah, but not through Dorothy's letter-box, it won't. 'On swift feet comes your death!' Now, that's much, much superior."

Pringle rose and stretched herself. "Plain daft."

"Not the way I shall do it. Come on, girl, we have no time to lose."

Duncan may have been a foolish man, but he was a very strong one. Pringle found herself flying downstairs, the sensation almost as delicious as in a dream.

They were out in Cork Street, under the steady stars. Duncan kept a maniac's grip upon his megaphone.

Immediately above the rooftops, the London sky was

burnt sienna, with an interior glow. Above the brown was a peaceful indigo, littered with stars as small and pure as they might have seemed in mid-Atlantic. Pringle's stockings were splashed by a passing taxi, but she did not swear: in her mouth was sweetness. She never would swear.

"Sh-sh-sh!" Duncan grasped her round the waist and tiptoed with her across the street, though there was no necessity for silence.

Before the shop, he paused. Delicately he prodded the slat of the letter-box, and seemed content.

"I don't know what you're up to," said Pringle, "but I want no part in it."

Distracted, for a moment he looked at her in enchantment. "I want no part in it." Hadn't she flattened the noun slightly, suggesting some charming provincial origin, some rustic birth, perhaps in a cottage on the outskirts of Strafford? Not that Duncan himself would have cared to be born on the outskirts of any town but London: he had all the Londoner's secret, heart-hugged vanity. But for a moment he had envisaged yeomen, clogs, peat, bannocks, shawls, rough red hands, the carrier's horn, places called Chases, thatches, patches, hedgings and ditchings, cowpats, ploughmen, rooky woods, and half a dozen different, ill-matching and often anachronistic concepts.

How little he knew of her! Yet, with a hint of a flattened vowel, she had opened her personality to him a little, a mere split in the bud, but showing a morning promise within, pink, satiny, sweet as clover.

"By the way," he said casually, "what part of the country do you come from? I never thought to ask you."

"Balham," said Pringle.

He dropped the subject.

He looked quickly up and down the street and saw no policemen.

"What do you think you're doing?" she demanded.

Bending quickly down, he thrust the small end of his megaphone through the letter-box, put his face to the big end and roared—"Prepare to meet thy doom!"

"Shut up!" Pringle cried, and putting her arms round his waist, tried to drag him away.

"On swift feet comes your—"

She smacked him hard on his backside, and he staggered.

The light in the shop went out.

"Just you do that again!"

"Yes, I will, if you don't come away."

She gave another wrench at him. This time he fell over. He sat on the pavement looking up at her in bewilderment. The megaphone was still stuck in the box: Pringle pulled it out, tore it up and threw it into the gutter.

A hand was fumbling with the door.

"How could you do that to me?" Duncan said reproachfully.

She helped him to scramble up. "Quick!"

She raced him into the shadow of the shop next door, into the porch of the hatter's.

"How could you, after all I've done—"

Her hand was over his mouth.

The shadow of Dorothy wavered across the pavement. They heard her cry fearfully—"Who's there? I'm going to call the police."

Duncan was breathing stertorously.

The shadow withdrew.

Pringle kept a grip on Duncan till she heard the door

close again. Then she went for him, in furious whispers.

"You horrible drunken brute! Don't you know that's as low as writing anonymous letters? She's terrified!"

"I hope so, you little beast. That was the whole idea."

"You should be ashamed of yourself. Come on, let's go back. I'm cold, anyway."

When they were in the flat again, Duncan slumped upon the sofa and sat with hands dangling between his knees. He turned upon Pringle a mournful, storm-blue gaze: when he felt ill-used, he seemed able to increase the size of his eyes by half as much again. "Now you're cross with me. You're against me, like all the rest of them."

"What rest of them? What do you mean?"

"I always knew you'd turn against me someday. No matter what I did for you. Not that I'm asking for thanks."

He expected protests, passionate and remorseful.

Instead, she looked at him for a moment without speaking. Then she said: "Yes, I believe I am turning against you. I didn't like your joke on Dorothy tonight. And I am always angry when you tell me what you've done for me. You know I didn't want it done. Anyhow, it was you who gained the most by it."

"Pringle! When you could be rolling in money, have a car of your own—a Jag—"

"I've never wanted a car. I'm afraid to drive, because I might run over a child. It's silly of me, but there it is."

"You hate me." Duncan, nonplused, sought refuge in a general statement.

"No. I'm very fond of you. I love you sometimes, in a sort of way, and I've worked quite hard for you just to prove it. But I don't like you as much as I once did."

He rose abruptly, lurching as he did so. Another man might have seemed menacing, but he did not, so Pringle did not blink an eyelid. To her he looked like some great clockwork toy with the sawdust leaking out. He seized the telephone and dialed.

"What are you doing now?"

"You wait and see. —I think she's gone, damn it. . . . Oh, is that you, Dotty? . . . Yes, it's me, Duncan. Look, Dotty, I rang up to apologize. It was me playing the fool just now. . . . No, I don't know why. I'd been to a party. . . . Yes, I know I shouldn't go to parties, that's beside the point. . . . I assure you it was me! If it hadn't been me, how would I have heard about it? . . . Listen, I have *said* I'm sorry! I'm groveling, aren't I?"

Pringle could hear Dorothy's angry screeching, but not her words.

"I will send you flowers tomorrow, Dotty, losh of beautiful flowers. . . . Look here, it's no good going on and on. I apologize, I said so. . . . Now Dotty, what you said just then was plain ungentlemanly. A gentleman always accepts an—"

He looked at the receiver, which he held in the air for a moment before replacing it. "Blast her, she's rung off. Still, I've taken a load off her mind. Pring, are you still against me?"

"Not so much as I was."

"*I know!*" This was the shout of one who has suddenly perceived the lie in life.

"What do you know?" she asked him, as she pushed her arms wearily into her coat.

"Peewee's put you off me! He's been saying things against me! He tried to take photographs once, and I told him he hadn't the talent for it. Damn Peewee and damn you! I always knew that man was a traitor. I—"

"You're being silly, and I've had enough of it. Peewee has hardly so much as mentioned you."

"Hah!" cried Duncan. "And isn't that significant in itself? When we were at school together, two twin cherries on a bloody stem? Can't I see the whole thing in all its caddish treachery?"

"You can't have been on a stem with Peewee. You'd left school about fifteen years before he got there."

"So you say." He spoke morosely: deflating. "So you say."

"Good-night, Duncan. Would you like me to take that bottle?"

"You leave it alone. I'm going to drink myself to death."

"Not you. You've got three debs for tomorrow morning."

She left him, before he could have another lightning change of mood.

She had done more good that evening than she knew, for, by forcing Duncan to the telephone, she had taken from Dorothy a frightful weight of superstitious terror. Perhaps such good deeds as Pringle's are on occasion rewarded instantly by some kind of sugar-plum, for, on her way downstairs, she met Tom coming up.

Though she longed to meet him, she had felt that it might be embarrassing. He did not make it so. He asked her if she had time for a drink—"For," he said, "I need one very badly and it would only sadden me to drink alone. You look extremely nice."

They sat together behind the lighted window she had so often watched with yearning from the street.

There may be, behind the veiled and glowing windows of our desire, something of the felicity we suspect: but never the total heaven from which we believe we are shut out. Even so much as two days ago, she would have thought it the most beautiful thing that could happen to her, to be with Tom thus, alone in his domestic radiance. Well, it was wonderful: but not quite so. . . .

It never is.

She told him about her trouble with Duncan.

"Poor chap," said Tom. "But then, he always was. If it's any comfort to you, he will get no worse. Even when he is an old man, he will still be precisely the same. I'm glad he rang Dorothy, though."

"I don't suppose it really worried her—the megaphone, I mean. But it seemed such a nasty thing to do."

"It's pretty nasty even to say 'Boo' to people when they're not expecting it. You are such a good girl, Pringle."

She glowed. Her closed lips expanded with satisfaction, her pug-nose wrinkled. She was not, however, at all egocentric. If Tom, who was a temperate man, wanted a drink so much, something must have gone amiss with his day. She made an enquiry.

"Well, I may get the sack. Or have to resign."

He told her the story.

"What has it got to do with them?" she cried in scorn. "Haven't you a private life of your own?"

"I couldn't have a private life of anyone else's. But I think I see their point."

She asked him if it would hurt much, if he lost his job at the university.

"Not financially. The trouble is, you know, I do enjoy it such a lot. Even when my students are as dense as mud. I like the way they lollop into class and sit with their chins in their hands. I like the way they invariably scowl and look insolent just when they're going to say something charming. I like all that mermaid hair, which is always clean. I like their sweaters and stockings with patterns on, and their terribly stuffy boots, so bad for the feet all day, and the way the engaged ones hold hands under the table while pretending they don't know each other. You see, I like it all."

Pringle left her chair and sat at his feet, an action he regarded nervously. She wished, by this dumb show, to convey a devotion of which he might make use in any way he pleased.

"Tom. I know you hate your play. But just suppose people say it's good—well, you could write a play you didn't hate, couldn't you?"

He shook his head.

"Tom."

"Yes?"

"I haven't told anyone yet, not even Duncan. I took my screen-test. They liked it. I don't know what happens next, only I don't want to be a film-star."

"Then, of course, don't be."

"When I got back from the studios I was so tired, and then Peewee rang up and I hadn't the strength to say don't come."

"So he came. Yes? Go on."

"He's always played at asking me to marry him. Now he means it. Shall I?"

"Good God, girl, how can I answer that for you?"

It was warm in the room, and the lamps were golden as sunflowers. It had the comfort of a hospital room to somebody who is very ill, a quiet place where people are officially kind and "no" is always said gently, and for one's good. She did not dare raise her eyes beyond the twin mountains of Tom's bony knees.

"You know how it is with me."

"Yes. It will pass away."

" 'And this, too, will pass away,' " Pringle said pathetically, remembering a film about Abraham Lincoln.

"Certainly."

She asked him then, straight out, whether he felt he would ever be able to love her: or even whether, if he could not love her, he might not be happy with the love and comfort she would offer him always, unswervingly, to the end.

Tom did not reply at once. Then he said in his light, firm voice, "Not ever in the world, my dear Pringle, though you are a darling. I always thought so. Not if the seas ran dry and the rocks melted in the sun—I am sorry for so wretched a reversal of the situation. You must accept this. I shall never be quite happy if you can't be a friend of mine. But I shall never get married, to you or to anyone else."

She drew in her breath and sat like stone.

(It is irrelevant to this story that within five years Tom, to his own astonishment, even disquiet, married a pretty and indigent widow with a son of two: yet it is the height of dishonesty to provoke, by a suggestion of lonely strength, pity for a character who, in fact, turned out neither to be lonely nor entirely strong. But all this has nothing to do with the sadness of the moment for Pringle Milton, and, though in a lesser degree, for Tom also.)

"All right," she said, and got up. She would not let him help her into her coat, nor see her down the stairs.

Her back was straight as a ramrod and it arched in a horizontal line just above her small buttocks. She left her drink untouched, and when she had gone Tom sat staring at it, thinking what a pretty color it was, because he dared not think of anything else.

26

IN RESPECT OF THE NIGHT BEFORE
FIRST NIGHT, AND OF A YOUNG WOMAN
WHO APPEARS IN THIS STORY ONLY
TO DISAPPEAR FROM IT FOR GOOD.

Rumors about Tom's play had been spreading for weeks, and chops were being licked. For the first night, the theater was of course sold out. Tom himself had asked only for one complimentary seat, but had stipulated that it should be in the third row of the little circle. He would not attend the dress rehearsal, saying that since there was no dress, it would be pointless.

By this time the director hated him. He usually did hate authors: firstly, because he did not believe they should even exist (his idea of a good play was something having no script at all, made up by the actors as they went along, no matter how brisk or how enfeebled their wits). He hated them secondly because they hung around all the time at rehearsals, trying to interfere, and when the time came for him to give his notes to the cast, were liable to leap up with silly notes of their own. One might have thought he would have been happy to be spared this nuisance for once: yet he felt bitterly resentful that Tom had refused to show even the slightest interest. He suspected a snub, and was all the more angry because he could not prove that one was being offered.

Rehearsals had not been going smoothly, since Grunt

and Roo detested their parts, and Babybaby had taken suddenly to Method acting, a technique with singular allure for him, since it enabled the practitioner to show off not only to an audience, but to his fellow-actors. In this case, it meant that everyone was hung up for five minutes at a time while he stood at the side of the stage, trembling, snarling, clenching his fists and making horrible faces. All this, he insisted, was done to get him into the skin of the character.

"But there isn't any discernible character," Roo said, "so why should you worry?"

Babybaby assured him, in a superior fashion, that his training had included impersonating a wheel-less bathchair, a stopped watch and a piece of chalk, and that his part had at least as much character as these.

Skipper, the fourth member of the cast, had tripped over the property goose and torn its head from its body. The director had had a frenzied search to lay his hands on another one and his temper was vile. Nobody dared even to think, much less to observe, that it would be all right on the night. The tension in the theater was like too small a rubber band around too big a box.

Meanwhile, on the very eve of opening, Tom's students had taken to greeting him with grins both lubricious and sardonic, which did little to improve the state of his nerves. After his last class of the day, he telephoned to Harold and asked him for a drink in a pub.

Harold appeared at six, wearing his usual air of lightfoot felicity.

"Old boy, you mustn't let this get you down. It's going to be fun, isn't it? Remember, you're striking a blow for the angels."

They were sitting at a table in the corner, gaining privacy by the press of standing bodies around them.

"I wish I'd left the angels to strike their own damned blows," Tom muttered, gulping at his beer.

"The trouble about that is, that they wouldn't have done anything of the kind. Angels are such awful asses, I think. They will keep on expecting human nature to improve. If they didn't carry on by a sort of idiot hope, they'd be descending all over the place with fiery swords. Not," Harold added, glancing around, "that they'd find much floor space if they tried it here."

"And their swords would get between people's legs," said Tom, brightening momentarily, then relapsing into apprehensive gloom.

The violet smoke wreathed and coiled in upon itself, a foot below the ceiling. It was hot and noisy in the pub, and comforting. "I wish," he said, "I could stop all the clocks and stay here forever."

"I have never known you in a state of funk."

"Call it first-night nerves. And yes, I am very much in a state of funk. I suppose it would sound conceited if I told you that it wasn't a familiar state with me?"

"I'm going to get myself a sausage-roll," said Harold, "they look nice and fresh. Can I get anything for you?"

"No, thanks. I couldn't eat a thing."

When Harold, who could eat, returned with two sausage-rolls and two turkey sandwiches, Tom said: "I can't help feeling glad my parents are dead. And, of course, my Aunt Daisy. Otherwise, I'd bring them in sorrow to the grave."

"Why your Aunt Daisy?"

"If you'd ever known her, you would not have to ask."

"Oh, by the way. Did you put in that bit of business about the shirt and the mangle?"

"Yes, I did. The shirt has an arm in it, as we agreed. Blood pours all over the place."

"Ketchup?"

"I told you, I'm not eating."

"Don't be a fool. I mean, ketchup-blood?"

"I suppose so. I haven't asked. I can't take the faintest interest in the mechanics of the thing."

"Whose arm is it?" Harold enquired.

"I don't know. I never said. The critics wouldn't respect me if I told them."

"That's more like you. I say, these rolls are good. They can't have been made more than half an hour ago. Come on, have one."

Tom drearily complied.

"We shall have another pint, old boy, and then we shall go for a walk."

"I don't want to. I want to stay here."

Tom slumped down in his chair. His face was strained, his eyes a little too bright. He looked like a man contemplating some action of an alarming nature. Harold did not like the look of him at all.

"A walk will buck you up no end," he said serenely, but with determination.

So they went out at last, the tall man and the short, and strolled along towards the trashy glitter of Oxford Street. Christmas was not far off, and the decorations were up. The over-all design consisted of reindeers, picked out in puce-colored lights, and holly wreaths, in scarlet and yellow-green, slung from side to side between the lamps. On a street corner two Father Christmases had jettisoned sandwich-boards and begun to fight. Harold and Tom joined the crowd of interested onlookers. A small child broke into a howl of grief for lost illusions.

"An unseemly spectacle," Tom said, but his smile was faint.

They paused in front of a hoarding to read the advertisements. A swami was going to put everything right somewhere in Holborn. A film called *Big Brown Bare* was boosted by the simple slogan, "Nude for a Giggle." A poster for another film showed a busty girl in a night-dress, her eyes protruding in a manner which might convey terror or pleasurable anticipation, strapped by her wrists to a bedpost. Richter was to play at the Festival Hall.

The gutters were filthy with fag-ends, scraps of news-paper, discarded sweet-papers. There was a queue a quarter of a mile long waiting outside the Academy Cinema to see a Portuguese film. Over it all, sparkled the horrible reindeers.

"London," said Harold.

"The march to the scaffold," said Tom.

Something disconcerting happened. He had been quite unable to keep his name and face out of the newspapers. A girl all in plastic leather, with back-combed hair and a remarkable visual memory, came to a halt in front of them.

"Oh, Mr. Grutch! May I have your autograph?"

She whipped out an empty cigarette packet, tore it open, and presented the blank side. Yes, she had a pen on her.

Tom, bewildered for a second, recovered. He looked searchingly into her large vacant eyes.

"Why, of course."

He steadied the piece of cardboard on a pocket edition of Chaucer which he carried round with him for comfort. "What is your name?"

"What, mine?"

"Yours, naturally."

"It's Iolanthe."

"What?"

"My mum was crazy about all that square sort of stuff. But my friends call me Lanti. I always spell it with an 'i,' because it looks more Continental."

Tom wrote carefully.

"To Lanti, imploring her never to be taken in by people like—Thomas R. Grutch."

She gasped at this, and giggled. "I say, you *are!*"

"What am I?"

"Oh, I don't know. What's the 'R.' for?"

"Rosamund," said Tom.

She blinked. "Get away!"

"My mother always—"

The moment he had begun the cheap and silly phrase, he was shocked into silence. It was as though a stranger had occupied his body and was pushing an insulting vulgarity out between his lips. He wanted to speak again, but found no words. Harold was looking away from him, down the street. Then he looked up at the reindeers, his mouth pursed as if he were whistling, but making no sound.

The girl's eyes became much the less vacant. "Thanks for the autograph, but there's no call to be superior. You may be a famous writer, but you needn't take it out on me."

He said then, in alarm and distress, "I'm awfully sorry. I didn't mean to say that. It was shoddy. Come and have a drink."

"Now that," she said, "whatever you may think, I don't do, not with people I've never met."

She tore the cigarette packet deliberately into four pieces, threw it into the gutter and marched away, with a strenuous movement of the hips.

"Dear God," said Tom, staring after her, "what a bloody awful man I must be!"

"With every Lanti, whether she has an 'i' or not, there is hope for this world. So lift up your heart."

"Don't you see that this is corrupting me? I've been feeling awful all the evening, and now I've behaved like a total stranger to myself."

He left Harold abruptly and broke into a run. Just by the tube station he caught up with her. "Please!"

"Stuff it," she said, "and don't follow me around, *if* you please."

"I wanted to say that I was sorry."

"Well, now you've said it. You've said it twice. And I've got to get back to Upminster, so if you don't *mind*—"

"I won't ask you again to come and have a drink with us, because you were quite right to refuse. But please, please let me give you another autograph."

In the moment of her irresolution he tore the flyleaf from the Chaucer and wrote on it, "To Lanti, with affection and respect, Tom Hariot." He held it out to her. She took it doubtfully, looked at it, then said, "O.K. That's a bit better."

The crowds battling to the ticket machines swallowed her up.

"Harold," he said, when they had made contact once more, "if I ever behave like that again, stop me. Just because I want to right a few things which look ugly to me, I am in danger of getting my nose up in the air."

"People sometimes stick their noses in the air in order to breathe better," said Harold.

"But if there's a fire, they crawl along with their noses to the floor, which is precisely where mine should be, and is now."

"Masochism," Harold said bracingly, "would not become either of us at this junction."

"Do you suppose that girl will come and see that ghastly play?"

"I am dead sure she will. But set your mind at rest. She will walk out during the first interval. Go home and think of her as your salvation, because, from one of these little ones, salvation is going to come."

"You think so?" said Tom.

27

A FIRST NIGHT.

Tom sat in the third row of the circle, looking down upon the rapidly swelling house.

There were the critics from every major newspaper. He surmised that at least two of them had composed their reviews mentally before coming to the theater. He looked with hope at little A———, honest as the sun is bright, determined to be unshockable, but quite capable of drawing the line suddenly, especially if blasphemy were involved, and there was, of course, the statutory amount painstakingly inserted into A *Potted Shrimp*. He noticed the handsome Miss D———, with her long black hair bouncing on her shoulders. She, he knew, was feverishly composing verbal squibs of high originality which she would somehow contrive to get into her article; he had little hope of her, since she clung to the petticoats of fashion with the frenzy of an infant terrified to be parted from its mother.

Tom also saw Pringle, in white, sitting stiffly next to Duncan Moss: Dorothy, in magenta, with Cosmo: Jane, in black lace, with Matthew Pryar: Miss Few, in full maternity fig, lavishly patterned. Six members of his classes. And the Dean.

There was, over the entire theater, an atmosphere of gleeful anticipation. There would not have seemed, to an observer from Mars, any obvious reason for this. The stage was, of course, already set: high dark walls with a strong suggestion of the jail, a urinal, two stools, a gas-meter and a wringer. The sight was not uplifting. But the glee was that of the cat who smells the fish cooking.

Even in his relatively inconspicuous position, Tom was attracting attention: all around him, there were whispers and nudges. He felt like the Marquis de Sade, let out of Charenton on a twenty-four-hour pass. His height worried him. He would have liked to resemble Harold who, he believed, might have been almost invisible if he kept his head down.

Where was Harold?

Just coming in, immediately below, with Zena holding onto his hand as they barged along their row of stalls. Harold looked up and caught his eye. For one terrible moment Tom thought he was going to wave, but his friend had too much delicacy for antics of that nature.

Someone put on a gramophone record. It is a remarkable fact that directors rarely pay the slightest attention to the music, if any, which is to precede the performance. One would have imagined that the establishment of atmosphere by this means was all-important: but it is almost invariably left to persons who are tone-deaf. Tom himself would have thought that a little Stockhausen might have been a good idea: but not a bit of it. The gramophone was grinding out "Narcissus," by Ethelbert Nevin.

Not that it mattered all that much, he supposed, since nobody was listening.

Dorothy turned, looked up and saw him. She had not Harold's tact. "Oh, To-om! To-om! Good luck!" She waved furiously, rearing half up in her seat. She looked hot and sweaty.

Tom gave her a sick smile and made an indecisive

movement of the hand. Cosmo looked up too, with his hyena's grin.

"Excuse me," Tom said. He pushed his way out into the passage and did not return till "Narcissus" was over, and the house-lights had been lowered. He fell over feet on his way back and was sworn at. But he was in the blessed dark.

A seedy yellowish glow lit up the stage and silence fell. His heart thumped painfully. He would have run away, had he not been frightened to pass all those feet again.

Here we go, he thought. Over the top.

Grunt, in dungarees, wandered onto the stage. He wandered for some moments as if he had come to the wrong theater and didn't know what to do about it. Then he advanced towards the audience and bellowed his single word.

Tom closed his eyes. What would happen? Would they start to riot already?

They did not. They tittered mildly, as they would still titter if they were to hear Eliza's "Not bloody likely" every week for the next ten years. Did this seem any more shocking to them? Certainly not. It was a different word, that was all. His opening shot had misfired.

Grunt wandered away again and began to bang on the floor with a piece of wood. He did this for quite a long time. Nobody seemed bored by this and no one fidgeted. Then Roo came on, dangling the goose by the neck in a suggestive fashion, hawked violently, and A Potted Shrimp was under way.

The play shall not be described. Since it was meant to be unspeakable, it is right that it should not be spoken of.

Tom could not catch the mood of the audience, and hoped it was boiling inwardly. Had he been experienced, he would have recognized a significant thing: nobody was coughing. Nobody at all.

When the first act came to an end no one clapped, since there was no means of knowing it had done so until the house-lights came on. It might have ended fifteen minutes earlier or fifteen minutes later, having no vestige of coherence. People began to drift into the corridors to smoke, and he drifted with them. What puzzled him were the snatches of conversation he managed to overhear.

"So I said, if you can't keep your clammy hands off her, I'll tell Alice."

"Oh, rheumatism, as usual."

"Well, we were in Hounslow that day, only it poured."

"I adore *Giselle*, I can't go too often."

"Twopence halfpenny on a tin of beans, no, really!"

"She would change at Charing Cross when I told her not to."

He stayed upstairs, hoping to avoid people he knew.

He had just heard the first reference to the play itself —"My dear, that poor goose!"—when the Dean sought him out. He was wearing his overcoat.

"I'm afraid I am unable to stay."

"I'm sorry, sir."

"Perhaps I am behind the times. We must try to think so."

"No. You're dead right."

"I shall want to speak to you tomorrow."

"Yes, sir, I thought you might."

There was, of course, no hope of getting a drink in the little bar, which was solid with struggling persons.

There was no hope of hiding in the lavatory, because there was a long queue outside. In the most inconspicuous corner he could find, which was not inconspicuous at all, he smoked rapidly, with bowed head. It was his first cigarette for six months.

Dorothy tracked him down next, Cosmo hard on her heels. "Didn't I tell you it was marvelous?" She was panting. "When I confess that I should have been proud to have written it, you'll know how I feel."

He looked at her miserably.

"A Philistine myself," said Cosmo, "I am having some trouble about the inner meaning. Do enlighten me."

"There isn't any."

Dorothy flared out at her husband. "Why do you have to look for meanings? This is *pure* art, with absolutely *no* meaning. Can't you just *accept?*"

"Excuse me," said Tom, and returned to his seat. He noticed that Jane and Matthew seemed not to have left theirs. Pink, clean, shining, they were talking together in a manner only possible to people in comfortable circumstances who have made a success of marriage. Pringle was just coming back. She did not glance up. Nor did she appear to notice the comment she provoked. She looked meek, sad and childish.

The play was so short that the director was dragging out the evening by means of an interval of twenty minutes. Tom stared at the set, at the wringer still dripping squalidly with tomato ketchup, at Roo's socks (much had been made of their odor), arranged side by side in the middle of a Union Jack. The gramophone started again: this time Percy Grainger, "Country Gardens."

As the second act proceeded, he became aware of a

change of mood around him. Laughter, when there was anything to laugh at, took on an edge of hysteria; the silences were filled with tension. Were they beginning to loathe it at last? How could they be content to sit there, listening to puerile and grubby assaults on all the values they would accept without question in their ordinary lives? There was nothing at which he had not jeered: before setting to work he had made a list of every conceivable social, political and religious value, and methodically overturned the lot. Yes, they were hating it now, fine people that they were. At any minute they were going to rise in revolt. He could feel it in his bones.

On the stage, Babybaby was kicking Grunt first in the teeth, then in the groin. A scared gasp and giggle arose from the audience, then a wave of audible emotion, the source of which was not in doubt.

They were not hating it.

They were loving every glorious moment.

Something happened to Tom. He was aware of adrenalin pouring through his system. His pulses were drumming, his cheeks were hot, and his forehead icy cold under a thick outbreak of sweat. He felt a tremendous thirst, as if he could have drunk the Round Pond dry. He was trembling, but not with misery, and not with funk.

He rose in his seat.

Behind him, people protested angrily and a woman next to him tried to jerk him down.

He stood where he was, silent, while the noise of agitation in the circle penetrated to the stalls. Heads were turned. Black ovals, the backs of heads, became pink ovals, which were faces.

"Will you siddown or get out?" a man said to him furiously, in a whisper so piercing that it reached the stage itself.

Roo was halted halfway through one of his appalling speeches and could not go on.

"Stop this degrading rubbish!" Tom called out in a strong, clear voice. "It is quite beastly!"

There was instant response. Half the people in the stalls were on their feet, trying to see the interrupter: the noise was terrific, *fortissimo* from the beginning.

"Sit down!"

"Effoff!"

"Stuff it, you fool!"

"Get the manager! Chuck him out!"

The play had stopped. Grunt, who had been dead, sat up and stared about him in bewilderment. The director had pounded onto the stage, and was, without result, holding up his hand.

"It is a disgrace for me to have written it and for you to listen," Tom said.

No fear at all in him now. He was having the time of his life, was even enjoying the force and clarity of his own voice. Perhaps he could have been an actor himself.

The lights went up. The manager was approaching, a little man plainly unfitted to cope at all with anyone so large as Tom.

Dorothy screamed out—"You idiot, you blind idiot! It is a masterpiece!"—and fainted. Cosmo merely heaved her back into her seat and let her slump there.

"Bloody wonderful!" This was Duncan, half drunk and inflamed. "Wunnerful play! Trific!"

At least half the audience was booing Tom. The

other half, confusedly, seemed to be cheering him, not as a protester but as a playwright.

Somebody behind him was heard to say, "Best first night since *Hernani*."

Tom now held up his hand and was much more effective than the director, for people now seemed to want to hear more of him.

He spoke to the manager first. "Don't come any nearer to me, please, or you'll regret it so much. I'm very sorry."

He addressed the house.

"I have put into this stuff, quite deliberately, every form of indecency, cruelty, blasphemy and plain inanity that I could devise."

An angry growl from the deceived.

Miss Few, smiling and bobbing, made her way out, projecting her stomach as she went.

"No, no, it wasn't to make fools of you. I thought you'd reject it in the first five minutes. I was dead sure of that. My play is an insult to this stage, or to any stage, an insult to the actors and an insult to you all."

Pringle was out in the aisle now, and for the moment attention was deflected to her. She had a scared, desperate look. When Duncan tried to put his arm round her she gave him a push that toppled him onto a man at the end of row E.

She screamed—"Tom's right! He's right! It is beastly. Can't you all see it's beastly?"

With a burst of hysterical tears she ran from the theater. By the time Duncan had succeeded in soothing the bruised and belligerent man upon whom he had fallen, she had gone, and he made no attempt to follow her.

Tom was never to know how much this gesture of support had cost Pringle, but he could guess. She had not really been shocked or insulted by the play; she was far too much a child of her time to feel that a sense of shock or of insult should even be possible, much less permissible. She had overcome her dreadful shyness simply to prove that she was on his side, that no matter if they never met again, she always would be.

People stared after her in amazement, and in that second of silence, the director regained control. Hulking, grubby, angry, he spoke to them.

"You all know that this is a wonderful play. Don't you?"

Cheers.

"I don't know what Grutch thinks he's up to. But he's written a fine play despite himself and we're going to get on with it, if he'll kindly take himself out of here and stop mucking up the evening for other people."

Cheers.

Boos for Tom.

Then Tom cried, "Boo!" and Matthew, very clearly and sweetly, but with the penetration of a steam-whistle, cried "Boo!" also.

"Boo! Boo!" Jane sang out delightedly. She waved her hand, and all her diamonds twinkled.

The noise was beyond anyone's power to check. The mere action of noise-making seemed to exhilarate. The manager had fought his way through to Tom's side and was giving him a series of small, despairing tugs.

Tom said, "You needn't bother. I'm going."

The audience watched him as he gathered up his neatly folded coat from under the seat and made his way without haste to the doors. Some people began to clap him and some to cheer. He did not know what aspect of him they were applauding—the playwright, or the moralist? He did not believe they knew, either.

The doors were well designed to exclude noise, and in the passage he thought, for a blessed and calm moment, that he was to be alone. He did not know whether the hubbub was still going on, whether or not they would be able to finish the play, whether Dorothy was still in a faint. Though the energy had left him, no renewal of fear had taken its place. He lit a cigarette and started down the stairs.

He was promptly engulfed by a dozen reporters.

Had they been there all the time? Surely not. Perhaps one or two. If they had been summoned when he first rose to protest, how had they managed to get to Holloway in so short a time? He was filled with admiration for them all and thought of them with kindness until, which happened almost at once, they made thought impossible.

28

ILLUSTRATIVE OF TOM'S TEMPO-
RARY COLLAPSE, AND SUGGESTING
A RAY OF HOPE FOR HIS FUTURE.

Tom awoke to find himself famous, which was
what he had expected: he had not, however, expected
to find that his play was not. Despite all the director's
efforts, they had not succeeded in getting going again
after the disturbance, and the critics were chary of re-
viewing an incomplete work. Although there were a
few smallish notices, using words like "audacity," "uneasy," "probing," "fearless," "contemporary," the reporters' version of the rumpus had squashed all critical
pieces into a miserable inch or two of space. His sole
remaining fear was that they would all go again tonight,
and that Miss D——— would be rhapsodic about it on
Sunday. If only, this evening, there had been another
first night to distract attention from it! But there was
not.

He did not go to his classes. He did not even get up.
He summoned District Messenger and sent his letter of
resignation to the Dean. Cosmo, not dishonest in one
way at least, had already slipped through the letter-box
an envelope containing two five-pound notes, in set-
tlement of a debt.

Now Tom lay in bed, drinking many cups of tea, the
newspapers sticking up like the tents of a besieging
army all over his stomach. He had taken the telephone

off the hook and had told the daily woman that she was to put the chain on the door before opening it and was on no account to admit reporters.

He tried not to look again at the numerous distraught, black-eyed Toms, made even more demented in appearance by the strange chiaroscuro of newsprint reproduction. He had even turned them face downwards. Yet whenever he moved, at least one of them, as if by some malign will of its own, obtruded itself again and glared hare-like back at him.

At the moment nobody was at war; that is, no more than usual, Royalty was not on tour in peculiar places, nobody had tested a new bomb, no footballer had sworn at the referee. The headlines of the popular papers were Tom's alone, and even *The Times* had given him nearly half a column on the middle page. Limp and lank in his striped pajamas, his heart hot and acrid, he thought he would turn his face to the wall: but soon found, like most people who try this desperate expedient, that walls, when a foot away from one's nose, present so boring a spectacle that it is better to sit up again and suffer in a less classic manner.

He was one of those who, with best meaning, had incurred the worst. Contemptuous of the moral quality of the age he lived in, out of a genuine idea to make others see how ugly it was, he had brought out from some dismal shed of his mind spiders, woodlice and dry rot. Like all people who act in perfect innocence and find themselves in trouble, he could only think on the side of the pack, and feel himself guilty. Little guilts, like bedbugs, sucked out their pinpoints of blood all over him. Had nobody but he felt the encroaching ugliness? Apparently not. There may have been many who, by turning their faces from it, pretended it did not exist:

but they were never the vocal ones. He was conscious of a horrible loneliness.

It had all gone for nothing. He had caused his detestable play to be ignored, he had not made his point at all, and he had lost his job. He felt an extraordinary impulse to cry. You can't win, he thought miserably, you can't beat them.

A horrible and violent noise assaulted his ears. At first he could not locate it. Then he realized that it came from his telephone. For a moment he had the wild idea that it might be about to explode, though common sense tried to insist that this was not something which happened to telephones. As he snatched it up, the noise ceased. A voice spoke his number. "Operator speaking."

"Do you realize this damned thing's been making the most shattering din?"

"Yes, sir. We were trying to attract your attention."

"You succeeded handsomely."

"Do you know that your receiver is improperly replaced?"

"Of course I know! I didn't replace it at all."

He persuaded her to disconnect him, for a couple of hours at least. She sounded disapproving.

The noise, though it had shaken him, had at least hauled him away from the brink of true accidie. He sat upright, punched the pillows to fit into his back, and took another look at the headlines.

DON DENOUNCES OWN PLAY. FIRST NIGHT SENSATION. BEASTLY! CRIES PLAYWRIGHT GRUTCH. And worst of all: PUBLICITY STUNT? AUTHOR BOOS HIS PLAY.

He studied the longest of the critical notices.

"The extraordinary uproar provoked by the playwright at the COBRA Theatre last night made it almost impossible to judge the work he himself denounced, since proceedings came to an end within ten minutes of the beginning of the second act. It appeared to be a singularly daring *comédie noire* in the style of ———"

Here an expected name.

"—and might well be calculated to shock and disturb. Yet it was obviously shock-therapy that the author intended, and though a mature and sophisticated audience seemed a little uneasy once or twice, there was no doubt of their general appreciation. All the more deplorable, then, that a freak on Mr. Grutch's part, designed, no doubt, as a 'happening,' deprived them of what must have been a most interesting evening."

"My God," Tom said aloud, "as if it wasn't interesting!"

Then he found, in a third paper, a phrase that made him lay his head upon his hands, not merely in a spurt of irony, or of lonely theatricality. ". . . Pervaded by beautiful menace. . . ."

The bell rang. The daily woman opened it, on the chain.

"I am quite sure Mr. Hariot will see us," said an astringent voice, "so please will you tell him that we are here."

"Let them in," Tom called, "it's all right."

Matthew and Jane came into the room, Jane almost obscured behind a bush of long-stemmed roses, which she dumped upon the bed.

"Well! Congratulations to the hero. We are on your side."

"Thank you, Jane."

"It really was an attractive evening," Matthew murmured, "we enjoyed it immensely. Jane says she's so glad she injured her knee, or we should have missed it. May I sit on the edge of the bed? Because it's not as though you're really ill . . . I hope?"

"I'm not really ill. Yes, do sit on the bed. Jane, that chair isn't too uncomfortable, though I'm sorry the room is so small. The flowers are magnificent—Mrs. Hill! Put these in water for me, if you'll be so kind?"

Jane surveyed him severely. "So you can't take it."

He felt very much like a prisoner at the opening of his trial, something anticipated for weeks, but impossible to believe in as a reality when it was actually upon him. He wished he had got up and dressed; he would have felt less defenseless.

"What do you mean?"

"Cowering in bed. You must have known what would happen, anyway."

"Yes. But when it does happen, it is quite different. I thought you'd gone back."

"Jane had a few things left to do," Matthew answered, "so we're flying to France this afternoon and picking up the boat at Cherbourg. Oh come, don't look like that!"

"Do you know," Tom said, with a savage push at the newspapers, "in all this mass of nonsense, *there is not one single suggestion that I had anything to protest about?*"

Jane straightened her hat and slid out of a sable coat. It fell from her arms like peat-water, and with no more noise. "You must not be impatient. All these poor people were taken by surprise and haven't had time to think properly yet."

"Oh yes, and I've resigned my job before they could

sack me. Such pitiful rags of dignity we gather about us," Tom added darkly.

"Poor little Pringle was superb. She was crying. I suppose you didn't notice."

"Yes I did."

"As a matter of fact," said Jane, her tone more rasping than before, "we met her as we came along the street. She gave us a message for you. Tell him, Matt."

Matthew smiled shyly. "She said we were to tell you that you were splendid."

"She said fab," Jane corrected him.

"And that she'd decided to come to terms with life."

"What terms?" Tom shot up.

"She is to star in a film about rape in a place called Worksop," said Jane, "and I am afraid all of it is your fault."

He looked at her for a moment. Then he said, "No. It is not my fault. You are not to think that."

She paused to take thought. This was something Jane never hurried. At last she said, "All right. I won't think it."

"Anyway," Matthew broke in, with a Brothers Cheeryble air which was just a little synthetic, "she is bound to make a terrific success which will transform her whole existence, and they will probably publish her book just because she is a film-star, which they would not do so readily if she were simply famous for being in mugs and boots."

Tom said, "Matthew." He searched, but not anxiously, for words. "I hope you are right. But there is no need to comfort me, since I am not at all guilty about Pringle. I live with a good deal of justifiable guilt, but I refuse to make myself miserable about things which are not my fault."

Mrs. Hill came in with three cups of bad coffee, nicely presented.

"How lucky you are to be able to make the distinction." Jane sounded tart: she had not enjoyed the unique experience of being outfaced. "Most of us can't," she added.

"Nice Jane, I assure you that I can."

Tom smiled at her, wanting her to like him, knowing that she did, but embarrassed by the knowledge that for a second he had worsted her. She had caught him in a state of resolution he was unlikely to attain again. Feeling himself oppressed by so many burdens, he had refused to take up Pringle's, for which he had not asked in the first place: yet, though his head was hard, and today his heart was, his heart would be nothing like so stony tomorrow morning. He was forced to make hay while the sun shone.

Matthew was steadily going through those papers which he had not already seen. He said, "It may be better on Sunday. Perhaps someone will hate the sight of it."

Tom swallowed his coffee in a scalding gulp. He meant to offer them the disappointing truth.

"I have failed completely. You realize that?"

"Oh, it's early days," Matthew replied, sounding vague and confident at the same time. It was one of his useful talents.

"No. And I have never felt so damned solitary in my life."

"Isn't that what one must be prepared to feel," said Jane, though not quite with her usual sangfroid, "if you go around challenging all the things smartyboots people accept? It isn't the challenge that hurts. It's what happens to you when the excitement dies down."

He did not answer, though he knew she was right.

"Where did you get 'smartyboots' from?" Matthew asked her, with curiosity.

"I had an English nannie. And I took from her everything that was best."

Meanwhile, several telegrams had arrived, including one from the Boultons. "DON'T YOU EVER REPEAT EVER THINK IT WAS FOR NOTHING FONDEST LOVE."

Mrs. Hill had turned away three reporters, who seemed very cross indeed.

"They won't be kind to you in future," said Jane, who had made a principle of keeping on good terms with the press.

"That's all right. I haven't a future."

Her eyes blazed alarmingly.

"Don't be spineless, Tom-Tom!" She had recovered her certainties. "Do you seriously believe you can fly against the wind—"

"Such an ill wind, too."

"—without being blown back a few paces, time and time again? I'm only sorry Matt and I have to go home. It is obvious that you need somebody to stiffen you. Get up!"

"I beg your pardon?"

"I said 'get up.' Get up and get dressed. Now. Immediately."

He hesitated. "I am in my pajamas."

"What does that matter?" she demanded with scorn. "You will neither shock nor allure me. I want you out of that bed."

"I'm sorry, no. But I will make you a promise. When you and Matthew have gone, and I hope you won't go for some time yet, as you are doing me a lot of good, I shall get up and dress. Will that do?"

"All right. In return, I will make you a proposition."

Whatever she might be going to say would certainly be news to Matthew, who was all ears.

"You have lost your job? Positively?"

"Yes, Jane."

"Then what I suggest is this." Draining her cup without a grimace, since she was nothing if not stoical, she got up and put on her coat. "As soon as you can, you will join Matt and me in New York—and you needn't rattle any tin can about the fare, because we are quite aware that you aren't poor. I shall then find you a job. You have good degrees—I know, because I took the trouble to look you up—and in any case, you will have the temporary advantage of being something of a figure in the English-speaking world. I can easily get you something to do, teaching your queer subject, or perhaps dramaturgy—what do you think? I might even manage a full professorship, if I gave some institution a new dormitory, or library, or psychiatric center. That is for the authority concerned to decide. You might go to Cobb College, in New Hampshire—yes, why not? I believe it is quite pleasant now, not difficult, as it was in poor Matt-Matt's day."

Tom said, "You're serious?"

Though he did not wish her to see it, he was inflamed by hope. Was it cowardly to dodge away from trouble across a wide sea? Well, yes. But if he stayed, what more could he do? There is little personal satisfaction in being a clay pigeon.

"I guess you need a good rest. If I were you, I'd sail on the *Mauretania* on Tuesday. It won't be full, liners never are. I often think Matt and I will be the last people to travel by them. I shall make you a booking before I leave London this afternoon."

"Jane, this is all very kind, but I'm not sure that I want—"

"Of course you do. You can't just be a layabout, can you?" She did not stay for an answer. "Well, we must go. And as I said before, congratulations. We are with you one hundred per cent."

She bent to kiss him, while Matthew hovered.

"No, don't call your lovely Mrs. Hill, we'll see ourselves out."

But Matthew stayed behind for a moment. "You know, Tom, when I first knew you, you were such a pale-looking chap."

"Aren't I now?" Tom sounded anxious.

"No, you're quite red in the face. I expect you're feeling much fitter."

"When I was writing that ghastly play I kept on blushing. It was a most peculiar experience. You wouldn't think it could have a permanent effect?"

Superstition touched them both, lightly.

"No, no, of course not," Matthew said. "That is— well, it simply couldn't, could it? I tell you what. I expect you've got a bit of a temperature."

"I hope so."

When the Pryars had gone, not out of his life, because he was pretty sure he would be on the *Mauretania* in a week's time, he kept his promise. He got out of the bed and began to run his bath. Then, for quite a long while, he peered and peered at his face in his shaving-mirror.

29

BRINGING THE FORTUNES OF NEAR-
LY EVERYONE MORE OR LESS TO
A CONCLUSION, AND COSMO TO A
CONVERSATION WITH A DOCTOR.

Cork Street: in the beneficence of one of those
douce mornings that sometimes precede Christmas.
The mildness of the air, the white-wine sun, the cloud-
less sky, spoke fraudulently of spring, as if, between it
and the heavy-gutted, commercialized Christmas, three
raw and freezing months did not exist. The bolder
women had abandoned topcoats, and in their neat suits
strolled, on long and insolent legs, in and out of the
galleries. In the hatter's, three people had bought hats
since nine o'clock and a fourth had ordered one of a
shape peculiar to himself. The razor-cut shadows were
the blue of hydrangeas.

The Pryars were back in America and Tom Hariot
had gone to join them, defeated at last by the successful endeavor of the Sunday press to praise the play
without mentioning its essential characteristics at all.
The honest little critic had not referred to it. Plainly he
had been shaken to the soul, but he still could not bear
to write with loathing of his fellow-man. He, alone, had
not attended the second night.

One review, however, nearly tossed Tom right back
into the depths of despair.

"This play helps to remove from our shoulders the
boring burden of mono-sexuality. Homosexuality,

heterosexuality, how stale it all seems, how trivial! Mr. Grutch would seem to offer the stage, at last, new horizons for the human condition."

But this he shut resolutely back into his mind, and consigned it from henceforth to the Freudian censor.

A *Potted Shrimp* would last its month with COBRA, but afterwards, since no commercial theater, not even the most advanced, was able to risk it, it would go to its death. (In order to spike the guns of a few theatrical paladins, Tom had made a short, firm statement to the newspapers that he would never permit any changes in it whatsoever.) People flocked into COBRA, giggled away as expected, gasped a little, on occasions said "Oo!" and immediately forgot about the whole thing. In the intervals, they still talked of their relations, their aches and pains, rising prices, and *Giselle*. During those four weeks, only two people walked out: a girl called Iolanthe and the head of a Russian trade delegation who had been misguidedly steered there by some organizing body without the faintest sense of the fitness of things. Since he understood English perfectly (though he did not reveal it) and since it was the only play he had seen during his visit to London, God alone knew what harm Tom had done to Anglo-Soviet relations. On his way out, the delegate had made one comment only: "ооράдок!"

In the bookshop, Dorothy toiled away at the accounts, snatching stray moments in which to burnish the prologue to her new play. It was quite natural, during these early days that the young assistant who had replaced Miss Few should not know where to find anything, but Cosmo had a dismal suspicion that she never would know, not if she stayed for half a century.

An era was crumbling away, and who could be cer-

269

tain that it wasn't all for the best? Since the incident of the paper megaphone, Dorothy would not speak to Duncan at all, nor permit him in the shop. He himself was negotiating the sale of his studio, having found more commodious quarters in Bond Street. Pringle was in Worksop and sent no news of herself—why should she? Yet on the hoardings the great eyes, the little muzzle, peered still over the rim of things, as if into the heart of them.

Dorothy improved her first few lines.

> Now we, enisled, encapsuled, cram the womb.
> Tomtom of heels upon the mother ribs
> > Throbs, sobs.
> > O let us out! Shout.
> > What is it all about?

Perfect. For the first time in months, contentment took her, the contentment of mind's genius incarnate. She closed her eyes, opened them with a snap because she felt so giddy.

"Now look here," said Cosmo, whose percipient gaze was upon her, "I've had enough of this. How can we accept even ordinary invitations if you're going to black out all the time? You go and get a check-up."

At first she resisted this, but her resolve slackened at last. It would not have slackened but for the blackouts to which Cosmo had referred with an indecent edge of asperity and a hint of inconvenience deliberately caused to himself. But it is one thing to feel under the weather and quite another to faint on two occasions, if fainting is not one's normal means of escape from the distresses of life.

She said one day at breakfast, "Well, who shall I go to?"

"Try that chap you last saw. Hubble, wasn't it?"

"A pig."

"Good as anybody else."

"To please you," Dorothy sighed, "not myself. For myself, I should never go crawling round doctors—"

"No need to crawl, my dear. They are more used to seeing people either upright or in bed."

"—but I suppose I owe something to you. And to our sons."

"You certainly do," said Cosmo, "because if you can get yourself really fit again, they needn't spend another holiday with Grannie. You're well aware that they hate it."

"You know how I adore them! But I have all your work to do now, and, though I know it's a petty thing in your eyes—"

"Not at all, my dear."

"Will you allow me to finish?—my own work. It is by *not* seeing them that I sacrifice myself to them. But will they ever understand?"

"I shouldn't think so," Cosmo replied, "none of them is particularly bright."

On another of these balmy days, she went to pay a second visit to Dr. Hubble.

The gardens of West Kensington were bare and twiggy now, but the pampered soil was breeding a premature spring. Already there were crocus spurs, pushing their green enamel through the crumbly black earth: in one garden, a couple of primroses had appeared. Little they knew, poor things.

The street, normally a quiet one, appeared to be singularly populated. Londoners, who privately detest their own climate while prepared to defend its over-all mildness, do not go out much when frost nips the toes, or the skies explode with rain. Give them a simulacrum of spring during the winter months and they will all be out, bright as buttons, as chattersome as starlings. The shops will be full.

The bare boughs threw a fretwork of shadow over walls of cream or grey, birds chirruped and hopped, lamb-like clouds trundled slowly across a permanent-looking vastness of blue.

"All right, Mrs. Hines or Miss Merlin," said Dr. Hubble, looking as unprepossessing as ever, and as much like some rhadamanthine beast, "let's have a look at you." He jerked out a screen and motioned her behind it. "Everything off the top half, please."

"I feel like Lady Teazle," she gasped, as she struggled with a zip fastener. It was an attempt at lightness, at insouciance, but it missed the mark. He did not mix medicine with comedy, and since he knew who Lady Teazle was (no better than she should be), a puritan streak kept him quiet. It had sounded too much like one of those familiar essays in flirtatiousness which, in a patient, he detested; though he was obliged to realize that Dorothy did not look the type.

"And your vest," he said brusquely, when she re-appeared.

He tested her for three-quarters of an hour, gave her a supply of pills meager by her standards, and told her to come back in three days' time. "Then we'll have another look. Friday at eleven, please."

After she had left him, she felt on better terms with the world than she had done for a long time past. Cosmo had been making a ridiculous fuss, and she would tell him so. All that commotion, and only a few miserable yellow tablets to show for it! Even her head didn't ache today, not even slightly. People screaming, howling, badgering her about! That was how she saw her husband, pluralizing him. Anger made her even more light-footed. She was angry with everyone and everything, and at the same time jocund.

She refused to think much about the past hour, since it had been a strain on her to endure it. Although she would not nowadays admit this to herself, Dorothy, free soul, earth-mother, had the greatest possible aversion to taking her clothes off, and Cosmo had always enjoyed her, if that was the word for it, in the dark. In her youth she had deliberately attempted to overcome this aversion by spending a week in the nudist colony on the Ile du Levant, where she had sat with new-found friends on the edge of the sea, making Frenchmen listen to her poetry. Despite the fact that the experience was a horrid one, she never ceased to smile and to emit little gay laughs: but it had cured nothing at all, and she never tried such drastic measures again.

"There's nothing the matter with me," she said to Cosmo, when she returned to Cork Street. "Why did you make me go to that awful man when you knew I didn't have to? All I got was half a dozen pills. It made me feel a fool."

"Delighted, my dear—I mean, that there's nothing wrong."

She bawled at him to take the damned ledgers out of her sight. She had sent off all the main bills and wasn't going to send any more; anyway, not that day. She was bittersweet to the new assistant, who had of course decided in her heart not to stay for more than another two weeks, and finding a distinguished poet wandering in the shop, forced upon him the draft of the prologue to *Enisled*. He assured her that it was a great privilege to have a first sight of it, for he was a good man who rejoiced in making happiness for others. His leg was still in plaster.

If Cosmo seemed out of spirits, she quite failed to notice it. She did not notice him often, except when she believed he was thinking of herself.

Next day, when the telephone rang, he happened to answer it. This was lucky, as it turned out.

On hearing the caller's name he said, "Excuse me, please, I'll take it on the other line," glided away to his sanctum, and closed the door.

Dr. Hubble was explanatory. He talked for quite a long time in language appropriate to the ear of the intelligent layman.

"Are you sure?" said Cosmo.

The doctor went on, explaining things all over again, carefully making the usual reservations.

It was quiet in this room, where the noise of traffic never penetrated. Cosmo could hear the gentlemanly tinkle of the bell in the shop, the rise and fall of voices: nothing more.

No expression whatsoever showed in his face: one might almost have thought he feared a hidden watcher.

Finally he said, "I see. Anyway, thank you."

"So there you have it," said the doctor. "Sorry."

"Oh well," said Cosmo.

He picked out one of the cigars kept for favored customers and lit it expertly with one hand. This was by way of a treat for himself, since he was far too parsimonious to smoke such things very often. "It can't be helped."

He hesitated.

He said: "It never has been helped, has it?"